THE PATH
Written By Tom Yelland

For Sara and Becki

CONTENTS

Prologue //
1st September 2012 // Silk Falls, Starr County, Wyoming //

Let him show you the path. Your soul will be free.

Hope stood alone in the pouring rain, tears spilling down her cheeks. It was her 21st birthday. She had no idea how she ended up like this or what the future might hold. So much had happened over the past few months and she felt overwhelmed trying to make sense of it all.

She drifted slowly along the darkest parts of the Emerald River. Her wavy blonde hair was soaked, her eyes were bloodshot red from all the tears but she didn't care. She wanted a new start. She wanted the world to swallow her. Again.

As she got to Kiwi Point, she saw her old house from a distance. She couldn't let him find out what she'd done through fear of how he might react. His temper could change instantly and she knew he wouldn't understand.

Things were so different less than a year ago. She had so much to look forward to. Then it all changed after one night out. That night led to so much suffering, so much hurt, so many tears. She was determined to make sure that no one else ever had to go through anything similar. She was determined to do what she could to change the world.

Just as she turned the corner near Alder Lake, she saw him walking towards her. She knew she couldn't turn back and she couldn't hide because somehow, some way, he would find her. She knew she wasn't the first and likely wouldn't be the last. She knew she had to put her heart and soul into the future, into his vision otherwise, she could end up like the others.

Without realising, she had started singing as she drifted towards him.

Amazing grace
Once lost now found
A wandering soul
My heart now bound.

PART ONE

Chapter One //
11th December 2011 – Walker Conservatory, Starr County //

Rachel Walker woke up smiling. Even though it was only a few weeks before Christmas, the sun shone brightly through her window and there wasn't a cloud in the sky. It was just past 9am MT. She sat up, stretched her arms then leapt out of bed and put MTV's 90s music channel on her phone. House of Pain's classic 'Jump Around' was blaring. She hummed the song as she showered then danced around the room at the same time as she got dressed.

The wallpaper in Rachel's room was pink with white unicorns on. She had a queen size bed with a duvet cover identical to her wallpaper. Her floor was carpeted white, the same colour as her bed frame and all the other furniture in the room. She had massive wardrobes for all her clothes and a bathroom attached to her bedroom. There was also another bigger bathroom opposite her room. Just down the hall was a living room next to the bigger bathroom, which housed her computer, a TV, a large couch and a fridge.

She checked her phone notifications and social media before going downstairs. There was nothing new that was of any interest on her Connect social media profile, just her best friend Hannah hyping the Gators game later on that day.

The Walker house was like a very large British cottage. It was three floors tall with some beautiful grounds attached. Rachel had one floor of the house all to herself, as her brother had moved out a long time ago. Her parents' bedroom and bathroom were on the top floor. The family living room, kitchen and another bathroom were on the ground floor. The roof was completely thatched which provided great insulation and soundproofed the entire house from all the aircraft that flew over, especially during the summer months.

Rachel danced her way downstairs, singing along with Shania Twain's song 'man I feel like a woman', which was blaring from her phone, and made herself mixed berries with syrup on pancakes for breakfast. She sat and ate her food by the log fire before going to find her dad in the conservatory within the grounds. As she opened the front door, she could feel the bitter cold, but crisp, fresh air and her eyes lit up at the thought of being outdoors all day.

****

Rachel's dad, Earl, was a doctor, who dedicated his life to experimenting with plants for medicinal purposes. His days were usually long and tiring. He worked hard to provide for his family and it wasn't easy. Plants, and their healing properties, fascinated him from a young age. His work had taken him around the US, including to North Carolina where he'd met Rachel's mum, Susan, in 1981. He was twenty-five and she was twenty-two at the time.

Earl Walker had married Susan Wilson in early 1984 and they moved to Starr County, Wyoming shortly after. Earl had bought land with a house and conservatory in the Silk Falls region and renamed the conservatory after the family.

Earl was shorter than Susan, standing at 5ft 4". He had blonde hair, green eyes and a very long beard. He could have easily been confused with one of the members of the band ZZ Top. He had a very antiquated dress sense, preferring to wear tweed tops with braces and worn jeans.

Susan, by contrast, was quite tall at 5ft 10". She was a stern woman with cropped, light brown hair, piercing blue eyes and had a stylish but practical dress sense.

Susan also had a professional interest in plants, particularly Orchids. She made a living by cultivating and selling them. While this didn't initially bring in much of an income, word spread and the residents of Starr County soon began buying these exotic plants from her in their droves before she was able to branch out and start selling them to other parts of the country too.

In January 1985, Susan gave birth to their first child, a son they named Mason. There were some complications and Susan ended up losing a lot of blood. She also developed severe postpartum anxiety, which caused many sleepless nights and put both of them off from having more children for some time.

On September 1st 1994, Susan gave birth to a second child, Rachel. The pregnancy wasn't planned and when Earl and Susan found out they were going to have another baby, they were initially scared due to what had happened with Mason. However, Rachel arrived quickly and without any complications. As he held her for the first time, Earl noticed just how beautiful her crystal green eyes were. She looked back at him and smiled. He knew his daughter was going to grow up to be someone very special.

As soon as both the kids were old enough, Earl taught them how to hunt. Starr County was rich with the most beautiful game money could buy. It was important to know how to survive from what the land provided and Earl was determined to teach his kids that. He had an extensive array of guns and other equipment that he'd purchased from Jefferson Canyon, a small town in the Owl Creek region, which was about a half-hour drive from where the Walker's lived in Silk Falls.

Mason was the more naturally gifted of the two kids. He seemed to enjoy the art and thrill of the hunt. He was also very interested in all the types of guns Earl had, as well as what different equipment could do to trap and kill any hunted animals quickly to ease their suffering. Mason's favourite weapon was a Winchester 70 Alaskan Rifle, which was also one of Earl's most prized possessions. It was particularly good for hunting grizzlies.

Rachel, on the other hand, got very upset when Earl tried to encourage her to hurt anything, so he promised to leave her to her own devices as long as she ꞏꞏꞏꞏ ꞏꞏ out with him. She was much more interested in plants and their uses, particularly their healing properties. This made Earl proud and pleased that he could teach her as much as he could about plants instead.

One afternoon, in a clearing just past Silver Oak Brewery, Rachel and Earl were out walking when Rachel suddenly spotted something and ran ahead. Earl watched in amazement as she approached a trapped cougar. He had been very careful to make sure she understood the dangers of particular species, such as the native moose and the pesky wolverines. Most of the time, this wasn't an issue as Rachel had a great understanding of the natural world and seemed to be able to communicate with the majority of animals on a totally different level than he could.

However, her naivety almost got her in trouble on more than one occasion and this time was no different. Rachel had calmed the creature down and was trying to release it from the trap when the cougar noticed a small weapon tucked away, which she would have only ever used in self-defence. Just as Rachel had opened the mechanism to free its trapped paw, the cougar lashed out with the other paw and caught her leg, before running away to tend to its wounds. After making sure his daughter was ok, Earl had tried to go after the beast much to Rachel's dismay, but lost its trail.

****

"Do you remember that day?" Earl asked Rachel in the conservatory.

"Yes, I can't believe you tried to run after the cougar to kill it. It was just trying to protect itself. They are very intelligent animals you know, Dad!" Rachel explained, smiling at the end. "Anyway, I just came in to tell you that I'm going over to see Hannah at Gators Stadium and I'll see you later. Love you!"

"Love you too sweetie. Stay safe."

The conservatory where Earl and Susan worked was massive. It housed a huge variety of different plant species and could be quite hard to navigate if you didn't know where the doors were. Earl's work meant that he took up the majority of the space inside but Susan still had a sizeable amount to grow her orchids as well as a greenhouse next to the rock garden, which she used as well. Susan also liked to keep the different gardens and maze within the grounds trimmed and watered but this became more difficult as she became busier with her orchid sales, so the family employed a part-time gardener who helped when she wasn't able to.

Rachel left the conservatory after fighting her way past a large palm. She skipped by the rose garden to the maze on the other side of the grounds. The maze was made of large topiary plants and covered a third of an acre with half a mile of pathways. It started at the end of the rose garden and came out by the woodlands at the edge of the property. It was a deterrent for any unwanted guests as it was very difficult to navigate unless you knew the route through it.

Gators stadium was home to the local baseball team and was a fair distance from the house but Rachel loved the walk. It gave her the chance to enjoy the everlasting fresh air and incredible views Starr County had to offer. Silk Falls was just one part of the vast and complex landscape, littered with mountains, lakes, farms, caves, animals and so many forests with a huge variety of different species of trees and shrubs.

To the south lay Owl Creek, a more rural, farming community. Rachel hadn't spent as much time there as Silk Falls but she knew Jefferson Canyon and liked to hang out there at the Great Mongoose bar. It had a pool table and there were guest bands every Friday night. It was also the best place to go to after a Gators game to relax with a beer or two. Even though Rachel was twenty, her best friend Hannah knew the bartender so she could always get a beer providing they behaved themselves.

To the north were the Phoenix Mountains, which stretched for miles around. Scenic walks and beautiful lakes in the mountains meant the area attracted many tourists. However, some of the different spots needed monitoring due to the animals that inhabited them and the danger they posed to those who were unaware. Anglers from all across America visited during the summer for the annual competitions that took place. The Phoenix Mountains were famous for mammoth fish that lived in the rivers and lakes.

Silk Falls was Rachel's favourite place in the whole world though. She'd lived there her entire life and knew the whole region by heart. From the beautiful vistas looking upriver to the Phoenix Mountains in the distance and the thick forests and vast caves, Rachel spent every moment she could outdoors and exploring. The area also had its own brewery which was ten minutes north from where the conservatory was, Murphy's grocery store which was pretty much an 'everything you could ever want' goods shop, a spa and sports facility as well as Gators Stadium.

Rachel was skipping along without a care in the world. About an hour into her walk, just after she'd passed Murphy's along the main road, Rachel felt like there was someone following her. She stopped and turned around but couldn't see anyone. Just as she was going to turn back and carry on, she felt something press against her neck.

"Don't make this harder than it already is. Gimme your money."

Chapter Two //
11th December 2011 – Silk Falls, Starr County //

He followed her from the conservatory, making sure he was far enough back that she didn't realise she was being tracked. She wasn't the easiest person to trail sometimes because she knew the area so well and was so flexible. He liked that about her. He liked everything about her.

He kept his distance up to Murphy's but then lost her once she'd walked past. He started to panic and jogged past the shop. She suddenly re-appeared almost in front of him, past the parking lot. He realised how heavily he was breathing from jogging, so he tried to hold his breath but she stopped. He ducked behind a tree just before she turned around.

He suddenly saw a large Caucasian male, approximately 6ft, appear out of nowhere and pull what looked like a gun out and pressed it against her neck. He didn't know what to do.

****

"WADE," Rachel shouted. "That's not funny! What if I knew karate and kicked your ass?"

Wade couldn't stop laughing. He loved playing what he thought were practical jokes, especially on Rachel.

"I'm sorry I'm sorry Rach. It's just... you're so easy to wind up!"

She hugged him.

"Aww its ok hun, but we better get a move on to get to the stadium before the game kicks off."

Wade Wheeler was 40, with a mental age of 16. He was 5ft 10", had dark black spiky hair, brown eyes and was overweight. He lived in the western area of the Phoenix Mountains region with his parents, Buck and Canberra. Wade hadn't been outside the county, let alone outside the state or country. He'd met Rachel and Hannah after a Gators game when he decided to streak after getting drunk. Hannah had almost thrown up but Rachel found him funny. Despite the age gap, they all became friends and regularly went to games together.

"How's things at home, Wade?" Rachel asked.

"Don't wanna talk about it! Mom's being a total bitch. I think she's gonna divorce dad soon. She hates him and keeps telling him he won't ever make it as a politician because he's lazy. Dad thinks mom is sleeping with someone else, but he doesn't care. He still thinks he can become president one day. He says that me hanging around you guys is bad for his image and that I should be hanging around people my age."

"Aww, I'm sure he'll come round. Invite him to a game. That way he can see how amazing we are!" Rachel winked at her friend.

"I don't want him coming anywhere near my friends. Friend life stays separate from parent life. Plus he thinks I like you."

"Silly!"

"Well, he's not wrong is he?" Wade raised his right eyebrow.

Rachel smiled. She knew Wade liked her but equally knew that both her dad and her brother would have something to say if anything ever happened between them. The age gap was also too much.

"Do you think we'll win today?" Rachel asked, changing the subject.

"Who we playing? It's those farmers from north of Montana ain't it?"

"Montana is as far north as you can go before you get to Canada! So no!" Rachel laughed. "We're playing the Boise Beavers from Idaho."

"I think we'll kick their ass!"

"I hope we do but they're top of the league at the moment so it's gonna be tough."

****

He felt the rage creeping through his body as he saw her hug the man. How could he pull a gun on such a sweet, innocent girl? He almost rushed out to beat the living hell out of this man but then he realised he knew him. It was her friend Wade. He'd seen him around the county before. He knew Wade was much older than Rachel. He didn't understand why he didn't hang around with people his own age.

He followed them round to the stadium and watched them for a bit until they went inside for the start of the game. He'd head off to the bar in Owl Creek for a few beers whilst the game was on before getting back home.

He just wished she'd notice him in the same way he noticed her. He sneaked into her room at night and just watched her sleep. He'd made… adjustments to the house so he could see what she was up to in different rooms. He felt like he needed to protect her from the outside world because she was so precious and pure.

He felt like no one else deserved to even to see her, spend time with her, to connect with her. Ever.

****

They got to the stadium just as the game was about to start. Gators Stadium was quite small in comparison to other baseball stadiums in the country. It could hold a thousand people but needed a major overhaul. The Gators were looking to move up a division to pay for renovations. They were currently sitting in third place in the northern mountain division, just two wins away from top spot, held by Boise who they were playing on that particular day. However, there were only three games left of the season, so they had to win to be in with any chance of overhauling the Beavers and being promoted.

Hannah was outside the stadium, waiting for them to arrive.

"Hey guys! Y'all look so cute together!" Hannah winked, as they walked over.

"She completes me," Wade looked over at Rachel, half lovingly, half mischievously.

"HANNAH! I feel like I haven't seen you in FOREVER," Rachel was beaming.

Hannah Taylor was Rachel's best friend. Born August 15th 1992 to English parents who had moved over to the US from Nottingham in 1987, Hannah had lived in Silk Falls since she was very young. She met Rachel in school and, even though she was two years older than Rachel was, they had so much in common that they clicked immediately and had remained friends since. At 5ft 5", she was a similar height to Rachel. She had auburn, wavy hair, brown eyes and a pale complexion.

"Rachel! It's so good to see you! It feels like so long and yet it's only been a few days!"

"I know but we get the whole day together today." Rachel said, excitedly.

"Have you heard? They are thinking of tearing down the stadium?" Hannah mentioned.

"Yeah but they're building a new one right?" Wade looked worried.

"Rumours are they want to build a jail instead. We have to do everything we can to stop that from happening. The only way to do that is to win today and the next two weeks to go up to the Premier League."

Despite the best efforts of the fans to cheer the team on and Wade, who tried to distract the Beaver players on numerous occasions by shouting and letting off an air horn, the Gators lost in the last few seconds to a home run. The entire stadium went dead silent once the Beaver player hit the ball out of the grounds.

After the game, they left despondent.

"We have to stop them from tearing down the stadium. Surely there is something we can do?" Rachel asked.

"I'll see what I can find out, my dad is tryin' to get into politics so he might be able to help," Wade said.

"I'm not sure if there is anything we can do," Hannah said, despondently. "Attendances will drop off now we're not going up. We sure could have used the money from promotion to build a new stadium. I think it's only going to be a matter of time now."

Some Beaver fans came over and started taunting them.

"Stupid Gators! You have no chance of going up this year now. Get used to your crappy stadium whilst we're living the dream in the premier league."

"Fuck You! You think you can just come here, run your mouth like that? I'll kick your ass!" Wade said, annoyed.

Before the Beaver fan could reply, Rachel interjected, "You won fair and square, congratulations. Can't we all just get along?"

"Stupid 'Starr County princess'. Enjoy YOUR league next year."

"Don't you DARE!"

"WADE – please don't start a fight with them, they did win fair and square!"

If Wade didn't have to leave right away to get back to his parents for dinner, he would have personally kicked them out of the county. But his dad threatened him with housework if he wasn't at the table and ready to eat at 6pm every evening so he begrudgingly left, ensuring the girls were right behind him.

Rachel and Hannah walked down to Jefferson Canyon to have a drink and a few games of pool to take their mind off the loss.

Jefferson Canyon was located right in the middle of Owl Creek. It was home to the Great Mongoose bar, a church, a garage, a plane shop and a gun store called New Frontier, which was part of a chain. The bar was a back-alley, dark building similar to many in rural America. It housed some of the region's finest beer and whiskey along with some of the grumpiest farm folk imaginable. The pool table was free to use but in need of some serious tender loving care. The ripped cloth and cushions needed replacing. The cues had no chalk, which had consequently worn the tips out.

The bar was also the only place in Owl Creek that provided a decent meal so it was usually very busy, especially on weekends.

"So, these guys I met in Battle Creek invited us to a gig over in Great Falls. You in?" Hannah asked, as she broke the second game of pool.

"When is it? I'm sure my dad won't mind driving us,"

"Next Saturday. Let me know?"

The girls continued to play a few further games before Earl met them outside to drive them back home. He dropped Hannah off first. She lived in a small shack down a mountain path right by the Emerald River that ran right through Silk Falls.

"See y'all soon, text me about Saturday," Hannah shouted, as they drove off.

"Dad, can you give us a lift to Great Falls on Saturday? It's for a gig,"

"Sure sweetie, I have a friend over in Great Falls so I can catch up with him whilst you're at the gig and then give you a lift back too?"

"You sure Mom won't mind? I feel like neither of us has spent a lot of time with her recently and she might be starting to wonder why?"

Rachel loved her mother dearly, but she was naturally closer to her dad, as he always seemed to be there every time she needed help or advice.

"She'll be fine. Christmas is coming so we'll get to spend loads of time together, as a family," Earl replied.

Chapter Three //
18th December 2011 – Great Falls, Montana //

Earl and Rachel left the conservatory at 5pm to collect Hannah. It was a two-hour drive to Great Falls. Once they got through the Owl Creek tunnel, there was nothing but country road the whole way. Hannah and Rachel passed the time by talking about the gig. The main act called themselves 'Cracken' and described themselves as a heavy metal meets hip-hop band. There was a support band first that neither of them cared about seeing so they had planned, without letting Earl hear, to get drunk during that time.

By the time they arrived in Great Falls, it was pitch black. Earl dropped them off by the western car park and made plans to collect them from the same location at 11pm.

The stadium was massive. It was home to the Great Falls college football team who had come close to winning the national championship last season. It had ten levels and was larger than most NFL stadiums. It could easily fit over one hundred thousand people inside and whilst this gig was going to be nowhere near a sell-out, there would still be a good seventy thousand there.

As they walked down Stadium Way, Rachel saw the pillars were lit green in honour of the band. About halfway down, she noticed two men sitting on one of the pillars, talking. Hannah veered off towards them.

"Rach – this is Bo and Chad. These are the guys I told you about. Chad is twenty-one and Bo is twenty-two. They are both from Missoula."

"It's lovely to meet y'all."

Rachel's eyes immediately met Bo's and she felt her heart flutter. She'd never even kissed a guy let alone had a boyfriend. She got the feeling her family wouldn't be happy with whomever she ended up dating or marrying.

"How was the journey?" Bo asked, smiling.

"Yeah, we made good time. My dad drove us."

Bo was about the same height as Rachel but height didn't bother her. He had black cropped hair, dark brown eyes that she felt she could stare into all night, and a pierced nose. He had very light complexion and looked like he worked out. He was wearing a Cranken T-Shirt, dark blue jeans and a pair of white sneakers.

In contrast, Chad was 7ft tall and looked like he was about five hundred pounds. He had odd shoes and socks on and long, wavy brown hair with pierced ears that were currently housing dagger jet-black earrings. They looked bizarre standing next to each other, Rachel thought.

"Have you got the stuff?" Hannah asked Chad.

"Yeah, it's hidden away. I'll get it out when we get inside"

Rachel was curious "What stuff?"

"Don't worry about it, Rachel. You'll love it," Hannah smiled.

They got into the stadium and split to go to the bathrooms. Hannah came out first. She was looking for the others when she saw a man across the room. He looked like he was standing on something and was talking to a small crowd. He wasn't wearing any kind of shirt and his body was covered in scratches and tattoos. The only items of clothing that Hannah could see where a pair of cargo pants and boots as well as a pair of aviator sunglasses, which covered his eyes. He looked to be mid-thirties and had his hair tied up in a top knot.

She couldn't hear what he was saying too well as the area was very busy and there was a lot of noise. Out of nowhere, he suddenly looked over her way. She felt him almost pierce her mind and felt herself stagger back.

"Hey!" Rachel had come over to find her.

"Do you see that guy over there?"

"Where?"

"Ther.."

He'd gone. Did she just imagine the whole thing?

****

There she was, my next princess. Not the first, nor the second, but hopefully the last. We had been on the lookout for too long now. Enlightenment needed Hope. I had finally found her.

****

"I can't see anyone there at all, Han. Just a crowd of excited people. Shall we get a beer? Come on, I can finally use my fake ID!" Rachel said, excitedly.

They got some drinks for themselves and the guys as well.

"Hey asshole, give me mine now!"

The girls turned around to see Bo and Chad arguing about something.

"What's up guys?" Rachel asked.

"He won't give me my candy!" Bo said.

"Candy? Can I have some?"

Hannah intervened "It's not… that kind of candy."

Hannah knew this would be a problem. She had taught Rachel so much but had so much more to do to help her understand the ways of the world. As much as she loved Rachel, she was so naive and trusting of everyone. The only times they had ever had issues were when fights broke out and all Rachel wanted was for everyone to get along, so she always tried to make peace. Hannah knew that sometimes, fights needed to happen to sort certain situations out properly.

"What kind of candy is it? I love candy!" Rachel said.

"She's old enough bro, she can have one," Bo said to Chad. "But you need to GIVE ME MINE!"

Rachel saw Chad give Bo a tiny bag, which had some kind of round green pills inside. She then saw him give the same to Hannah as well. Rachel excited snatched the bag from Hannah. She opened the bag, took two pills out, sipped her beer, put them in her mouth and swallowed. Chad just smirked.

"RACHEL! WHAT THE HELL?" Hannah cried.

"What? They're candy, what's the problem?"

"They're not candy Rachel!" Hannah rolled her eyes.

Bo whispered in Rachel's ear "You just double dropped two ecstasy pills."

"Oh. OH! I've never touched drugs before! Am I going to die?"

"Very possibly," Chad smirked.

Rachel looked at Hannah and Bo, terrified.

"Don't be a dick!" Bo said. He turned to Rachel. "You're not going to die, we will look after you. Just enjoy it. You'll start to feel alive in about an hour and we'll be having the time of our lives by then anyway."

"Rachel, you'll be fine. Let's just find our spot," Hannah said.

****

Just as Cracken were about to come on stage, Rachel started to feel a very strange but nice sensation come over her entire body, almost like she was free and released. She felt so much love for everyone around her and wanted to express that. She hugged Hannah, then hugged Chad and then grabbed Bo and kissed him. She didn't know what she was doing but didn't care. Hannah and Chad smiled as they knew the 'candy' was working. They danced the night away, drinking and chatting in between songs about how good the band was.

Halfway through the penultimate song, Hannah realised she hadn't seen Rachel for a while.

"Chad, have you seen Rachel?"

"I was just going to ask you the same thing about Bo."

"Do you think we should look for them?"

"I'm sure they'll be fine, Bo will look after her."

About a half-hour before, Rachel had wandered off to try to find the bathroom. Bo had followed, wanting to make sure she was ok. He caught up with her and found her hugging a man in the corridor. The man walked off and Rachel turned around after Bo whispered in her ear.

"Oh hey… BO! What does that stand for? Bo-lin? Bo-lieve? Bo-Iwannafuckyourbrains out? You're so cute. I just wanna rip your shirt off."

Bo looked into her eyes and could tell she was being genuine despite not being sober. He grabbed her hand and took her into a cubicle in the bathroom, where he kissed her passionately. As he proceeded to unzip his pants, followed by hers, she didn't have a care in the world, all she felt was pure joy.

****

Not long after, Hannah and Chad eventually found Rachel and Bo sitting on a bench near the exit just laughing and making out.

"Rachel, are you ok?" Hannah asked.

"They've had a great time!" Chad said, slyly.

"It was everything I ever dreamed it would be," Rachel smiled. "You were amazing" she turned to Bo, still smiling.

"SHIT – we've gotta meet your dad in ten minutes. We need to get you sobered up NOW!" Hannah said, suddenly starting to get anxious.

"You don't look like you're even remotely close to coming down. You've only taken the two at the start of the night, right?"

"She took another one before we…" Bo said. "I'm sorry, I couldn't stop her! I don't even know where she got it!"

"Couldn't or didn't want to?" Hannah said, rolling her eyes. "Why are you boys all the same? She's going to come up again right in the middle of the drive back. I'm going to have to tell her dad she was drugged and we don't know who by."

Hannah got some drinking water from one of the food outlets as well as a burger and some fries to try to help sober Rachel up but, despite eating and drinking, it didn't work.

She tried to get Rachel to stand up but she kept falling back down and started laughing. Hannah wasn't impressed and kept getting more anxious as they had to almost drag Rachel downstairs and outside.

****

He watched them from over the other side of the parking lot. He could see she was intoxicated but he couldn't tell if she was drunk or had taken drugs. If it were the latter, there would be severe repercussions. He felt the anger boil up inside of him. He couldn't believe she'd be so naïve. The two guys that were with them said their goodbyes. She was in no state to even stand up, let alone talk but he saw the shorter of the two guys bend down. She whispered something to him and he kissed her then walked away smirking.

A thought flashed through his mind. Kill them. KILL THEM NOW! He shut that down because he knew he'd never see her again if he did. No, their time would come. Soon.

****

Earl met the girls as planned. As soon as he saw Rachel, slumped on Hannah's shoulder, he rushed over.

"What the hell happened?" Earl asked, alarmed.

"Mr Walker, I'm so sorry – we kept telling her to cover her drink with her hand but she just didn't listen and we think someone slipped her something. She is ok, I've been making sure she's been drinking loads of water," Hannah said.

Earl didn't acknowledge Hannah's words at all. He noticed her eyes and beads of sweat on her forehead and knew she'd taken some kind of drugs as well.

"Let's just get home. I'm not best pleased, but I know you kids will do what you will do and whilst I don't believe you are old enough to take care of yourselves, you need to learn to."

They got Rachel into the back seat of the SUV. Hannah sat next to her and looked after her on the drive back. By the time Earl dropped Hannah off, Rachel was asleep. Hannah said she would check in on Rachel in the morning then walked down to mountain path to her shack.

A couple of miles down the road, Rachel started to stir and mumbled something Earl couldn't hear. As Earl started to pull over to check on her, he heard a sound, which he thought could have been a snake outside. He stopped the SUV, checked the area then opened the back door. He noticed Rachel's trousers were wet and the back of his SUV was too. They were about ten minutes south of the border of Owl Creek and Silk Falls so he turned the vehicle around and drove to Murphy's as quickly as he could to try to find something to clean up the mess. He got to the store, parked up and got out of the SUV in such a rush he forgot to lock it.

****

"Stupid old idiot," he thought. What was it that he taught them when they were younger? Safety first. Forgot his own rule and now he'd put her in danger. She was alone, unconscious and vulnerable.

He approached the back of the SUV and could see that she'd clearly had an accident but that wasn't a problem. It was perfect. He quietly opened the door and slid onto the back seat. She was fast asleep. He knew Earl would be at least ten minutes in Murphy's, which was plenty of time. He unzipped his jeans…

****

Chapter Four //
19th December 2011 – Silk Falls, Starr County //

Rachel stirred. She could feel she was lying down and something soft was propping up her head, which was pounding. She remembered she'd mixed a lot of alcohol and some drugs the night before. She also realised that she was also in a lot of pain near her pelvis.

She thought about being with Bo at the concert so she thought it must have been something to do with it being her first time having sex. Then she remembered that Bo had been gentle so it surely couldn't have been that either.

She thought about the ride home and realised she had stirred a few minutes prior. Whilst she hadn't fully woken, she remembered feeling like something was wrong. She suddenly felt very uneasy. She could feel there was a hand in a place it shouldn't be. Her legs must be bare as it was freezing cold and she felt her pants at the bottom of her feet. What was going on?

She slowly opened one eye to see her dad was touching parts of her body that he shouldn't. Had he raped her? Was he now trying to clean up any evidence? She knew she had to stay deathly quiet. She couldn't let him know she'd seen him as it would tear the entire family apart. She tried to fall back to sleep, perhaps this was just an awful nightmare?

****

This was perfect. The old man didn't even realise anyone had been anywhere near his precious daughter.

He'd made sure that he didn't 'make an even bigger mess' by using protection then quickly got out of the vehicle as soon as he'd finished and heard the shop door open. He made sure to leave everything as he'd found it and exactly as it was when the old man left her.

As he walked away, he felt ambivalent. At the same time of the thrill of FINALLY getting what he wanted… what he felt he DESERVED, he also felt sheer anger because he wasn't the first and now never would be.

He vowed to make the guys from that gig pay. He knew that if Rachel saw her dad trying to clean the urine up, she'd assume he was trying to abuse her, would likely never want to see him again and try to find somewhere remote to go away from Starr County. He knew that Hannah would contact those guys from the gig and that would be when he would make his move.

Rachel woke up the following morning in her bed. She had no recollection of how she got there and memories of the previous night were hazy aside from the one image she couldn't get out of her head. Her dad.

As she lay there, she realised all she was wearing under the covers was a t-shirt and immediately felt sick.

She picked up her phone, which was on the dressing table next to her bed, and messaged Hannah straight away on Connect saying that she needed to meet urgently, then went and had a shower.

As she was in the shower in the en-suite connected to her room, she noticed something she'd never seen before; four holes in the wall. They were fairly small but big enough to be able to see through and were at the right height to be able to see enough of someone showering.

Horrified, she realised that a decent size ladder could be put up against that side of the house without anyone knowing. The window in the bathroom was a small one at the end of the shower and there were no windows on the ground floor on that side of the building.

At that point, she couldn't hold it in any more. She got out of the shower quickly and vomited. She composed herself then, after a minute or so, she cleaned up, brushed her teeth and got dressed. She checked the bathroom across the landing and found the same four holes on the same side of the house. How could she have been so stupid and not seen them before?

She left the house quietly via the back door just in case her dad was in. Hannah hadn't replied to her message so she decided to go to her brother's house.

Mason lived with his heavily pregnant wife, Abi, near the Tyran Gorge, which was up by Jericho Ridge in the Phoenix Mountains. Rachel knew her dad wouldn't follow her because he found the journey difficult. She was finding it tough herself that morning. She still felt a lot of pain, both physically and mentally. She couldn't get the image out of her dad touching her out of her head. She was terrified of having to see him again and to confront him.

When she arrived near the ridge, she saw Mason in the garden, mowing the lawn with a cigarette in his hand. His short blonde hair glistened in the morning sunshine. His house almost felt more like a barn but there was a log fire, decent sized kitchen and living room. Out back, there were two bedrooms and a bathroom. Mason had converted the second bedroom ready for when the baby arrived.

Mason was 6ft 5", well-built and wore massive denim dungarees. Rachel thought they were goofy and wondered how he managed to sweet talk his wife whilst wearing them.

"Oh hey! How's it going?" he asked, as he saw her walking over.

She burst out crying.

"It's dad. I caught him… touching me last night."

"WHAT? I'll kill the old man! I don't care if he is my own pop! What happened?"

Rachel went through everything that she could remember and mentioned about the pain she was currently feeling. She broke down in tears again.

"I don't know what to do. I can't go back, I just can't. I've tried messaging Hannah but she's not answering me. I didn't know where else to go. I just want to die."

"Did he rape you, Rachel?"

"Yes."

"Are you sure?"

"I felt someone… doing… things they shouldn't… to me, minutes before I opened my eyes and saw him. It had to have been him."

Mason threw his cigarette butt on the ground and lit another. He made his own roll-up smokes that were unique as they had his initials stamped on the tobacco papers.

"Ok Sis, hang here as long as you like and get Hannah over once she messages. Do you want me to call the doc? Do you want a soda or something? Can go shoot some ducks if you want? I just bought a new Remington 870. Best gun I ever owned!"

"Soda would be nice. Please don't harm the ducks and yes I think it would be best if I saw the doctor."

Mason went into the house whilst Rachel sat down one of the chairs in his garden. She checked social media and could see Hannah hadn't been on Connect or Bat-of-an-Eyelid, a social media site which focused on its users uploading pictures, so figured she must still be asleep. Bo had accepted her friend request on both which made her smile through the tears. Mason came back out from the house with a can in his hand a few minutes later.

"I called the doc, she'll be here soon. Here's your soda."

Hannah eventually called at around 3pm and came up to the ridge as quick as she could. Rachel told her the whole story when she arrived.

"I can't face him, Hannah, You know I can't."

"You HAVE to Rachel. You have to confront him." Hannah said angrily.

"What good will it do? He'll never admit to it and I can't face seeing him."

"If you don't then I will and I'm telling you now Sis, I won't ever forgive him for this!" Mason chimed in.

"We need to get away, for good," Hannah said. "I've heard about this group who live in the mountains out of town. I'll see if I can get more information, but you HAVE to talk to your dad. If you don't, I'll report him to Sheriff Fowler."

"You can't Hannah! It's my word against his, no one has any evidence. I can't see him go down, he's my daddy!" Rachel sobbed.

Mason was furious.

"Dammit Rachel, he's my pop too but the old man cannot be allowed to get away with this."

"Ok, fine you guys. I'll talk to him. Alone."

"You can't trust him, Rachel. How do you know he won't attack you again?" Hannah asked.

"Why don't you come over then and wait in the next room while I talk to him?"

"Mason should come too," Hannah said. "I've just messaged Chad. He said he and Bo can help us find this group and said they'd come with us."

"Oh awesome, I'd love to see Bo again!" Rachel said excitedly. She looked over at Mason, catching a flash of disdain in his eyes so she thought better of saying anything else.

There was a knock at the door. Mason opened it.

"Oh hey Doc, this way."

The doctor came in. She was a very short woman with black hair, which she wore in a bob. She had worked in the Starr County Clinic for years. SCC was located in Owl Creek and was a tiny medical facility but housed enough equipment to be able to do proper exams.

The doctor took Rachel into the spare room in Mason's shack.

"Hi, Rachel. I'm Doctor Garcia. So what seems to be the problem here?"

"I had sex for the first time last night and I've woken up this morning experiencing a lot of pain."

"Where are you specifically experiencing this pain, Rachel?"

Rachel pointed to her vulva.

"This can be normal after your first time. However, I'd like to check you out just as a precaution."

Doctor Garcia examined Rachel and could see the area Rachel had pointed to looked sore.

"This does look to be significantly sorer than it should be. I'd need to examine you properly to be able to make sure you are ok internally. Can you come by the clinic at some point over the next few days?"

"Thank you, Doctor. Of course, I will. The guy I was with was so gentle. He knew it was my first time. We used protection so I can't work out why this is so painful."

"We will get to the bottom of this Rachel, but I'll need to perform more tests that I can only do at the clinic."

"Thank you, Doctor."

Doctor Garcia left. Mason immediately wanted to know what happened.

"Well, she said it was normal to feel like that after your first time but she wants to run more tests at the clinic. I'm worried now after what happened with dad last night that he might have seriously hurt me."

"I'll take you down there next week, Sis. We will get to the bottom of this."

****

Two days before Christmas, Mason drove Rachel to the clinic in Owl Creek. As they walked in, a man and woman were just leaving. They both smiled at Rachel who smiled back. She could overhear the man excitedly say to the woman "I can't believe it Aurora, we can finally start trying."

Rachel walked to reception, registered and sat down in the reception area.

"Mason, who were those two people we passed on the way in?"

'Mike and Aurora Raye. They live just down the road, south of the clinic. Good people. He's a pilot and services planes. She's a vet, served our country for ten years in Iraq and Afghanistan.'

'RACHEL WALKER – EXAM ROOM 1 PLEASE,' the tannoy system announced.

Rachel went to the exam room alone after telling Mason she'd be fine. The clinic was tiny so the room was easy enough to find.

"Hi Rachel, how are you doing?" Doctor Garcia asked.

"I'm feeling better overall. The pain has gone down a lot."

"I'd like to give you an x-ray and perform a few further tests just to make sure you are ok and there is nothing internally we should be worried about."

"Thank you, Doctor."

All the tests took about an hour to complete then another hour to confirm the results.

"I'm not going to lie, Rachel. I was worried. But all the tests have come back negative. You aren't pregnant and there is nothing wrong internally. This looks like it was a case of your partner being too rough. Are you sure you've only slept with him once?"

"Definitely and he was very gentle."

"If this is the case, we need to consider the possibility that someone has abused you. My suggestion would be to talk things over with your brother or someone you know you can trust, and try to figure out if there is any situation you can remember where that might have happened."

Rachel looked uneasy.

"If you can think of something or someone, don't hesitate to contact Sheriff Fowler. He's fairly new but he's been great at sorting out any trouble so far."

Rachel walked out of the room. Mason stood up and asked how it went. Rachel remained quiet until they were out of the surgery.

"How did it go?" Mason asked again.

"I'm pregnant."

Chapter Five //
8th January 2012 – Owl Creek, Starr County //

Christmas had come and gone. It had been a subdued affair at the Walker household. Rachel had agreed to get the holidays out of the way before confronting her dad. This also allowed Hannah more time to get all the information they needed to leave Starr County and find the group she'd heard about. Mason had said he would drive them out to meet Bo and Chad in Sioux Pass.

Since Rachel's revelation, Mason was desperate to do everything he could to help her in any way, with anything she needed. He'd message her twice a day to make sure she was ok and had everything she needed. If she didn't reply or said she needed something, he'd rush over. Rachel knew that she had lied to her brother however, she wanted to make her dad feel awful for what he'd done so she needed Mason to be as authentic as possible. She probably hadn't thought it through too well but she just decided to go for it once she left the doctors room.

Rachel had become increasingly anxious in general so Hannah had recommended turning to marijuana to help her relax. Hannah arranged to meet Bo and Chad in Owl Creek one evening just after New Year celebrations were over.

The girls arrived at the Great Mongoose bar in Jefferson Canyon to find the boys waiting. Hannah noticed that there was only one other man in the bar, who looked like he might be from out of town. Aside from his slick, combed ginger hair, he wore a loud shirt with palm trees on, which had the top two buttons open, and a pair of dark aviators on his head. He had tattoos covering the majority of his arms and he had a very full ginger beard. He was drinking a pint of Guinness and smoking. He smiled over at her. She smiled back in politeness but then focused on the boys. Chad was smirking as usual. Bo smiled as Rachel caught his eye.

"How's it goin' ladies? I've got more than you asked for Hannah," Chad bragged.

"Thanks, guys! Pretty good. How were the holidays?" Hannah replied.

"I'm just glad it's all over. Hate this time of year as I have to spend time with my folks. I just want to leave and start again. That's where FREEDOM come in. Everything is set, all you have to do is send word and we'll be ready to meet you in Sioux Pass," Chad said.

"They are amazing!" Bo chimed in. "They are totally open, chilled out and relaxed. They believe in the power of positivity, the power of being free."

"Sounds exactly what we need right now," Rachel was looking into Bo's eyes. "Something happened after the gig which I need to deal with but once I have done that, we'll be ready to leave. Until then, let's get drunk and try out this weed!"

"Hope it's nothing too serious?" Bo asked, concerned.

"Just family stuff," Rachel smiled.

The four of them had a great night drinking in the bar, playing games and telling jokes but knew they wouldn't be allowed to smoke the marijuana in there so ended up staggering to the church which was a few hundred yards away. As they departed, Hannah noticed the man from earlier had gone.

****

As soon as I saw her at the stadium, I started preparing to begin the new chapter. I sent word to Brother James and Brother Joel to keep an eye on my new prize, our new Hope. After following her to a bar in Owl Creek, Brother James reported the terrible news that she would soon depart Starr County. My heart was shattered but I knew God had a plan. I knew that one day soon, she would return and come to me.

****

Hannah knew the Pastor was out of town. With the whole church shut, it would be the perfect place.

When they got there, they sat down on the bench in the courtyard outside. Bo taught Rachel to roll a joint whilst Hannah and Chad rolled their own.

"How do I… smoke it?" Rachel asked Bo.

Bo laughed. "You're so innocent."

"You like that, baby?" Rachel had seen women in old movies use that line. She wasn't sure she managed to pull it off.

Bo laughed. "Stop it! You just smoke it like a normal cigarette."

"I don't smoke cigarettes though?"

"Well, first you need to light it," he pulled out a lighter. "Now drag in on the non-lit tip and hold it for a few seconds before exhaling."

Rachel tried but kept coughing. The others laughed.

"You'll get the hang of it," Hannah said, offering encouragement.

After a few minutes, Rachel felt slightly more comfortable and could feel the effect the marijuana was having. She felt calm and relaxed.

It was starting to get a little bit cold as the clock ticked ever closer to midnight. Bo took his coat off and put it around Rachel's shoulders. She kissed him then whispered into his ear.

In a loud voice, Bo said, "We're um… just gonna go… um."

Rachel laughed, so hard that she snorted a bit. This in turn made the others laugh.

She led Bo around the back of the church and found one of the windows slightly ajar. She managed to wedge it open and climbed through.

The church looked abandoned. The white walls needed a serious lick of paint. The pews looked like they all needed replacing. Rachel wondered how Pastor Gore coped with doing sermons like this every week.

Bo followed her in and they shut the window. Rachel instantly jumped on him, pressing her lips up against his, whilst simultaneously unzipping his jeans and cupping his neck with her other hand.

"Should we… be doing this… in here?" Bo asked, hesitantly.

"Do you believe in God?"

"Well, no but..."

"Unless you want to have sex in the middle of a field of cows, we're doing this."

Bo didn't need any further convincing.

Chapter Six //
28th February 2012 – Silk Falls, Starr County //

She knew today was the day. She had to face him then leave Starr County forever. This was going to be the hardest day of her life. She was shaking from the moment she woke up, knowing that Hannah and Mason would be arriving around 11am.

She went downstairs at 9am. He was already down there, sitting on the sofa, reading his paper.

"You ok sweetie?" Earl said, peering over the paper as she walked down the stairs.

"Fine."

"Are you sure? You've been very quiet recently. I feel like I've hardly seen you."

"Do you remember the night you took us to that gig in Great Falls, Daddy?"

"Of course!"

"Do you remember what happened after the gig?"

"I drove you both home."

Earl knew what Rachel was getting at but he couldn't tell her. He knew how ashamed she'd be about what had happened.

"What else happened, Daddy?"

"I don't think I like your tone, young lady! I took time out of my weekend to drive you to a gig at which you proceeded to get involved in illegal activities. I was then the one who had to deal with the aftermath!"

"YOU TOUCHED ME, DADDY, YOU RAPED ME."

Rachel burst out crying. Earl's face turned to thunder. He slammed his paper on the table and got up out of his seat.

"EXCUSE ME? YOU ARE MY DAUGHTER. HOW DARE YOU ACCUSE ME OF THAT?"

Rachel saw he was shocked and had no idea how she had come to such a conclusion. Rachel could see his eyes were the colour of fire and he was both angry and upset she had made such an accusation.

"I caught you, Daddy, in the back of the SUV. You had unzipped my pants and you were..."

"I WAS CLEANING UP THE FUCKING MESS. YOU HAD PEE'D ALL OVER THE BACK OF MY CAR."

Rachel didn't believe him.

"You're my daddy. Why did you HAVE to do this? You have RUINED my life."

"Next time you go around accusing people of such serious crimes, you better get your GOD DAMN facts right. After we dropped Hannah off, you were mumbling something. I then heard a sound so I stopped the vehicle and had a look round as I thought it might be a snake. I opened the back of the SUV and found the whole DAMN seat wet as well as your pants. I HAD to take them off to clean up the fucking mess!"

"I don't believe you, Daddy."

"What the HELL do you want me to tell you, Rachel? I did what you said. That would be a lie. I left you for ten minutes to go into Murphy's to get some wipes."

"I SAW you, Daddy. I FELT you inside me. I've been sore for weeks because of what YOU did."

She stopped for a second, struggling to compose herself.

"I'm pregnant."

"GET OUT OF MY HOUSE RACHEL. NOW! HOW DARE YOU LIE LIKE THAT! GET. OUT."

Earl picked up the lamp from the sideboard and threw it against the wall opposite to Rachel. It smashed into a thousand pieces. Rachel had never seen him like this. She was fearful of what else he might do so she ran out of the house.

Once she was far enough away, she sat down next to a tree and phoned Hannah.

"Babe, I'll be there in about twenty minutes."

"He tried to kill me, Hannah. I stood up to him like you guys said I should and he tried to kill me. Where are you? I need to come round."

"WHAT? We have to tell Sheriff Fowler now and have him arrested!"

"No. I just want to leave, forever. I never want to see him again."

"What did he do though? You said he tried to kill you?"

"He didn't touch me. But after I told him I knew he'd raped me and saw what he did, he flew into a rage like I've never seen before. He picked up the lamp on the side and threw it against the wall next to me. He shouted at me to get out of the house. I've never been so scared, Hannah. I can't face him again."

"I wish you'd have waited for us to come round. I'm at home. I'll call Mason and tell him to grab your stuff so we can leave today."

"Thank you."

Rachel put down the phone and started crying uncontrollably. She'd never asked for this. She'd never wanted her life to end up so hopeless that she couldn't even trust her own father. She picked herself up and walked over to Hannah's house, sobbing.

Trees covered Hannah's shack with mountains stretching behind. It was perfectly located as the shack was hidden from anyone standing above or on the opposite side of the Emerald River. There was a great fishing spot outside too, which helped give Hannah everything she needed.

Rachel saw Hannah waiting for her at the top of the mountain trail.

"I'm so sorry Rachel."

Rachel just ran into her arms sobbing again.

"I've never seen him get that angry, Hannah. Never. He destroyed that lamp. I was terrified. I thought he was going to throw it right at me."

"I've spoken to Mason. He's going to go round to get your stuff shortly. He sounded really angry on the phone when I told him what happened though."

"I wondered where Mason got his temper from, now I guess I know. I can't believe Daddy had that all these years and I never knew."

****

Earl was in the house still cleaning up the mess of the broken lamp when Mason arrived to collect Rachel's stuff.

"What are you doing here, Mason?" Earl asked, as his son walked in to the living room.

"I think you know Pop. Rachel is so scared. She never wants to see you again. Heck, Pop, I don't want to see you again. I can't believe you'd do something like this."

Earl was tired. He had done nothing wrong. He had tried to look after his daughter. He knew he shouldn't have to explain himself like this.

"Your sister never gave me any chance to properly explain what happened, Mason. Do you really think I'd abuse her? That I'd rape her? She's my daughter for god sake. She had taken something at the gig she went to, so had her friends. I was furious but I know kids will be kids so I didn't say anything and just drove them home.

After I'd dropped Hannah off, Rachel started to mumble something which I couldn't hear. I then heard a sound, which I thought might be coming outside the car, so I stopped to take a look. I then checked the back of the car, I found the back seat soaked and her pants were wet too, so I stopped off at Murphy's to get some wipes and clean the mess up. I was in there ten minutes, no more. When I got back, I took her clothes off because they stank. I used the wipes to clean her up before driving her back and getting her into bed at home. I guess she stirred and saw me."

"She said she felt you inside of her. How could you do that, Pop? How could you? You know she's pregnant, right? How the hell is she going to raise a kid at 20?"

Earl could see the fury in Mason's eyes but wasn't in any mood to bite back.

"Look Mason, I am not going through this again. If you don't have anything else to say, please just leave."

"You don't get it do you, Pop? Rachel never wants to see you again. She's leaving Starr County for good."

"Then I suggest you get her stuff. I will not have my own children accusing me of something so disgusting. I raised you both to think better and judge based on fact. I loved you. Dammit, I STILL love you."

Now it was Earl's turn to break down. The pure raw emotion of both arguments and feeling like he was going to lose both his children was too much for him to bare.

"Perhaps you should have thought of that before you molested her, Pop."

"JUST GET HER DAMN THINGS AND GET OUT MASON."

****

Mason arrived at Hannah's about an hour later. He had packed all of Rachel's clothes and possessions into two suitcases. The girls met him at the top of the mountain path.

"What happened?" Rachel asked.

"Well, Sis, he hates you for what you said. He maintains he never did it and can't believe you don't trust him. He said he was wiping you to clean up all the mess when you woke up. He never wants to see you again either and said you broke his heart."

Rachel burst into tears.

"You… do believe me that this happened… don't you?"

"Of course, we do! The doc phoned me last week, she's really worried about you."

Rachel's eyes widened.

"What did she tell you?"

"Nothing, just that she was worried and wanted to make sure you're ok. You know, doctor-patient confidentiality n' all that – she can't tell anyone shit without your permission."

Rachel wasn't sure how she'd be able to tell Mason that she wasn't pregnant. She knew he'd be so angry she'd lied to him.

"So what else happened with Dad?"

"He got really angry again and started smashing more stuff. I just got your shit as quickly as I could and got the hell out."

"Thank you so much," Rachel hugged her brother. "I'm sorry you had to go through that for me, but I'm so grateful."

"Anytime, so long as you and the baby are good," Mason said. "Are both you ready to go?"

"Yup," Hannah said. "You good Rach?"

"Can't wait! Let's get out of here."

Mason put all the bags and suitcases in the back of his truck. As he was doing so, Hannah whispered to Rachel,

"When are you going to tell him you're not pregnant?"

"I'm not," she whispered back. "He'll never forgive me for lying to him. Let's just get to the mountains and I'll figure something out."

"All done. Ladies, let's go!" Mason said, lighting a cigarette.

As Mason pulled out of the layby onto the road to get to Owl Creek, Rachel looked at her Connect timeline on her phone. She noticed a strange advert come up for something called 'Enlightenment'. She noticed they were based in Starr County, which she thought was odd as she'd never seen or heard of them before. The website showed they were near the Phoenix Mountains but didn't give an exact location.

'Oh well,' she thought. 'It's not like I'm ever going back there now'.

PART TWO

Interlude //
14th February 2013 // Phoenix Mountains, Starr County //

One day, you will find the path and everything will become clear.

Hope stood over the body feeling ambivalent. She felt pure relief that it was finally over but equally sad that it had to come to this. She had searched for him for months to no avail but as her mind had become clearer and the Messiah had trained her to use the Myst to her advantage, she'd sensed his presence numerous times before tracking him down to the Phoenix Mountains where she had laid a trap she knew he couldn't refuse.

The awful things that he'd done both to her and those closest to her would scar her for the rest of her life. She would never forgive or forget what he did.

Hope turned to Roland.

"Burn the body."

Roland signalled to two of the Enlightened. Hope watched as they did as they were told; firstly getting logs from the pile in the rail yard, stacking them to form a table then picking up the body and placing it on the pile of logs. Finally, they lit the ends and the bottoms of the logs with lighters.

Watching them closely, Hope could see tears in their eyes and she understood why. The body was that of their son.

Chapter Seven //
28th February 2012 – Sioux Pass, Wyoming //

He knew she wasn't pregnant. He couldn't work out why she'd lied to him. He hated that she felt she couldn't tell him the truth. He wanted there to be no secrets between them and he felt angry that she did not trust him. However, he wouldn't take it out on her. He would make that guy, Bo, from the gig, pay. Then no one would ever touch her again.

****

Mason dropped Rachel and Hannah off at the Walmart, east of Miller Creek in Sioux Pass.

"You got all your stuff, Sis?" Mason asked. "Happy to drive anything out to you if and when you need."

"Thanks, Mason, but I have everything plus FREEDOM are real secretive about their location. I promise you we'll be fine. We can look after ourselves and the guys will be with us. I like Bo a lot and want to see where things go with him."

"Ok. Promise you'll message me when you can, especially when the baby is born."

"I will and promise me you'll check in on mom and dad when you can too. I'll never forgive him for what he did but he is still our daddy." Rachel said.

"I will for you, Sis. But I will tell mom what that asshole did and I won't ever forgive him. I don't want him to have any part in Mason JR's life."

"You're having a boy? Congratulations! Promise to send me pics via Connect, Mason?"

Rachel was so thrilled she was going to be an aunt but also heartbroken that she wouldn't be there to see her nephew grow up.

"Of course I will, Sis! Right, I gotta go. Stay safe, tell the guys that if anything happens to you, I will find out and I will make them pay."

"We'll be fine! I'll message you soon," Rachel said, hugging her brother.

They watched Mason drive off, back towards Starr County. Five minutes later, Bo and Chad arrived in Chad's banged up 1988 Chevy Tahoe. It was almost falling apart and neither of the girls was particularly thrilled about being driven anywhere in it. However, Bo assured them it was very reliable.

"So where are we going, guys?" Hannah asked.

"FREEDOM are currently based near Mount Moran in Purpleshell National Park. We have to drive to Elk, park the car and then hike for a day or so to get there. We brought two huge tents with us and plenty of food," Bo said.

"Plus plenty of weed and shrooms!" Chad added.

"Shrooms?" Rachel asked.

"Mushrooms! Shroom trips are amazing. But you have to be in the right frame of mind and with the right people otherwise they can freak you the fuck out!" Chad said, laughing.

"You'll be fine," Hannah added. "If I can handle them, anyone can. Plus, Chad knows a few tricks to make sure the trips aren't too weird."

"Sounds like fun, I'm in!"

It took about an hour to get up to Elk. The roads were narrow and winding through the park. Rachel could see the snow on the mountain peaks glistening in the winter sun. She wondered if there was another place in the world equal in beauty to the mountains and lakes of Wyoming and Montana. She had visited other parts of the US such as Florida and Santa Monica in LA but she didn't really like either. Rachel's parents had also taken the family to London when Rachel was thirteen, which she had enjoyed more but it was still a very congested, built-up city. Rachel decided she wanted to explore more of the world one day and see if she could find any other places with such vast and beautiful landscapes like Starr County.

Once they reached the car park in Elk, they parked up and got their bags out. The guys carried the tents and they started the long walk to Mount Moran. Just as they crossed the river, the sun began to dip in the distance.

"There's a ridge up on that smaller peak over there. That looks like a good spot to pitch the tents," Hannah was pointing to a smaller mountain, a mile ahead of them.

Once they got there and put the tents up, Bo and Chad went to get some wood to start a fire. Hannah and Rachel sat just above the tents on the peak of the mountain, overlooking the river below. The sun was setting and the view was beautiful.

"Do you think we made the right decision to leave Starr County?" Rachel asked, turning to Hannah.

"We had no choice. I know how hard that was for you and I'm so proud of you for standing up to your dad. What he did was awful and we should have reported him to Sheriff Fowler."

"I'm just worried I made a mistake," Rachel said, apprehensively.

"What do you mean?"

"Well, like I said Han, I caught him touching me. But what if what he said was true and he was cleaning up the mess when I opened my eyes? What if dad was in Murphy's at the time and what I felt was someone else?"

"I thought you said you were sure it was your dad?"

"I thought I was, but I just don't know any more, I was completely out of it at the time. I've felt like I'm being followed sometimes, before and after everything that happened, when I'm out but I never see anyone when I go to look around."

"Well, we can put all of that behind us now, regardless of who it was. Time for a fresh start," Hannah smiled and hugged her friend.

****

He watched them from a distance, sad that he couldn't hug her and tell her everything was going to be ok. He had thought about trying to get rid of Bo immediately, to make him pay for drugging her but decided to wait to find out where this FREEDOM group were so he could continue keeping an eye on her. He knew that if he acted too early, he'd ruin things. It had to be at the perfect moment.

****

Bo and Chad got back with some firewood and got the fire going. Hannah went into the tents and grabbed four beers. Both tents had two large sections, one which had room for a double mattress or two sleeping bags and the other which housed two seats, a mini cooler and enough room for clothes. Hannah opened the beers and they all sat watching the last remnants of the sunset.

"Who wants some shrooms?" Chad already had a small bag out with some dried mushrooms. "Grew them myself."

"I'm not sure it's a good idea for Rachel considering what she's just…" Hannah started to say before realising Rachel had already taken the bag from Chad and had consumed the entire contents.

"RACHEL! You have to stop stealing all our drugs!"

"Huh? Oh, I thought those were for me." Rachel said, innocently.

"Hannah, chill, there was hardly anything in there," Bo smiled.

"You're a freaking monster!" Chad laughed at Rachel. "I'm glad I put a small amount in that bag now. Here are the rest and YOU'RE NOT HAVING ANY!"

Chad pulled out another bag and gave the others the same amount Rachel had.

"You've got an innocent demeanour but boy, you don't half use it to your advantage sometimes, Rach," Hannah laughed.

Rachel blushed.

About an hour later, the four of them were lying on the ground, staring at the sky and chatting when Rachel started to feel a very strange sensation. She felt herself lift up and out of her body, into the sky. She started to fly over the mountains and rivers. She saw Hannah flying next to her. She felt herself expand to be able to see the whole state from far above her body. They started to fly back towards Starr County, over to Rachel's family house in Silk Falls. She could see her father was on the couch and looked upset. She heard him say to her mother that he wished he could turn back time and get his daughter back. Hearing that made Rachel feel upset. Whilst she hated him for what she thought he had done, he was still her dad. She wanted to fly in and tell him that she was sorry and she missed him but she had no control over her body.

Rachel and Hannah then flew north and saw a group of people gathered outdoors, praying to a man who was standing at the front of the congregation with a large cross. The man looked to be mid-thirties and had his hair tied up in a top knot. He wasn't wearing a shirt. As they passed over, he looked up right at them and Rachel felt him pierce her mind. Hannah immediately fell to the ground and into his arms before disappearing. Rachel shrieked but she couldn't do anything. She felt helpless as she floated away.

Rachel then flew up to the Phoenix Mountains over to Wade's house. She saw Wade's parents shouting at him for being a useless, lily-livered man-boy who was good for nothing.

Rachel's journey then took her back up to Tyran Gorge, to Mason's shack. No one was in. She thought that was weird as her brother said he was driving straight home and she was sure his wife would have been in as she was pregnant.

Rachel finally floated back over the mountain peak in Elk, where she'd left her body. She saw an SUV in the distance that wasn't moving. Its headlights were on. She flew closer and saw why her brother wasn't home. The SUV was on a hill about a mile away from where their tents were. Her brother was sitting there, in the truck, watching them with a pair of binoculars. She saw him look up at her in the sky. As she blinked, he was suddenly flying next to her. His face was like thunder.

"How could you do this to me, Rachel? How could you lie to me about the baby? I loved you, dammit, I STILL love you!"

Rachel tried to fly away but he grabbed her, forcing himself on her by kissing her and touching her in places that she didn't want him to. She couldn't do anything to stop him.

Finally, she felt herself evaporate and open her eyes. She saw Bo and Chad standing over her looking worried.

"My head hurts. Guys, where's Hannah?" Rachel said, slowly sitting up.

"She's here, next to you. She's not finished her trip yet, so don't touch her. I was worried about you, Rach. Your body started convulsing. You don't have epilepsy or something, do you?" Bo asked.

"Not to my knowledge. I'm fine, honestly. It was an amazing experience, thank you."

She kissed Bo. He smiled.

"I'm glad. I didn't know what to do for a second. You were out for five hours!"

"Is that normal?"

"Well, we were out for three," Chad said. "Anything between three and six is standard."

Hannah suddenly bolted straight up.

"That was AWESOME! Chad, you're the friggin master."

Chad blushed. He was beaming ear to ear.

"Han, can I... talk to you? Alone?" Rachel asked.

She looked at Bo and said "It's nothing bad, I promise, it's just... something I saw during the trip which happened just before we drove out here. I will tell you everything soon."

"Sure. It's no problem at all," Bo said. "I just hope you're ok."

"I am," Rachel smiled.

She turned her torch on and they walked back up to the peak where they had been sitting to watch the sunset.

"That was so amazing wasn't it? I just closed my eyes and was immediately in Gator's Stadium watching a game that we needed to win to get promoted and we smashed it out the park," Hannah excitedly told Rachel. "Once the game was over, we went dancing, I got wasted and I might have… fucked Chad. It was so good. It's kinda making me think differently about him now though. I've never been attracted to him before."

"Sounds like so much fun."

"You don't sound too enthusiastic, Rach?"

"I'm sorry! I am, of course I am! It's just my trip was a bit different."

"What happened?"

"So it started well. I saw myself leave my body and you were by my side. We flew so high we could see the whole state. It was amazing. We flew back home and I saw my old house. Daddy still was upset. He just wanted to turn back time and for me to come home."

She started crying. Hannah hugged her.

"Then we flew west and saw a group of people praying. There was a man at the front of the congregation who then looked up at us and you fell. I couldn't stop it and I was so scared."

"What happened when I fell?"

"You fell into his arms and disappeared. I shrieked after you but don't know what happened after because I then flew up to the Phoenix Mountains. I saw Wade being shouted at by his dad then flew to Mason's but he wasn't home so I flew back to where we are now and I saw why Mason wasn't home."

"Why?"

"He was sitting in his SUV on a mound about a mile from where we are now. He saw me flying above him and as soon as I blinked he was next to me, shouting at me that he couldn't believe I'd lied to him and that he loved me?!"

"WHAT?"

"He started kissing me and… touching me. I eventually evaporated and woke up after that."

"Wow, Rach. I mean… trips can do some fucked up things but that is another level cray."

"I don't think it was."

"What do you mean?"

"Do you remember I told you that I was worried I'd made a mistake about my dad and that maybe he was doing what he said? Well, what if I was right and when I did stir that night and felt someone… it was Mason?"

"That's crazy, Rach, he's been so kind and helpful to you and he's got a kid on the way! He'd never do that?"

"Exactly. He's been too kind and over helpful. I have to know. Before we carry on tomorrow, I'm going back to have a look over where I saw him. I won't wake you and I'll be back before you're all up. I have to know, Han."

"What do you think you'll find?"

"Tyre marks are good enough. No one would have parked where he was. If we find any marks, when we then get to FREEDOM, I'll lie and tell him they weren't there so we've gone to track them down further north."

"Don't you think telling him when we get there will be too late?

"Good point. I'll message him before we leave for Colter Bay."

"I'll come with you in the morning. We'll get back before the boys wake up. I don't want you going anywhere alone in case Mason or someone else is there waiting to attack you."

"Thank you," Rachel said.

****

He watched them for a few hours from a distance. He could see them sitting, then lying next to the fire. He assumed they were just talking. He wanted to make sure Rachel wasn't going to sleep with Bo again and that the guys weren't feeding her any more drugs. However, he was too far away to see properly and the girls had their backs to him most of the time. He decided to call it quits for the night and go back to the hotel before tracking them again in the morning. He knew Rachel was a heavy sleeper so likely wouldn't be up until at least mid-morning, which gave him plenty of time to get some rest. He threw his half-smoked cigarette out the window and drove off.

****

Rachel had set her phone to vibrate at 7am. She opened her eyes immediately and quietly woke Hannah. The boys were in the other tent so didn't hear them moving about softly. Unfortunately for them, it was teeming down with rain. They put their coats and waterproof trousers on then started to walk over to the mount, which Rachel had seen in her trip.

When they got to the area, Rachel recognised the mound immediately. They walked up there and had a look around. Due to the terrible weather, any tyre marks that could have been there had washed away.

"It's useless Han, there's nothing here! Let's go back."

"I'm sorry you didn't find anything Rachel, but trips can take you to some seriously fucked up places."

"Wait a sec, what's that?"

Rachel walked over to look at something on the ground. It was a burnt-out cigarette. She picked it up and inspected it.

"It could be anyone's Rachel. How do you know it's his type?"

"It's a roll-up. He smokes roll-ups with MW printed on the outside paper. This one is too far gone to see any letters. But why would anyone ever walk or even drive up here?"

"It could have been the cops. This is perfect for them to sit, unseen, so they can keep law and order on the roads. Or it could have just been blown up or down here by the wind, we'll never know."

"I guess. Let's go back. I'm sorry I dragged you out here."

Chapter Eight //
1st March 2012 – Colter Bay, Wyoming //

Once Bo and Chad were awake, all four of them packed up the tents and started to head north in search of Colter Bay, which was near Mount Moran. When they left, it was still pouring with rain but eventually, the wet weather disappeared and they were able to take their rain clothes off.

They arrived in Colter Bay late afternoon, grabbed a very late lunch at a local burger shack, and sat by the lake. Hannah told Rachel she wanted to talk to Chad alone so Rachel asked Bo to go for a walk. They left their bags with Hannah and Chad then began to walk around the right-hand side of the lake. The sky had completely cleared and the sun shone over the town.

"This is so beautiful, I'm glad we decided to leave Silk Falls and come here," Rachel said. "I've had a really difficult time since I first met you."

"What's happened? I know you've mentioned it before but you've not gone into any detail?" Bo asked.

Rachel told Bo about everything that happened after her dad collected them the night of the gig. She started by telling him about her waking up and feeling her dad's hand in a place it shouldn't be to telling her brother she was pregnant, then her trip and the feeling that she might be wrong about everything she previously thought about her dad. Bo listened and looked shocked by what she said.

After Rachel finished talking, Bo looked her in the eyes.

"It's going to be ok, Rachel. We're away from both of them now and can start again, together."

He kissed her then they walked, hand in hand, for a few minutes before stopping at a nearby bench to sit down.

"I get how hard that was for you and I can promise you that I will do everything in my power to make sure that no one hurts you ever again."

Rachel smiled.

"Thank you, I couldn't have asked for better friends or a better boyfriend. You're so sweet and so kind. I'm glad we're here now and not back home because I wouldn't want you anywhere near my family, knowing what both my brother and my dad would say about you or do to you."

"You're welcome. I just want to be there for you whenever you need me and I can hold my own against anyone."

Bo walked over to a pair of binoculars that were at the lakefront and put a coin in.

"Let's have a look and see if we can see Chad and Hannah!"

He moved the binoculars back toward the direction they'd walked from.

"He's kissing her! Looks like tongue, the works."

"WHAT?" Rachel said, excitedly. "Let me see!"

"Wait, someone else is using another pair of these binoculars on the lakefront not far away from them. Looks like a dude. Tall with blonde hair and wearing denim dungarees? Who wears those these days? He's looking over here, has been the whole time since I spotted him."

Rachel went white.

"Bo, I need to see. I think that might be Mason unless it's a very strange coincidence."

"Ah dang it, he's walked off down a street into town. But he had a moustache? We can try and run to see if we can follow him?"

"Ah in that case, maybe it wasn't him. He doesn't have any facial hair at all, but without seeing whoever you saw, I'm still nervous he could be tracking us. We need to get to Mount Moran as quickly as possible and find FREEDOM to ask if they can help protect us," Rachel said. "I know Hannah thinks it was the trip that has made me feel this way but I'm really nervous that what I saw was true, especially after you noticing that guy."

They walked back and found Chad and Hannah, who both had massive smiles on their faces.

"Look, we already know, so you might as well just tell us!" Bo laughed.

"Yeah we kissed! I'm totally digging the Chad!" Hannah laughed.

"Happy for you guys! Y'all are so cute!"

"Thanks, I'm going to bring him out of his shell."

Bo and Chad just looked at each other and laughed.

"I always liked you Hannah but I thought you thought I was some stoner dude," Chad said.

"Oh, I did. You have the shrooms to thank for changing my mind!"

"Score!"

"Han, sorry to change the subject but did you see Mason anywhere near you guys whilst we were away?" Rachel asked.

"Huh?"

"I put fifty cents into a set of the binoculars dotted around the lake and first, I saw you guys kissing but then I saw this tall dude with blonde hair and denim dungarees," Bo said. "But he had a moustache so Rachel doesn't think it could have been Mason. But this dude was staring over where we were standing the whole time I was looking through the binoculars before he walked off."

"No, we didn't see him anywhere but granted, we weren't paying too much attention to anyone else, not gonna lie! But I'm sure it wasn't him Rachel, I think you're just being paranoid because of the trip."

"All the same, I'd just rather get to Mount Moran and find FREEDOM as soon as we can," Rachel said.

"We'll go first thing in the morning seeing as we have the hostel tonight. Once we've left Colter Bay, we won't stop until we get there. It shouldn't be much further as I was told they are just over Mount Moran," Chad said.

They got to the hostel around 6.30pm and decided to share one room to save money. The room itself had two double beds and a large shower bathroom, as well as the TV, which picked up all the major news channels and a host of local stations.

One of the local news channels had a report on Starr County about Christ's Day and showed local churches from all around the area celebrating. Three or four from Silk Falls and Phoenix Mountains all had large white banners up all around them with a strange symbol. It had a black cross with two lines striking through the centre of the cross then horseshoes on the left and right sides of the cross that looked like an E on the left and three on the right.

"I don't remember ever seeing those at any churches in Starr County, Han?" Rachel asked.

"No idea, they've probably just put them up for Christ's Day," Hannah replied.

They stayed in the room for the rest of the evening and played games after turning the TV off. Rachel hoped that the following day would be the last trekking so she could try to relax a bit and not worry about any unwanted attention.

****

He woke up and made sure he was ready to go on time. He saw them pack the tents up and get ready to leave from the hotel window so rushed out to make sure he wasn't far behind. Once he'd followed them for a little while, he figured they were heading for Colter Bay so he went back and got the SUV then drove to town instead. He parked up, found a place to stay the night then found a fancy dress shop. He bought a blonde moustache, hoping that was enough to hide his identity in case either of the girls saw him in town.

He walked to the side of the lake, ducking into a shop as he saw them not far away. He watched Hannah and the taller guy split from Rachel and Bo who went for a walk along the right side of the lake. He went to the left side of the lake, not far from where Hannah and Chad were and used the binoculars on the lakefront to watch Bo and Rachel. He didn't trust Bo at all. Rachel could do so much better. He'd show her that when this was all said and done.

Chapter Nine //
2nd March 2012 – Colter Bay, Wyoming //

Just after they woke around 9am, Rachel sent Mason a message to check in. She thought her brother would get suspicious if she didn't. He didn't reply straight away but twenty minutes later, she felt her phone buzz. She didn't want to answer but the others encouraged her to.

"Hi Mason, how are you?" Rachel asked, trying to disguise any nervousness in her voice.

"Hi Sis, just making sure you're good and the guys are looking after you both? How are y'all getting on?"

Rachel could hear the noise of a baby crying in the background.

"Mason, what's that noise?" she asked, surprised.

"Well, I was going to tell you but Mason JR arrived at 3am this morning. Abi's doing real good considering he was born at home. I can already tell we're gonna have matching pairs of dungarees. This is the greatest day of my life."

"I'm so happy for you both! That's amazing! Can you send me a picture?" Rachel replied, relieved.

"Sure! He can't wait to see his aunt Rachel at some point soon."

"I can't wait to meet him at some point too. We gotta go but tell Abi I said hey and give her a hug!"

"Speak soon, Sis!" Mason said, hanging up the phone.

Rachel locked her phone then looked up, smiling at the others.

"He's home, he said Abi's just given birth to Mason JR. I'm so happy for them! At least it means I was wrong about what happened."

"Are you sure you trust him?" Hannah asked, concerned.

"There is no way he would have missed the birth of his son. I know my brother well enough to know that Mason JR and Abi are everything to him. At least we can now move on to get to FREEDOM without having to split up."

They had originally planned to separate with Hannah and Chad going on towards FREEDOM and Rachel and Bo walking further north for a few days to try to lead Mason in the wrong direction.

However, after talking to him on the phone, Rachel was satisfied that her brother was home, looking after his wife and baby. So they packed up their stuff, paid the hostel then set off towards Mount Moran for what would hopefully be the last part of their journey.

Chapter Ten //
2nd March 2012 – Mount Moran, Wyoming //

They crossed over the peak of Mount Moran and looked into the distance at the Matsuri mountain range. In the pass beneath, they saw tents and huts everywhere. At the bottom of the path down the mountain, they could see an entrance to FREEDOM. There was a banner with the town name running across the top of a huge wooden archway, made from branches and logs.

They climbed down Mount Moran slowly and reached the path to walk down to the entrance of the town. As well as the banner across the archway, there were two large freestanding banners on either side, which said WELCOME TO FREEDOM. Three men and two women were standing underneath the arch to meet them.

"Hey dudes! Welcome to FREEDOM!" the younger of the two women said. She had long auburn hair and blue eyes, which sparkled in the sunshine. "I'm Emily, the head of FREEDOM Town. This is Kayla, Matt, Jonny and Wes. We are here for the needs of all our citizens. We'll provide everything we can to help you fit in here."

"This is amazing!" Bo said. "We've been trying to find you guys for ages. We've just wanted to get away and start over. I'm Bo, this is Rachel, Hannah and Chad. We have our own stuff. If you'd be happy to give us a plot so we can pitch the tents, we can work or do whatever you need us to."

"That's awesome Bo. We'd love to have you guys join our community. We're totally chilled out, there's a very relaxed vibe here. Everyone does what they can and helps when they want. We only have a few small rules, which we ask you to follow. Whilst we permit the use of marijuana, we do not allow hard drugs. We don't operate a search policy, but we do ask and trust that everyone sticks to this rule. Also, assuming you guys are two couples?"

Rachel nodded.

"The only other thing we ask everyone is to be mindful of your surroundings and neighbours in terms of knowing what time they go to bed and making sure you stay quieter after that time."

"No problem at all. Thank you for agreeing to take us in," Hannah said.

"Follow us through. We'll take you to a spot that you can set up the two tents. Everyone pitches in a bit in terms of money for food and then we pool everything together to buy enough for everyone."

Emily and the others took them to an empty spot near the Matsuri Mountains. There were three tents to the left of where they were and much higher number to the right. Further to the left, past the tents, there was a shower and toilet building which Johnny explained was open all hours and cleaning the building worked on a rota basis. Then further back from the building, outside the town walls were woods as far as the eye could see.

"I wouldn't go into those woods though if I were you," Wes explained. "They are supposed to be haunted. There's a cabin in the middle, which is home to a sheriff who ran Tuscaloosa County in Idaho in the 60s and 70s. We've never seen him before, but we heard that he keeps himself to himself and doesn't like visitors."

Matt then ran through the current work schedule that included cleaning the toilet and shower room, cleaning the town entrance archways and taking turns to go and buy supplies from a local town.

"You should have enough room here," Emily said. "You've got really lovely neighbours on either side of you. Settle in, get your tents up and I'm sure they'll come and say hey."

Emily, Kayla, Matt, Jonny and Wes said their goodbyes and promised to check on them later. Rachel, Hannah, Bo and Chad set up the tents then Chad got some marijuana out. They spent the night smoking and chatting, watching the sun go down. None of the people living in the tents around them were around so they went to another part of the town and introduced themselves to some of the locals to find out more information about what it was like living in FREEDOM.

One couple who lived in a tent over on the Mount Moran side of town told them that they'd heard all the town heads were involved in open relationships, mostly with each other and that was also the case for a lot of people in the town as they were a very open community.

Once they got back from their walk, Chad and Hannah decided to retire for the evening. Rachel and Bo sat and watched the last remnants of the sunset before going to into their tent to chill.

Chapter Eleven //
28th June 2012 // FREEDOM Town, Mount Moran, Wyoming //

It took them a few months to settle into FREEDOM town and get used to living in tents and the daily routines that came with staying in the town. They got to know all their neighbours surrounding the tents fairly quickly.

To the left, there were two men called Willie and Ralph. Willie was around 7ft and was scrawny, with a moustache. He had scraggy brown hair that looked half-cut. Ralph was 6ft 5" and had a blonde bowl haircut with a full beard. Willie looked wrecked every time they saw him and Ralph usually encouraged Willie's behaviour. They were outcasts from New York who moved to Montana but eventually got kicked out of their rental home for bad behaviour. Ralph was a trained lawyer who graduated from Harvard but had fallen on tough times in the worldwide recession in 2008. Willie moved from state to state, never having a fixed abode or a job but was qualified biological sciences. They had been living on Ralph's saved wages to get food and score drugs.

In the tent to the right were Hayden and Sean, who had left home at sixteen with no plan and very little money. Sean was well built and worked out a lot. He was tall with brown hair and big bushy eyebrows. Hayden was short, coming in at 5ft and had beautiful long blonde hair. They had been dating since they were fourteen and were originally from Seattle. They had travelled to LA to work and hang out for a while. Sean got a job as a waiter and Hayden as a car sales woman. Hayden took to her role naturally and made a lot of money very quickly. They ended up travelling to Wyoming after hearing about FREEDOM so they could chill out for a bit with some like-minded people before moving on to another state.

In front of Hayden and Sean's tent were Amy and Carrie who were ex-army. Both were tall, at 5ft 8" and had long brown hair. Wearing sunglasses, they looked like twins. Amy was a sergeant major and Carrie a corporal. They'd both been dismissed from the army for misdemeanours relating to drugs so they decided to take some time off and try to relax with FREEDOM before finding a permanent place to live and start working again.

They all liked to hang out as much as possible as a group and had a lot of fun doing so. One night, Emily and the leaders had gone away to stock up on supplies. Willie was fooling around as usual when a man from another tent approached them.

"Hey y'all. I'm Dan."

"Hey Dan, how's it going?" they all said in chorus.

Dan was almost as tall as Chad but was stick thin. His long bright blue hair looked like it hadn't been washed for at least a week. He wore ripped trainers on his feet and was wearing ripped clothes too.

"Eh Yo, Willie, I got that shit you've been asking for."

"Yo, it's my main blud, sleepy Dan! Yo, man, that's awesome. How much do we owe you? Ralph, pay the man!"

Ralph did as he was told and in return, Dan gave Willie five packs of white powder.

"Willie, what's in those bags?" Rachel asked.

"Willie, please don't answer. She's a fiend and will steal them," Hannah said, jokingly.

"Well, my dearest Rachel," Willie said, in his poshest voice. "Sleepy Dan has procured us five backs of the strongest cocaine you'll find anywhere west of the Mississippi."

"I thought we weren't allowed anything like that?"

"As if I care, this stuff is far too good not to go up my nose!" Willie was already opening one packet and pouring some of the contents out. "Anyway, it's not like Emily would ever find out. She's far too busy with her boyfriend's Wes and Jonny."

"Boyfriend's?" Hannah asked.

"Yeah, she's fucking both of them. She calls it being in 'open relationships'. I call it being a dirty…"

"We get it, Willie, you're in love with her," Rachel smiled.

"No way dude! The only thing I'm in love with is this coke!"

"I saw your pupils dilate when her name was mentioned, Willie! And now you're turning bright red," Rachel laughed.

"AM NOT!"

"You are! There's nothing wrong with that at all though. Why would Emily not be open to having a third open relationship? You should ask her out."

"Ask her out? No! Who wants some uncle charles?"

"Not Rachel!" Hannah glared.

"Oh come on Han, she can have a bit if she wants!" Ralph said. "It's really good stuff, paid top dollar for only the purest and the best. Totally worth it."

"I wanna try it, Han, I'll be good I promise. Pinky swear!" Rachel laughed.

"Fine. But don't blame me if she snorts it all."

She smiled and hugged her friend. "Only kidding, kinda. Just don't go overboard."

Willie cut Rachel two small lines, which she then proceeded to inhale using a one-dollar bill.

"I don't know what that is supposed to feel like or taste like but my nose is tingling," Rachel said, sitting back.

"Sounds about right, it almost feels like you have a cold but so much better! Can you feel the hit yet?" Ralph asked.

"It feels nice," Rachel lay on the floor. She looked at Willie and fluttered her eyelids "Can I have some more, Willie?"

"I told you guys, she's a fiend!" Hannah said, cuddling Rachel. "You don't need any more right now, Rach. Give it time."

They chatted as a group for a bit then one by one started to go off to bed until Willie, Rachel and Bo were the only three left.

"I'm going to bed, you coming Rach?" Bo asked, yawning.

"I'll come in soon babe, just finishing my drink."

Bo kissed her on her forehead then went back to their tent.

"You want more coke don't you?" Willie sniggered.

"Not here," Rachel whispered. "Tomorrow night, meet me at the peak of the White Mountain. Night!"

She kissed him on the cheek then walked over to the tent she shared with Bo. Just before she went inside, she looked back and smiled.

Bo sat up as Rachel staggered into the tent.

"You ok, Rach? You look a bit drunk!"

Rachel lay down next to Bo on their mattress and kissed him.

"You know how much I love you, Bo, babe?" she said, slurring her words. "Time to show you…"

She went to kiss him again but fell on his chest and started snoring. Bo laughed to himself and rolled her on to her side.

Chapter Twelve //
22nd July 2012 – FREEDOM Town, Mount Moran, Wyoming //

She could see him waiting for her, the closer she got to the top of the mountain. As she approached the summit, he saw her and smiled.

"Come, my child. There is much to achieve. You have reached the summit of the holy mountain but now you need to prove your belief in our cause and walk the path of ascension. Follow me."

In front of her was a statue of the Messiah. Anyone a hundred miles away could see it due to the size. There was a door at the bottom of the right foot, which he opened and went through. She followed him.

In front of them, she could see a large circular staircase. He walked to the bottom and started to climb. She followed. There were over three thousand steps before they reached the summit. She was silent as they drifted through the door at the top.

The view in front of her was incredible. She saw the entire county, in every direction. She turned around and could see they had come out of a door in the arm of the statue.

"My child," he said. "You are not the first to undertake the path of ascension and you will not be the last. Some took the path before you and did not make it because they failed to believe in us, in me. The path takes no prisoners. This is the ultimate test of your loyalty and your faith.

I am asking you to trust me, believe that I will look after you and take care of you. What I am asking you to do is to walk across the stone book of Enlightenment where we now stand. Once you step off, you will ascend, higher than you've ever been before."

"Surely, I will fall to my death?"

"Not if you truly believe, my child."

She did as he asked. As she reached the edge of the stone book, her heart was pounding. She stopped and looked back. He smiled and said, "Go on, my child. I believe in you. Do you believe in me?"

"Yes."

She stepped off the edge of the book.

****

Rachel woke up sweating. She didn't understand why she'd had such a vivid vision of jumping off a statue with no parachute or wingsuit. She remembered she'd seen that man before in her trip. He was at the head of the congregation when Hannah had fallen from the sky. She didn't understand why this man seemingly was following her around in her subconscious.

Bo had made her some breakfast and a mug of coffee, which she gulped down.

"Baby, do you remember I told you about that weird church congregation in my 'shroom trip and how that man who was at the head of that congregation almost pierced my mind? Well, I saw him again."

"Oh? Where?"

"He was in a dream I had last night."

Rachel then proceeded to tell Bo what happened in the dream and how she woke up as soon as she had stepped off the end of the book.

"Rach, it was just a dream. I'm sure he's probably not even real. Everything will be fine."

"But..."

"Rachel. Bo. Could you come outside please?"

The voice sounded like Emily's. Rachel got dressed quickly and they unzipped the tent. Emily, Kayla, Matt, Jonny and Wes were standing outside with Hannah, Chad, Willie, Ralph, Hayden, Sean, Amy and Carrie.

"We've had some unconfirmed reports that this group were involved in taking illegal hard drugs last night," Kayla said. "We've just come to remind you that is strictly forbidden. If we hear about anything like that again, all of you will have your tents searched."

"I know how hard you all worked to get here, so please don't throw this away," Emily said. "We don't feel unreasonable setting a no hard drugs rule, it is there for everyone's health and so we can all enjoy each other's company. If you don't agree, you are free to leave at any time and we won't hold it against you. But if we hear any more reports, or find any evidence that hard drugs have been used, we will be forced to search your tents then if we find anything, evict you for good."

They all stayed silent as the group of town heads left. Most of the others scattered to go and do other things. As Rachel and Bo were about to head back to their tent, Rachel heard her name. She turned around to see Willie beckoning her back.

"Yo Rach, how do you feel this morning? Still up for later?"

"Rough as hell, but definitely up for tonight. Can I tell the rest of our group? I don't want to keep anything from them."

"Sure."

"Awesome. Was that what coke should feel like by the way?"

"Yeah, it was great wasn't it? Sleepy Dan's shit is usually pretty pure but that felt like it had acid in."

"Is it possible to mix drugs?" Rachel asked. "Like acid or mushrooms and put them in with cocaine? Even though I've never had acid before, I knew it must have had something like that in it because I had the craziest dream."

"Yeah man, definitely. That shit had acid cut in. It was so good. What was the dream you had about?"

Rachel then proceeded to tell Willie about climbing the statue and jumping off the book.

"That was when I woke up," she said. "Whilst I know that's a good thing, the dream was still super weird because I've seen that man before."

"What d'ya mean?"

"Do you remember I told you about the trip I had when I first tried 'shrooms before we got here?"

"Yeah, the one where you thought your bro was groping you? That was messed up man."

"So, this guy was head of the congregation in that church we flew over where Hannah fell. I've never met anyone like him in my life before and somehow he's infiltrating my dreams?"

"He's probably not even real, Rach. Chill. Have some of my smoke."

Rachel shared the rest of the joint with Willie, which made her feel worse, then went back into the tent she shared with Bo.

"Baby, Willie's just invited us out later to White Mountain so we can get away for a bit and enjoy ourselves without feeling like we're being watched. What do you think?"

"Hell yeah, I'm up for that."

"Awesome, I'll tell Hannah and Chad too then we can all go up together later."

Bo kissed her forehead and cuddled her.

"I told Willie about it that dream too and he said that the stuff we had last night was possibly laced with acid. I'm a bit nervous for later though because I don't understand why I keep dreaming about this man considering I've never met him and don't know who he is."

"Honestly Rach, he's not real, he can't hurt you."

Bo smiled at her then, to take her mind off it, they played a strip drinking game.

****

They walked up to the peak of White Mountain together that evening. On the way, they met Emily and Wes, who had been for a walk to Moose, a town near the border of Idaho and Wyoming.

"Hey guys. Where y'all going?" Emily asked.

"Just going for a walk into Idaho," Hannah said, lying. "Or is that not allowed too?"

"Of course it is. I hope y'all have a wonderful evening."

Emily smiled then walked off back to FREEDOM with Wes. Hannah rolled her eyes.

"Does anyone else really not like her?"

"She has to enforce the rules Han, otherwise they'd be no FREEDOM," Rachel said.

"Yeah I get that, but I dunno, I just wanna slap her."

"Forget about her," Chad put his arm around Hannah. "Tonight is gonna be all about getting as messed up as possible."

As they climbed to the top of the mountain, the few clouds left in the sky disappeared. The view was beautiful. They could see into Idaho looking north. Looking south, they saw Mount Moran and right below them, FREEDOM town.

Willie was waiting for them up top. He'd set up tarpaulin which created a shelter from any wind. There was a stack of rocks directly behind him then a large area of trees behind the rocks, which lead through to the other side of the mountain, overlooking Idaho.

Willie already had lines of cocaine waiting for them, which they eagerly devoured.

"Well, at least we won't get disturbed up here by any of those killjoys," Hannah rolled her eyes.

"And we don't just have charlie," smiled Willie. "Say hello to my little friends."

He pulled out some needles.

"Hell no!" Hannah said. "No way, there is a limit Willie and we're not touching that. I never would try heroin."

"Why not?" Rachel asked.

"It's seriously dangerous Rachel! It can mess you up worse than anything you've ever tried before, please don't do it, ever."

Rachel didn't say anything as Willie put the needles away again.

By the time they were ready to go back, the sun was starting to set to the east. They packed everything up and were just about to start to walk back down.

"I'll catch you guys up," Bo said. "Need to go to the bathroom."

Bo walked through the trees, towards the Idaho side of the mountain range. He put his drink down against the base of a tree. As he did so, he noticed a mobile phone on the ground by the other side. He decided he'd pick it up after relieving himself and have a look after, just in case he could then return it to its rightful owner at a later point. He stood against a different tree facing the cliff edge and unzipped his pants. He smelt a faint smell of tobacco so he had a look around to see if anyone else was nearby.

Within a split second, he felt something sharp slide across his throat and blood start to pour out. The last thing he ever heard, whispered into his ear before he collapsed to the ground was,

"You will never touch my sister again, asshole. Payback's a bitch."

Chapter Thirteen //
29th June 2012 – Matsuri Mountains, Wyoming //

Mason's plan had finally worked. He used a second device when he phoned Rachel back in Colter Bay, which she didn't know he had, to play the sound of a baby crying. He always kept a second phone just for tracking her, which is where he also kept the photos and videos he'd taken of her.

Once he had allayed any fears she might have had about someone following her, he tracked them up Mount Moran and saw the tents below. It took him time to prepare a plan. He sneaked in to FREEDOM to listen in on their conversations from time to time.

Mason had been staying in Colter Bay. He had no idea if his wife had the baby or not, she'd left him two months ago. She left a note saying that she was leaving because he was never around and he needed to seek help for whatever he was so obsessed with that he couldn't be home to be with her.

Once Mason had overheard Rachel making plans to go up to White Mountain, he knew that was the right time to strike. He'd arrived on the mountain top with little time to spare after leaving the hotel late in Colter Bay and without going to the bathroom. He'd been using his second phone to navigate his way up the mountain and had put it down at the side of the tree whilst he relieved himself. He lit a cigarette but realised after doing so that someone was coming.

After he'd slit Bo's throat with his trusty knife, he stubbed the cigarette out on the tree where Bo now lay motionless and started to make his way down the mountain quickly, making sure he stayed away from the trail he knew the girls and Chad would take.

He'd done it. He'd finally got rid of Bo. He couldn't stop smiling to himself knowing that Bo would never touch Rachel again. Now, she'd finally realise how much she meant to him.

****

Rachel started to get nervous that something had happened to Bo after they had been waiting a while for him to come back.

"He said he wouldn't be long. Do you think anything's happened to him?"

"He's probably just got lost or fell asleep, he's done this before," Chad ask. "He'll come back in the morning and will be fine."

"I'm going to look for him, it's almost dark and I don't want him having to find his way back later or in the morning if his hangover is really bad. Come with me, Han?"

"Let's all go," Hannah replied.

They walked the same path they saw Bo take through the trees, towards the edge of the mountain. Rachel was the first one to notice the blood. She screamed when she saw Bo lying against the tree motionless. The shock caused her to burst into tears and fall to the ground.

Chad didn't see the body at first.

"Rachel… What's wrong?"

Rachel pointed at Bo's body, her hand shaking.

"Bo?" Chad said, staggering back in shock, seeing his friend lifeless.

"Bo?" Hannah asked. "What do you mean? Where…"

She then saw the body and almost collapsed against one of the trees, before going over to Rachel and hugging her. Rachel was trembling.

"This can't be real, we're gonna wake up soon right?" Chad said, in pure disbelief.

He stepped back, away from the trees, not being able to comprehend what had happened. He didn't realise how close he was to the edge of the mountain. He put one foot too far back and before he or the others realised, he'd lost his balance and fell from the top of the mountain, shrieking until he hid the ground with a thud.

"CHAD!" Hannah screamed, before sinking to her knees in despair.

For the first time in his life, Willie realised the gravity of what had just happened. He walked over to both Hannah and Rachel who were on their knees, tears flooding down their faces and hugged them. As they were all kneeling, he noticed something out of the corner of his eyes.

"Yo, look at this," Willie said, pointing to the bottle of beer that was on the ground, next to the tree where Bo's body lay. "There's a cigarette near it too."

"What?" Rachel yanked herself up from the ground and grabbed the cigarette. She saw it almost brand new so she turned it over. It had the markings MW on the side.

"Oh my god. Han, its Mason. I can't believe I was right."

Rachel turned around to show her friend. As she did, she noticed a phone near the tree where Bo's body was. She picked the phone up and pressed the home button. There was damage to the screen and it was asking for a passcode. There was a picture in the background that she couldn't see as it was out of focus because of the passcode request. She was trembling as her fingers typed 722435, her name. The phone opened and had a naked picture of her in the shower at her parent's house as the background.

She felt the colour drain from her face as she turned around and showed Hannah.

"Mason," she repeated, shaking. "How is this possible? How could the trip have possibly been right? I need to go back to the tent. I can't..."

She broke down again in floods of tears. Hannah gave her another hug, not being able to stop crying herself.

Rachel slipped the cigarette and phone in her jeans pocket. Willie helped them both back to FREEDOM and the tents. When they got back, Rachel collapsed.

"Han, I can't...," Rachel sobbed.

"I know," Hannah said. "I can't either."

They both burst out crying again. Amy and Carrie heard the noise and came out of their tent.

"What's happened? Are you ok?" Carrie asked.

"Where are Bo and Chad?" Amy noticed. She saw Willie mouthing 'NO' but it was too late. Rachel and Hannah couldn't hold it in anymore and both screamed in agony.

"Yo, not tonight," Willie whispered.

"Come sleep with us tonight if you want to," Carrie gave them both hugs.

"That's kind of you," Rachel sobbed. "But we need to be alone tonight."

They said good night to the others then went into the tent Rachel and Bo shared and started crying again. They'd both lost two of the most important people in their lives and were struggling to deal with the shock.

"I... I don't understand. How can any of this be real? How could those 'shrooms show me something so real, yet something I wasn't even aware of till that point? This is freaking me out." Rachel said, still in total shock.

"If there is any way possible, I think we need to try and get some sleep tonight, Rach. We've so much we need to figure out tomorrow morning and I can't..."

Hannah broke down again. They both curled up in each other's arms and eventually managed to fall asleep.

The following morning, Rachel and Hannah woke up and decided to go for a walk on their own, back towards Mount Moran.

Before they left, they spoke to Hayden and Sean who said they'd get some help and get both bodies back so they could give Bo and Chad the funerals they deserved.

As they walked around the mountain, back towards Colter Bay, Rachel realised that Bo must have seen Mason along the lake that afternoon.

"I still can't believe you were right about Mason," Hannah said. "I'm sorry I didn't believe you."

"I messaged him this morning. He said he's been looking after the baby and Abi's been resting a lot. I asked him to send me a photo. He hasn't replied yet.

I also contacted Abi who told me that she'd left him months ago because he was never home. She said she'd been worried he was either seeing someone else or completely obsessed with someone or something. I told her everything that had happened and to make sure she didn't let him anywhere near the baby."

"What do you wanna do now? Do you wanna stay here with Willie, Ralph and the others or move on?"

"Where are we gonna go if we don't stay here? Everyone's so nice and I don't wanna leave," Rachel said, almost pleading.

"What about your mom and dad?"

"I need to go back at some point and talk to my dad but I can't face him yet."

They walked back around to the tents in FREEDOM and found the town heads waiting for them along with their other friends. Emily walked over to them and gave them both a hug.

"We just heard. I'm so sorry for what happened to Bo and Chad. If there is anything we can do within the rules, please just let us know."

The other town heads all gave them hugs then they all left.

"She just HAD to get that dig in didn't she?" Hannah said, wiping away the tears furiously. "Fuck your fucking rules, bitch."

"What did you tell them?" Rachel asked the others.

"Just the truth," Willie said. "We didn't mention anything about the drugs obviously but aside from that, the truth."

"Thank you," Rachel smiled.

****

It took a couple of days to arrange the funerals for Bo and Chad. Rachel and Hannah decided to cremate them. They found a small space on the other side of the mountain range from their tents, where the wind flowed over the border into Idaho. The town gathered at dusk and helped create a large log pile then laid both bodies on top. There was silence as Rachel and Hannah lit a smaller log then threw it on to the middle of the pile.

They stepped back and watched the fire engulf the two bodies.

Neither of the girls said anything as the others slowly walked back to FREEDOM. Once the fire had completely burnt out, the remainder of the town headed back to FREEDOM. Hannah saw Rachel walk towards the burnt embers of the logs and laid a necklace at the side that Bo used to wear. She saw Rachel mouth something but couldn't make out what.

"What did you just say?" Hannah asked.

"That's between Bo and me," Rachel smiled, through the tears. "Let's go home."

****

Mason knew he'd ruined everything as soon as he got back to the hotel and realised his second phone was missing. He couldn't believe he been so stupid to leave it there. He thought they'd find it but hoped none of them would be able to guess the passcode. The cigarette was dumb luck but leaving the phone behind was a fatal error.

Now he was worried that if Rachel did find it, he'd lose her forever.

Chapter Fourteen //
18th July 2012 – FREEDOM Town, Mount Moran, Wyoming //

Over the next few weeks, Rachel and Hannah found themselves spending more and more time with Willie, Ralph, Carrie and Amy. One evening, Willie and Rachel were walking in the mountains, further than Rachel had explored before.

"Where do you see yourself in a year from now, Willie?" Rachel asked.

"Heck, I dunno where I see myself in a week, Rach!"

"Do you think you're gonna stay in FREEDOM or move on?"

"I'm a drifter," he said, staring into her eyes. "I just go where life takes me. I enjoy drugs and getting messed up but I don't need them. I can stop whenever I want."

"Do you still have that Heroin?" she looked at him. "I need a proper escape. I can't stop thinking about what happened to Bo and about everything with my brother."

Willie took a pair of needles out.

"Do you trust me?" he asked.

"Yes."

"These are clean, sterilised needles. I know the risks and I'm not ready to risk myself or anyone else to getting infected by shit, dodgy needles. The drug is pure grade. Once we do this, we lie down and don't move. Just enjoy the experience."

She saw him prick her skin then inject the drug into her vein. She felt the drug rush into her bloodstream and she lay back as he told her to.

Before Willie did the same, Rachel softly said his name.

"Yes, Rachel."

"I don't want you to take this the wrong way because you know where my head is right now, but kiss me."

"What?"

"Don't overthink it, just kiss me."

****

Three hours later, Rachel and Willie lay on the ground, naked.

"That… was… AMAZING," Rachel said. She looked at Willie and smiled. "Thank you."

"I… don't know what to say," Willie looked confused.

"You don't have to say anything. You helped me out in a time when I needed a friend and I am very grateful for that."

"I almost feel… manipulated, used. But on the other hand…"

"See! We don't need to tell anyone about this!"

"Yo, that works for me" Willie said, smiling.

They put their clothes back on and headed back to FREEDOM. On the way, back they met Hannah, Amy and Carrie who had all been for a walk to Moose.

"What have you two been up to then?" Carrie winked.

"We've been for a walk ourselves. Just needed to clear my head and think things through," Rachel said. "Ralf was gonna come but said he had a few calls to make so it ended up just being us."

"What have you taken?" Hannah asked.

"What do you mean?"

"I can see your pupils look really small and you don't seem to be able to focus properly."

"Mason contacted me, Han, he said…"

"Don't change the subject Rachel! What drugs did you guys do?"

Rachel went very quiet just as Willie threw the needles away in the trash before they got back to FREEDOM. Willie then walked ahead with Amy and Carrie whilst Hannah took Rachel's arm and saw the mark where the needle had penetrated her skin.

"RACHEL! I can't believe you did that! Heroin is so dangerous," Hannah said, looking worried.

"Please stop shouting at me, I needed an escape and it was awesome. Willie looked after me," Rachel started crying.

"I'm sorry, it's just I'm worried about you."

"Then come with us next time, Han. You'll enjoy it and it'll take your mind off Chad and everything that's happened too."

"You said Mason contacted you?"

"He asked me how I was and if I'd had the baby yet so I told him that I lost the baby. He asked what happened and if Bo had done anything to hurt me. I told him what happened, how we found Bo and how we'd also discovered the cigarette in the bottle of beer with Mason's initials on. I told him that I'd found his phone with naked pictures of me on and that I was going to get it tested by the police for fingerprints. He didn't reply and blocked me."

"Wow. Do you think you'll ever see him again?"

"I don't want to think about him. Let's just get back and get some sleep."

****

As soon as Mason read Rachel's message, he realised he had no choice but to block her. He was mortified she'd found out it was him who had killed Bo.

He had to make sure she didn't know where to find him as she would probably tell the cops. It broke his heart thinking about not being able to see her but he had to protect himself. It would be worth it in the end. He would make her see that he was the right person for her.

Chapter Fifteen //
19th July 2012 – FREEDOM Town, Mount Moran, Wyoming //

Rachel opened her eyes. She was standing in a field of yellow flowers as far as the eye could see. The only other thing in front of her in the field was a tree with a swing. She saw a person sitting on the swing, rocking back and forth. It was Bo.

She nervously approached the tree. Bo eventually stopped swinging when he saw her walking towards him. He got up and hugged her for what seemed like an eternity.

"Why Bo? Why did you have to need to go to the bathroom right then? Why couldn't you have waited until we got back to FREEDOM?" Rachel cried, helplessly.

Bo just stood there in silence.

"I have to go on without you. I can't... do it. I need you. I miss you so much."

Bo just stood there in silence.

"I know it was Mason, I wish you'd never met me so you and Chad would be safe somewhere, instead of both dead. I love you with all my heart," Rachel sobbed.

Bo just stood there in silence.

"Having to get over you has been the hardest thing I've ever done. I... I slept with Willie. I needed the release. I couldn't cope. I'm so sorry."

Rachel lowered her head in shame as Bo walked away in silence. As he walked away, Rachel could see arcus clouds forming in front of him.

"Bo! Please don't leave me. I can't... please!"

It was too late. Bo disappeared in the distance. Rachel felt the hailstones hit her head. The Derecho storm had already started. She ran as fast as her legs would carry her but it wasn't fast enough. She heard Mason's voice in the clouds, laughing before a gust of wind blew her off her feet and a fork of lightning hit her chest.

****

Rachel woke up crying. The enormity of everything that happened had finally hit her. She'd never get to see Bo again, never feel so happy being held in his arms, never feel his soft lips caress against hers or never stare into his beautiful eyes.

"Rachel, are you ok?" Hannah asked, after Rachel's sobs woke her up.

"I gotta go. I don't think I can stay here much longer, Han," Rachel said through the tears, as she got dressed then left the tent and ran down towards the street out of town.

"Rachel!" Hannah shouted after her, but it was no use.

Rachel messaged Willie and asked him to meet her in Moose. She booked a hostel on her phone then walked into town. She sat by the river and thought about how it had all gone wrong after that one night out at the gig. She wanted the world to swallow her.

Willie joined her half an hour later.

"Yo! Sup?"

"You, me, private hostel room. Let's get messed up."

"Game!"

They walked through Moose to the hostel. Moose was a small enough town with one grocery store, a New Frontier gun store, the hostel Rachel had booked, a restaurant, a local police station and a gym.

They checked in to the backpacker's hostel and got their private room. Within five minutes, Rachel was lying on her back on the bed completely zoned out in a euphoric state.

She opened her eyes and saw she was in the middle of a desert. She felt herself spring up from the ground then hurtle back down towards the surface headfirst. She burrowed deep down, beneath the ground. She saw the remains of what looked like a huge boat that was buried deep beneath the surface. She continued burrowing through the mantle then the outer core. She got hotter and hotter the deeper she went until her body evaporated from the heat.

Her eyes pinged open again. She looked like she was in a void somewhere. Everything was completely white surrounding her except she saw a lot of people staring at her from a distance. They were all shouting 'RACHEL' in chorus. As she looked closer, she saw Bo, her family including Mason, Hannah, Chad and Wade all standing with their backs to her, refusing to join in. Despite her trying to get them to turn around, none of them moved, but the chanting kept going, getting louder. 'RACHEL RACHEL RACHEL RACHEL." Willie then appeared and she realised he was the one shouting her name louder than anyone else. She saw him start shaking her so hard that she shattered into a million pieces.

She opened her eyes again and saw she was back in the hostel room. She saw Willie wasn't the only one in the room. Emily, Kayla, Matt, Jonny and Wes were also there.

"I'm sorry, Rach. Someone knocked at the door and I stupidly opened it not thinking." Willie said.

"We warned you. We warned you that if we found evidence of hard drug use, we would expel you from FREEDOM without ever being allowed to return," Emily said.

She picked up an empty bag with the needles in. "I know you have had a really difficult time recently Rachel, so I will not report this to the cops, but the pair of you have two days to pack your things and leave FREEDOM for good."

"How… how did you…?"

"How did we know you were here?" interrupted Jonny, pacing up and down. "Emily works here. She happened to walk past your room outside and saw Willie injecting you with Heroin then proceeded to… take advantage of you. Did you know he was doing that Rachel? Bo's been gone for less than a month!"

Rachel stayed silent until they gave up trying to ask her questions about the relationship she was involved in with Willie.

"Two days, both of you," Kayla said. "If we find you're still around town, we will call the cops and have you arrested."

PART THREE

Interlude //
4th July 2016 // Silk Falls, Starr County //

It's the end, but the moment has been prepared for.

She heard him behind, following her. She knew he was intent on bringing death and destruction to all who opposed him in Starr County and despite her best efforts, she wasn't sure that she had enough Enlightened in the region to help stop him.

She looked behind and saw him a few hundred yards back through the trees. The only way she could lose him was by hiding in the caves. She had to use everything the Messiah had taught her, so she concentrated her mind on the caves and almost felt the Myst envelop her but heard a huge explosion at the last second. She looked round briefly, breaking her concentration. She knew she didn't have time to mourn, she had to keep going to get to the caves. Not far now.

She was at the caves within a couple of minutes. She went deep into the darkest cavern, taking the most complicated route she knew in order to lose him. She waited until dusk then crept out of the caves slowly and carefully, making her way to the border of Silk Falls and the Phoenix Mountains. She knew if she could make it across the border, Brother Joel would protect her the short distance she then needed to travel to get to The Haven.

She could see her brothers and sisters guarding the checkpoint. She closed her eyes as she ran and prayed the Messiah would keep her safe to the border but as she carried on running, she heard a shot from a distance.

She fell to the ground. She could see blood start oozing out of her shoulder. She was in agony, trying to crawl closer to the checkpoint and trying to shout to her brothers and sisters. But it was no use. No sound was coming out of her mouth.

He walked up and stood by her side, looking into her eyes as she lay on the ground, crying.

"Goodbye Hope," he said, pointing the gun to her forehead.

Chapter Sixteen //
20th July 2012 - FREEDOM Town, Mount Moran, Wyoming //

"So what do we do now?" Hannah asked. "I don't think we've any choice but to head back to Starr Country. There's nowhere else we can go for now."

"How do we get back?" Rachel asked. "Neither of us can drive."

"I'll drive you," Willie offered. "Chad's banger is in Elk, right? That gives us two nights camping where we get can get fucked up."

"I'm not getting in a car with you whilst you're on drugs, Willie," Hannah rolled her eyes. "Plus I think Chad must have had his keys on him as I can't find them in the tent. I couldn't touch him after they found him, I just couldn't."

"I won't be on drugs, I'll make sure I'm sober. I can hotwire a Chevy easily so chill about the keys. It'll be fine, babe," Willie grinned.

"Don't call me babe," Hannah said, looking disgusted. "Rachel, where are we going to go? What are we going to do?"

"Have you ever heard of 'Enlightenment', Han? I found them online before we left Starr County. I've just had a look and it could be the place for us! They are a group who are looking to bring peace and harmony to the world."

"Do we have any other choice right now? Let's do it."

"Is Ralph coming?"

"Hell yeah! He's our back up driver in case I do get trashed," Willie laughed.

Once they had packed away all their gear, they said goodbye to Hayden, Sean, Carrie and Amy. Willie lit a joint, which they passed between the four of them, then headed off through the town and up towards Mount Moran. Just before they walked through the entrance of FREEDOM town, Hannah threw the end of the joint to the side of one of the huts.

****

They got to Chad's Chevy a couple of days later in Elk. Willie and Rachel had been shooting up both evenings so were both fairly worse for wear. Ralph had joined in on the first night and Hannah stuck to smoking weed. When they got back to the Chevy, Ralf offered to drive, at Hannah's request. Willie managed to hot wire the vehicle, after almost electrocuting himself, then promptly crashed out in the back seat along with Rachel who was looking very gaunt and her speech was slurring badly.

"Rach, you've lost a lot of weight over the past few weeks, I'm really worried about you," Hannah said.

"Ok, Mom! I'll eat more junk food," came the reply from the back seat.

Hannah didn't say anything.

"I'm sorry, Han, this is my way of coping. I have nothing else in my life right now."

"I'm just trying to help you and I'm worried about you getting hooked on Heroin. It is such a destructive drug. I'll always be here for you but I can only help so much if you won't help yourself," Hannah said, turning around and smiling at her friend.

"I'll get over it".

Ralph drove them back. As they got close to the tunnel that connected to Owl Creek, they stopped to fill up the Chevy with gas and get some groceries. They left Rachel asleep on the back seat. Ralf filled the vehicle with gas whilst Hannah and Willie grabbed some food.

"Sixty bucks for the gas and twenty for the groceries," the store attendant said.

"Ralph, pay the man!" Willie said, twirling his finger in the air.

Ralph did as he was told.

"Hey, you folks aren't going to Starr County are you?"

"Yeah, we're going home. Why do you ask?" Hannah queried.

"Strange things going on there, child. The Owl Creek farmers lost a lot of their land, weird new radio stations all over the county, Sheriff Fowler suddenly getting a lot of his deputies quitting and these strange banners in churches. Something ain't right."

"Thanks, mister. We'll keep our eyes open."

"That's such a load of scaremongering, fake news!" Willie sniggered. "There is no way any farmer I've ever known would give up land for anyone and police jobs always have high turnovers. I don't know why people make such a big deal out of it."

They all got back in the car. Rachel was finally beginning to stir from her slumber.

"Hey... guys..." she slurred. "Are we there yet?"

"Rachel, sort yourself out. Enlightenment will never let us be part of their community if they see you this messed up. Gosh!" Hannah said, clearly frustrated.

"She'll be fine by the time we get there," Willie said, confidently.

They got on the freeway and drove through the tunnel. Before they entered, Hannah noticed the beautiful weather. Ten minutes later, they exited the tunnel into torrential rain. The clouds were so dark, it was impossible to see very far ahead.

Within an hour, Ralph had driven through most of Owl Creek. They hadn't seen many farmers out and no cops but they put that down to the bad weather. All the churches they had past had no banners up at all.

"So where exactly is it we're heading to, Han?" Ralph asked.

"Rachel said they were on one of the islands but she didn't know which one. From what I know, there is nothing on Christmas Island except a disused bunker and an abandoned church. The only other island I know is tiny so it can't be that. Let's just drive past Christmas Island towards the Phoenix Mountains and see what's there."

Ralph did as Hannah suggested. They got to the north of Owl Creek just as it was starting to get dark. The rain was still coming down so hard it was barely possible to see more than a hundred yards down the road. Thick clouds enveloped the entire car.

Directly in front of them, Hannah noticed the start of one of the lakes. She'd not ever done much travelling around the islands of Starr County. She could see a huge road built over the lakes that linked Owl Creek to the Phoenix Mountains. As they started to drive down the road over the lakes, she noticed Christmas Island was on the left and a small island to the right, just as she had thought.

They saw a signpost on the right as they drove past Christmas Island.

"Enlightenment - next left"

"That's weird, there's a turning I can just about see in the distance but there is nothing there but a road," Ralph said.

"Take it and let's see where it goes," Hannah said.

Ralph took the left turn and saw that the road went right up to one of the mountains and became a tunnel. They drove for another ten minutes through the tunnel, looping around a few bends before they saw light at the end. When they came out, they noticed the rain had disappeared, the clouds had thinned significantly and they could see they were on another road, driving across another lake right in the middle of the mountains. In front of them were some large white gates with a banner hanging across the top saying:

"Welcome To Enlightenment"

As they drove up to the gates, two guards stopped them from going any further. Ralph wound the window down to talk to the guard. They noticed the most beautiful, relaxing music fill the car. They couldn't tell where it was coming from.

"Welcome to The Haven. Proceed to the Church of Souls and ask for James and Joel. They are expecting you," the guard on the left said to Ralph. "Please have a drink of water, y'all look thirsty."

The guard passed through four cups of water. Willie took two and gulped his down. Ralph also drank his. Hannah had a sip then left hers in the cup holder.

"Expecting us?" Ralph asked Hannah.

"How do they even know who we are?" she replied. "We'll soon find out I guess!"

Rachel had stirred just as the guards passed through the water to Willie and Ralph.

"My head hurts, where are we?" she said, sluggishly.

"Enlightenment I think," Hannah said.

Willie passed Rachel her cup of water, which she gulped down. She immediately began to feel a lot better.

Ralph drove through the gates. Hannah looked to the left and the right side of the road. She could make out what looked like vineyards that had some strange plants growing and ran for half a mile on both sides ahead of them. Due to little remaining daylight, she couldn't see more than a few yards on either side however the road was well lit with bright white lights which made the slow drive down the pathway easier.

Once they had gone by the plants, they could see a building to the right that had some white vans and pickup trucks parked next to it, then further on from that was what looked like a Swiss-style church.

Surrounding the church, they could see trees with the purest, whitest flowers on. Then further, a few more developments that had scaffolding up and looked almost built. All the trees and buildings had white lights surrounding them at the bottom as well.

They parked the vehicle near the church. As they got out of the Chevy, they heard the same calming music playing as they'd heard when Ralph wound down the window by the gates.

"It's all so angelic, so beautiful," Rachel said. She walked closer to some of the trees and smelled the flowers. "Where is this place?"

"Home," a voice from behind her said.

Chapter Seventeen //
20th July 2012 – The Haven, Starr County //

I watched from the church tower as they arrived. As soon as I saw her, I knew God had kept his word and returned her to me. Everything I had prepared had worked and now Enlightenment could have Hope. She was finally here.

****

Rachel turned around and saw two men standing outside the church. The man on the right was the shorter of the two by a good few inches. He had ginger hair, slicked back with a comb and gel, a full beard that was also ginger and tattoos covering his arms. He wore a black waistcoat with a navy blue shirt underneath which had the arms rolled up. His trousers were grey and his shoes were black.

The man on the left was well over 6ft and had dark brown hair that was long on top and grade zero on the back and sides. He wore a bright green jacket with a darker green shirt underneath, combat trousers and walking boots.

The man on the right spoke.

"You are home. We have been expecting you. Please follow me."

"Who are you?" Rachel asked.

"I am James Eve, this is Joel Eve. We are here to welcome you into our community."

"How did you know we were coming?" Hannah asked. "Wait a sec, I know you. I've seen you before, in the bar in Jefferson Canyon earlier this year."

"The Messiah has foreseen your arrival for some time. He is very much looking forward to meeting you all in due course. And yes, I was in the bar in Jefferson Canyon," James smiled.

"But who are y'all? What is Enlightenment?" Rachel asked, confused.

"The Messiah founded Enlightenment because he saw much sickness in the world. The sick need hope and to be free from sin. We offer a place within our community to help the sick find themselves again, to free them from their transgressions and help them understand why sin is wrong. As you walk around the island, you will talk to individuals who joined our community previously and can tell of their own experiences as to how the Messiah has helped them personally. However, all that is to come. For now, we will take you into the Church of Souls to meet our brother, Joshua before finding you a room so you can rest for the night."

"Thank you so much! That's so kind of you," Rachel said.

They all walked silently behind James and Joel who led them into the Church of Souls. As she entered the church, Rachel saw two white doors on either side of the hallway right by the entrance. The corridor ahead was also completely white with tiles on the floor, lights at the bottom of the wall and white paint on covering the ceiling and walls.

James opened the door to what he called the inner sanctum and they stepped through. Rachel immediately felt a strange sensation. It felt as if she belonged here and she'd finally found a place she could completely be herself. She just hoped they would accept her.

In front of them were twenty pews on each side. The hall was large enough to fit at least five hundred people. They could hear the same calming music playing that they'd heard all around The Haven. Near the front, a man was sitting with his back to them, with his head drooped, looking at the floor.

"Brother Joshua. They have arrived," Joel said.

Joshua stood up. He had bright long blonde hair, with no facial hair. He was wearing white robes that covered his whole body and his head.

"My children. Welcome to Enlightenment. Welcome to The Haven. Welcome to the Church of Souls. I am glad you have found us. The Messiah talks highly of you all. He is looking forward to meeting you in due course. First, you must rest. Brother James will take the women to the Ashbrook. Brother Joel will take the men to the PIT. We will reconvene in the morning."

"Can we not stay together?" Hannah asked.

"I'm afraid that is impossible, my child," Joshua said. "The Messiah forbids men and women sleeping in the same room who are not married as it is a sin. Rest well, tomorrow is a new day."

Joshua smiled at them then turned and walked to a room at the back of the church. James and Joel led them out through the same corridor to get their things from the Chevy. Once they'd collected everything they needed, Rachel and Hannah headed north with James to the Ashbrook which was just in front of the buildings in the final stages of being built. The girls turned around briefly and saw Willie and Ralph walking off in the opposite direction with Joel.

Once they arrived outside the Ashbrook, James stopped and turned to Rachel.

"Please take this key. You are in Room 4673," he took out a key from the inside of his waistcoat and gave it to Rachel.

"Hannah, you are in Room 3323," he took a second key out of his other waistcoat pocket.

"The rooms should have everything you need including en-suites in case you wish to wash in the morning. We serve breakfast between 8am and 9.30am at the building to the right of the church before daily prayer at 10am. Sleep well."

"Where are Willie and Ralph?" Hannah asked.

"They have gone to the PIT which is through the trees behind the church. They will see you at daily prayer tomorrow. Sleep well."

James left Rachel and Hannah and walked back to the church. It was pitch-black outside, so the girls went up to their rooms and found they were next to each other with a connecting door in between the two rooms.

"So what do you think of this place?" Hannah asked.

"It's beautiful. I feel so relaxed here, so at home. It's like this was always where I was meant to be."

"I don't trust 'em. It's all too... perfect."

"I think they seem like lovely people, Han. They have given us everything we could want, completely free. They have offered to help us. What more could we ask for?"

"Nothing is ever free Rachel. Ever. Please remember that."

"Ok, well, I'm going to bed. Night!"

Rachel hugged Hannah then closed the door in-between the two rooms.

Hannah wasn't tired so she waited until she thought Rachel had gone to sleep then snuck out of her room. She tried to get out of the front door to the building but found it locked. She circled round to the back and found another door, which, luckily for her, was open. She crept back to the Church of Souls. There was still a light on inside so she carefully opened the door. Once inside, she closed the door behind her then opened the white door on the right-hand side of the hallway. Behind the door was a winding staircase. She went up the stairs and found a pair of sliding doors open, which led to a balcony overlooking the inner sanctum.

She crept through and heard voices. It was Joshua, Joel and James below her.

"Are the women safely asleep Brother James?" Joshua asked.

"They are, Messiah."

"What of the men, Brother Joel?"

"They are in the PIT as you requested."

"Good. We will use them all to further our plans. The boy Willie was the one I sold the scopolamine to, which he believed to be heroin. All four of them should be ready for purification. Very soon, once Hope is ready and willing to embrace my vision, everything else will fall into place."

Hannah looked over the balcony carefully. She was shocked at what she saw. Joshua was a completely different person. He had brown hair and a full beard with pale yellow aviators covering his eyes. He now wore a silver jacket with a turquoise grey shirt. She crouched down again as she knew they could not find out she was there or they'd likely kill her.

"Brothers, soon we will be in a position to take over this wretched county, to start purifying the sick and take out the demons who oppose our vision. It has taken us time to find the place we needed and our Hope but God has always had a plan. I knew she would come to me."

"She?" Hannah thought. What did they mean? She looked over the side of the balcony again at Joshua. The more she looked at him, the more she thought she recognised him. Where had she seen him before?

Suddenly, it came to her, that night at the gig with Rachel, Chad and Bo. She saw him standing on something, elevated from a crowd of people who were watching him speak. He was the one who she felt pierce her mind and had then disappeared in a flash.

As that thought crossed her mind, she realised that Joshua had stopped talking and was staring at her with a psychotic grin as she peered over the balcony. She collapsed to the ground, gasping for air. She couldn't breathe.

Chapter Eighteen //
21st July 2012 – The Haven, Starr County //

Hannah woke up in her room in the Ashbrook gasping for water. She saw a couple of bottles on the side, which she assumed must be for guests. She opened one and gulped the contents down before immediately spraying as much of the liquid back out again as quickly she could. She had no idea what was in the water but it tasted vile, different from any kind she'd had before. She looked at it and noticed a strong blue tinge to it that she hadn't seen when she'd opened the bottle.

She got a flask from her backpack, which she knew had water in which had not been tampered with as she had filled it from a spring near FREEDOM. She finished that off before opening the curtains. The sun was shining over the Church of Souls. She could see a building behind the church in the distance that she assumed must be the PIT. She looked to the left and saw the two buildings in the last stages of being built. Further away to the right of those buildings, there was larger building, which was mainly made of glass and then further right of the glass building was a large forest that covered right up to and including the PIT. She could see the sun glistening on the lake which surrounded the island and then beyond that, the mountains that rose high into the sky.

She knocked on Rachel's door.

"Rach, you up?"

She saw the door handle start to turn and Rachel walked in, still looking like she was half-asleep.

"Morning, Han. How did you sleep?"

"Rachel, we need to get out of here. This place is fucking psycho."

"What are you talking about?" Rachel asked, bleary-eyed.

"Last night, I couldn't sleep so I went downstairs to go for a walk. I also realised I forgot my makeup bag from the Chevy so I wanted to get that. I tried the front door but I couldn't get out. I found another door open so went through that and walked to the Chevy to get the bag. I went to come back but realised there was a light on in the church so I went to take a look. I went through and tried one of those two white doors, which ended up taking me upstairs.

I heard Joshua, Joel and James talking. They are planning to take over the whole county and 'purify' all of us. I looked over the balcony and saw Joshua looked nothing like he did when we were there yesterday evening."

"What do you mean?" Rachel looked at her, confused.

"He had dark brown hair. He wasn't the same man, Rachel! I also realised I've seen him before, at the gig we went to in Great Falls. When I came out of the bathrooms, a man was standing on something, talking to a large crowd of people. Do you remember me asking you if you'd seen him when you came over?"

"This was before we'd taken anything right? I think I was too excited about using the fake ID for the first time, to be honest. What happened next?"

"Just after I remembered where I'd seen him, I realised that they'd stopped talking and Joshua was looking at me. I collapsed on the floor. The next thing I remember was waking up in bed in my room."

"Sounds like you had a really bad dream, Han. Let's get dressed and have some breakfast. I hope they have sunny side eggs!"

"It wasn't a dream, Rachel! I know what I saw. I wanna go... go home."

"This is my home now, Han. I've never felt happier. I feel like they can help me overcome my addictions and help me get my life back. I want to try to give them a chance."

"Rachel, what I overheard last night... I can't put myself in danger and I feel like staying here would be doing that. I heard Joshua say that he was the one that sold Willie the heroin you have been injecting. He also said to them that it wasn't heroin. Then I heard Joel call Joshua 'the Messiah'. Joshua also said once he'd purified us, he was going to turn one of us into something. He called one of us 'Hope'?"

"All that time you called me crazy because of the trip I had and the weird dreams afterwards? Well, now it's my turn. You had a dream, Hannah. A DREAM. It wasn't real. Did you inject some of Willie's heroin?"

"God no! Rachel, you HAVE to believe me. We need to get out of here."

Hannah was almost pleading with her friend but Rachel wouldn't have it.

"I'm going to have a shower then go down for breakfast. I messaged Willie and he said that he and Ralph will be going down soon so would see us down there. Please, Han, come down for me. Try little bit longer. We've only just got here."

They got dressed, walked out of the Ashbrook and saw people going in and out of the building on the right of the church, so they walked over to have a look.

As they arrived, they saw James and Joel at the entrance.

"How did you sleep?" James asked.

"Very well thank you," Rachel smiled. "The air is so clean here, so pure and fresh. It's wonderful."

"I'm glad you are happy here, Rachel. Enjoy your breakfast and we will see you at daily prayer," James smiled. "How did you sleep, Hannah?"

Hannah looked at James and noticed his eyes had changed from smiling at Rachel to an evil glance at her as she walked through into the room.

"Good, thanks."

She felt a hand on her shoulder.

"If we catch you outside after curfew again, the Messiah will not be so lenient," James whispered. He removed his hand and she carried on walking.

Hannah caught up with Rachel who was walking past the long tables inside to the breakfast buffet. There were a good few hundred people in the room, eating or queuing for the buffet.

"Oh my gosh, they do have sunny side eggs!" Rachel turned to Hannah, looking excited.

"Did you hear what James just said to me?"

"No?"

"He warned me that if they caught me out after dark again, Joshua would do something to me."

"Are you sure you heard them right?"

"YES! My god, Rachel!"

"Let's just sit down and have something to eat and get some strength back, Han, I'm famished!"

"Rachel! Are you listening to me?"

Rachel turned and faced Hannah with tears in her eyes, clearly frustrated.

"Look, I need this, Hannah. I need this to work out. I have nothing. My brother raped me and then killed my boyfriend. My family hate me because I accused my dad of abusing me and even if he didn't, I can't go back there. I need this to work out. I need something to believe in. Please, I don't have anything else left."

"I know you've lost things and I know how much you've been through, Rachel but I have too and I can't stay here. I do not trust these people."

"Give it the rest of the day, Han. Please? For me?" Rachel pleaded.

"Fine, but if I still feel the same way tomorrow then I'm leaving, with or without you."

They got some breakfast from the buffet. Rachel got waffles, syrup, bacon and the sunny side eggs she had been craving. Hannah grabbed a breakfast burrito with some orange juice.

They went to sit down at an empty table but there wasn't one available, so they approached a table with only one man sitting there.

"Hey, do you mind if we sit here?" Rachel asked the man.

"Not at al... Rachel?" he replied.

"Do I know you?"

"You probably won't remember me, I'm Pastor Frank E Gore."

"Oh my god, I had se... never mind," Rachel had to stop herself from telling the Pastor about what happened with Bo in his church in Jefferson Canyon. "It's really good to see you, Pastor. What are you doing here?"

Pastor Gore was a tall, slim man in his early fifties. Rachel remembered that her mum and dad had taken her and Mason to church when they were children but they had stopped going once they became teenagers.

The pastor lowered his voice.

"I'm spying on this sect. They seem so wholesome but I don't believe they are for a second. The Eve family are up to something. I can't put my finger on it yet but I'll be damned if I let some religious sect take over our county."

"See, Rachel!" Hannah hissed. "I told you they were evil!"

Rachel ignored her.

"Pastor, what makes you think they are up to something, what have you seen?"

"I've seen them doing some work on manufacturing some kind of substance. I don't know what it is yet but I'm determined to find out."

"Well, I am happy to help you, Pastor. Rachel here thinks the Eve family are angels and are going to cure her of all her worries," Hannah rolled her eyes.

"Have you seen any members of Enlightenment in the community, away from The Haven or doing anything strange though, Pastor?" Rachel asked.

"Not before I came in here but I know they've been slowly trying to work their way through encouraging as many people as possible to come to The Haven and they've taken over a couple of local radio stations. The previous owners have strangely disappeared without a trace. Something big is goin' down."

"So you've no concrete evidence regarding what happened to those radio broadcasters though?"

"Well, no but I'm close to finding some."

"Rachel, HOW can you be so naive?" Hannah asked. "Pastor Gore has confirmed what the shop attendant said just before we got back to Starr County about the radio stations, I also told you what happened last night…"

"What happened last night?" Pastor Gore asked.

Hannah told him everything that she had seen in the inner sanctum of the Church of Souls. Pastor Gore looked horrified.

"So you think they're planning to take over the entire county?"

"I think there is every chance they could be looking to do more than that, eventually," Hannah said. "We have to stop them. I'm going to use today to see what else they have to say as they've promised to give us a tour of the island."

They finished eating breakfast and cleared their stuff away. The Pastor told them that because they had only arrived last night, they wouldn't be expected to help clear up yet but they still took their plates out back. They went to walk to church but James stopped them.

"Hannah, Joshua has requested your presence. Please follow me. Rachel and Pastor Gore, you may join the others at daily prayer with Joel."

Hannah watched as Rachel and Pastor Gore walked off.

"Where I am going?" she asked James.

James didn't say anything but started walking towards the other end of the church. Hannah followed, as she didn't want to put any more suspicion on herself. James went to the back of the church and opened a door. As Hannah walked through, James told her to go up the stairs on the left-hand side of the building. She saw the back room in the church looked like an office. There was a safe, a desk, with a chair and table at the back, which had a phone on it with a pad of paper.

Hannah also noticed on the sidewall, there was a large white banner with a symbol on it. The symbol was one she'd seen before. When they were in the hostel in Colter Bay, it was on the news article about churches celebrating Christ's Day. It was a black cross with two lines striking through the centre of the cross then horseshoes on the left and right sides of the cross that looked like an E on the left and three on the right.

"James, what is that banner supposed to represent?"

"You ask a lot of questions Hannah. Too many questions."

James opened the door at the top. Hannah walked through and saw Joshua sitting in a room overlooking the inner sanctum. She heard James close the door behind her.

"Why am I here?" she asked. "What are you going to do to me?"

Joshua turned his head. His long, blonde hair glistened as the sun shone through the glass panes.

"I'm not here to harm you, my child. I am here to help you," he smiled. "Enlightenment isn't what you think. Let me explain.

We started with just a few. Brother James, Brother Joel, the Messiah and I. We want to help the sick and make this world a better place. Greed, lust, immorality, sin and temptation have taken over every part of life in America today. What we are offering is a way out, a way to learn to control your urges, let go of your immoral behaviour, realise that money isn't everything and atone for your sins. We want to help free America.

We are slowly showing the sick that they can be better by listening to and trusting our teachings, changing their behaviour and believing in this project. I am not here to take over the county or to hurt you despite what you believe."

"So why am I being threatened by James and Joel?"

"We are not threatening you, my child. We have strict rules here. You were outside after Brother James had left you at the Ashbrook for the night. An hour later, you were walking near the church. It became clear you were sleep walking but Brother James heard you talking in your sleep and saying some awful things about the Messiah, that he wants to hurt people and take over the county. The Messiah is a truly peaceful person. He is here to protect us all."

"But you are the Messiah, I saw you last night, in that room," Hannah pointed down to the inner sanctum. "You had dark hair, a dark beard and aviators on. It was almost like..."

"I was a different man?"

"Yes. But your voice was the same."

Joshua put his hands on Hannah's cheeks and kissed her forehead.

"You were dreaming. Having, what sounds like, a nightmare. Please believe me when I say, you are so important to our plans, Hannah. I need you to invest in us, in me, so we can get the buy-in of everyone in this county. Give me time after daily prayer has finished today to take you all around our island and show you what we are doing to help those who have chosen to join us. Hopefully, I can help you realise that we mean you no harm."

Joshua smiled at Hannah.

"You may re-join the others for prayer."

The door opened and James signalled for Hannah to leave. Hannah got up and went to walk downstairs. As she got through the doorway, James put his hand on her shoulder.

"You may join your friends through the main entrance, prayer is about to start."

He took her through the main door and let her find Rachel, Willie, Ralph and Pastor Gore.

"Are you ok?" Rachel asked her as she sat down.

"I'll tell you after," she whispered, looking up at Joshua who was still in the room above the inner sanctum. He was staring down at her with that same sadistic grin from the previous night.

Chapter Nineteen //
21st July 2012 – The Haven, Starr County //

After daily prayer, they all went to leave the inner sanctum but were stopped by Joel.

"Joshua will meet you in ten minutes inside the front gates. Pastor Gore, you may join them if you want."

Joel wished them a good day then walked over to carry on overseeing the building projects near to the Ashbrook. Hannah saw James walk out from the back of the church then get into one of the white vans and drive off the island towards Starr County mainland. They followed the van on foot towards the gates to meet Joshua.

"So what happened to you, Han?" Rachel asked, as they walked.

"James took me to see Joshua. He was in a room looking down on the inner sanctum of the church. He just told me that what I believed about Enlightenment wasn't true and that they hoped I would change my mind once they've shown us around. He said they weren't threatening me and had strict rules regarding going out after dark not being allowed."

"See, I told you there was a reasonable explanation for it!"

"Except after I joined you guys, I saw him staring down at me and he had the same evil, sadistic smile, which I saw last night. I just don't trust any of them, but I will go on the tour."

"Thank you," Rachel smiled. "Willie, how was your evening last night?"

"Pretty gnarly, we got taken to this PIT place and left to fend for ourselves pretty much so we just ended up shooting up."

"You did, I didn't," Ralph said.

"You know that's not heroin right?" Hannah said.

"What do you mean? Of course, it is," Willie smirked.

"No, it's not. Who did you get it from?"

"I dunno. Some dude with some funny glasses that had dark brown hair and a beard."

"What did you just say?" Rachel asked, looking alarmed.

"The dude had yellow-tinted glasses, a beard and long dark brown hair which he tied up in a bun on his head. He was some random guy we met on the way to FREEDOM before we arrived there."

"Han, that's the guy who was in my trip and my dream."

"Rachel, that's Joshua. That is the Messiah. I saw him last night in the church."

"Joshua has blonde hair and no facial hair at all. That's not possible."

Hannah ignored her, turning back to Willie.

"That man you saw who sold you the heroin, did he say anything weird?"

"Nope, just that he heard I was looking for gear and he had the best stuff available. Oh and he said he give it to me free if I shared it with others because it gave him hope."

"Gave him hope?"

"Yeah, I thought that was weird as well."

Hannah turned to Rachel.

"I think Joshua has been following me somehow, he's been using you to get to me. He has wanted to infect all of us and I think he plans to kidnap me. Think about it, in your trip, I fell into his arms as soon as he looked up. I think he's obsessed with me."

"Han, Joshua has been nothing but nice to us since we got here. Please don't get us all kicked out. Let's just do this tour, spend the rest of the day observing and then you can sleep on it and if you really wanna leave tomorrow, I won't stop you. But I'm staying here. I told you, I need this to work out."

As they reached the gates at the end of the island, they could see Joshua waiting for them.

"Welcome my children," he said, with open arms. "What you see in front of you is the start of something really special. For too long, the good people of Starr County have been calling out for help and we are here to answer that call. We are developing a Haven, an island of peace and tranquillity.

You can see plants on either side of you. We are using these to work on getting a formula for a purely plant-based substance, which clears the mind and allows us all to think more freely. We are looking to help the sick who have had their thoughts clouded by sin, abuse and darkness.

We want to show the sick what it is like to be truly free and feel truly blessed by this wonderful gift that God has bestowed upon us; life. We want the sick to feel empowered and to work together for the greater good of both themselves and the human race.

We are building and developing the tools to help the sick to become better versions of themselves. As you know, we have the food hall to the right. We only import the best and purist ingredients for all, free of preservatives and impurities.

You have all seen the Church of Souls just behind that. Opposite the church, we have built a meditation and confessions chamber called Sync. This is for those wishing to confess their sins privately, should they feel the need to. No one shall be forced if they do not want to.

We are also building housing for the ever-growing number of sick coming to The Haven to seek Enlightenment's help. Behind the residential buildings, you can see the Garden of Babylon. This is a place of tranquillity, relaxation and peace.

At the end of the island, we have a school with an auditorium for optional teachings from the Messiah's book of Enlightenment. Classes are daily at 11am and 2pm.

Do you have any questions so far?"

"Yes," Hannah said, "What's in the forest at the back of the church?"

"That is what I was moving on to next," Joshua smiled. "The Forest of Eden has two buildings, the PIT and the holy temple of Gethsemane which is only available to those who truly need God. No one is allowed in there but the Messiah and the sick individual who needs 1-1 help."

"Finally, further at the back of the island, to the south is where Joel, James and I have our biosphere quarters."

"So what are we expected to do whilst we are here?" Hannah asked.

"That's entirely up to you, my child. We are a community so everyone pitches in to help however how much you do per day plus what classes and prayers you attend is your decision."

"So what if we decide not to do any?"

Joshua smiled.

"We will only provide help for those who embrace our vision and invest as much in us as we invest in them. There are those who have joined us in the past who took the tour and decided Enlightenment wasn't right for them. We held no feelings of ill against them and let them leave as they wished. If you decide this place isn't for you, you too are free to leave as you wish."

"What kind of things does the Messiah teach?" Rachel asked.

"James, Joel and I take it in turns to present teachings from the book of Enlightenment and work on both individual and group challenges. Topics range from mindfulness, awareness, sin, critical thinking and anxieties. I'd very much like you all to come and join the class this afternoon."

"We'd love to," Rachel said.

"That is excellent news. I shall mark you all down as attending and will leave you to look around until then. We serve lunch between 12.30pm and 1.30pm. See you later."

Joshua smiled at them and walked back to the church.

"So? What do you think?" Rachel asked Hannah.

"I don't trust this place at all and I don't trust any of the Eve's. However, I will stick around for one more night. I want to see what these lessons are like."

"I don't feel so good, guys," Ralph said.

"What do you mean?" Pastor Gore asked.

"I feel sick and woozy like I've got a really painful headache."

"Have you taken any drugs, Ralph?" the Pastor asked, concerned.

"Not since we left FREEDOM. I wonder if it was something I ate?"

"What did you have for breakfast?" Hannah asked.

"Just fruit and pancakes?"

"Did you try any of the bottled water?"

"Yeah – had a whole bottle of it and then slept the whole night without waking up once. It was a nice deep sleep as well, haven't slept like it for ages."

"Did it not taste funny?"

"It tasted a little bit off but didn't think anything of it, to be honest. I was just thirsty."

"How did you feel when you woke up this morning?" Hannah asked.

"Refreshed, but had a bit of a headache right on top of my head."

"Hannah, what's with all the questions? Why are you so suspicious of everything that's happened since we all got here?" Rachel asked.

"You just don't get it, do you, Rachel? That water tasted like they've put some kind of substance in. I can only assume it's whatever they are growing here. It was foul. I tried some but spat it back out straight away.

Do you still have a headache Ralph? Come back to our rooms later and we'll have a look and see if we can see anything."

"They're not allowed in our rooms remember?" Rachel said.

"Screw their dumb rules!" Hannah screamed.

Luckily, there wasn't anyone around to hear Hannah's outburst. Rachel looked embarrassed.

"Han, if we break their rules, we will be kicked out and I told you, I can't afford to let this opportunity go, I have to make this work and I want to help make the world a better place. I believe Joshua's vision and want to help him succeed.

Ralph, do you think you can make it through until after lunch and the class at 2pm?"

"Yeah, I think so – so long as I can get something decent to drink."

"Here," Rachel said. "I've got one bottle of water left from the spring outside the tent we had in FREEDOM."

Ralph drank the bottle, which helped him feel a lot better. They went for lunch then helped clear everyone's dishes away into the dishwashers before heading to class.

They arrived at the auditorium and took their seats. Rachel looked around. The auditorium was massive. It could easily fit a thousand people inside. Joshua appeared at the head of the class.

"Welcome," Joshua said. "Welcome to those who have just joined us and those who have been with us from the when we launched the Enlightenment Project. Welcome all. Today we are going to be discussing mindfulness, how one person's words and actions can have an effect on another's wellbeing. Let's start with an example of criticism."

Joshua turned to a man who was sitting about halfway across the room, right in the middle of the group.

"Todd, if I sat with you each morning at breakfast and was vocally critical of your choice of food every single day, how would you feel?"

Todd stood up. He was about 6ft tall, had black wavy hair and a goatee. He had a vest tank top on, which had the American flag on.

"I'd be pissed off Joshua. No one pisses off the Todd," he said, with a very strong northern accent. "And, if you kept doing it, I'd smash your face in."

"Todd, we've spoken about this. Violence is never the answer."

"Sorry Joshua but I get angry when someone calls me fat."

"No one is making any kind of negative comment towards you, Todd. We'll talk about this after," Joshua said. "Can anyone else tell me what they'd feel if someone called out what they were eating all the time?"

Rachel stood up.

"I'd feel upset and anxious. I would think about it a lot and worry that I am in the wrong all the time about what I eat. I'd be much more aware of others looking at me whilst I'm eating and constantly think I'm too fat or not good enough as a person because of what I'm eating."

"Thank you, Rachel," Joshua said. "Whilst there is no right or wrong answer to this conundrum, what Rachel has just said is what most who come across this kind of behaviour would find they start feeling. Even if the individual who had said the comments to begin with didn't mean anything by them, the person on the receiving end could feel personally attacked and paranoid by what was said to them."

"This is ridiculous," came a voice with a deep southern accent from across the room. "If you can't take a little criticism, you're a god damn hippie snowflake."

"Carl, there is a big difference between constructive criticism and being critical to the point of nasty," Joshua had turned to the man who had spoken.

"People get so upset over everything man. I'm so sick of this cry baby culture. Everyone's so god damn sensitive."

Rachel saw Carl had a red, angry face. His eyes were dark brown, which just added to the look of anger. He was a big man, but built well, certainly not someone she'd want to be on opposite sides of a fight with.

"The world has become a much more critical place, Carl. We're all different. There is also a difference between having a laugh and constantly criticising people for the sake of it."

"So what do we do to change it then, Joshua? How do I get around these god damn pussies who can't take a harmless comment?"

"For starters, Carl, the comments you're making aren't harmless. They can have a large impact on someone's mental wellbeing. Have you ever heard of the English proverb 'if you've got nothing nice to say then don't say anything at all?' I believe that rings true in many situations today. However, if you want to try to help someone and give them more motivation, why not try positive reinforcement. Complement the choice of food then ask if they've given thought to a healthy option to go with it and see what they say."

"So pussyfoot around them?"

Ralph and Hannah sniggered. Rachel stood up again.

"Hi Carl, I'm Rachel. I'm new here but I just wanted to say that I understand where you are coming from. However, for us to become a more positive society and help everyone feel better about themselves, positive reinforcement is a really good first step and has been proven to work in many communities."

Joshua looked at Rachel and smiled.

"Thank you, Rachel. That was pretty much what I was going to say, word for word. Society has become sick and we need to help everyone to heal from that sickness. That starts with changing the narrative. Therefore, I want each one of you to go away from today's lesson and focus on coming back tomorrow afternoon with an example of how you have tried to be more encouraging or promote positive reinforcement. Tomorrow we will discuss some individual situations, what you said, what they said and how changing your own narrative left you both feeling."

Joshua went to give more examples of mindfulness before finishing the class by talking about some projects that were ongoing and needed some extra help. He wished everyone an enjoyable rest of the day.

"Carl, Todd, Ralph and Hannah. Please can you remain please?"

Everyone started to file out of the auditorium.

"Rachel, what the hell was that?" Hannah asked.

"Huh?"

"Why are you sticking up for Joshua? He's obviously lying and doesn't legitimately care about helping society. I can't believe you can't see it."

"I believe he does Hannah and I want to help him."

"Have you been on drugs again?" Hannah asked, looking deep into her friend's eyes.

"We got rid of everything before we arrived, you know that." Rachel dismissed the accusation.

Hannah looked at Willie.

"Not sure what you're looking at me for Hannah, we haven't had any since…"

"I can see it in both your eyes. I'm telling Joshua."

"Do you think that'll do you any good?" Rachel hissed. "Why does it matter if you're just gonna leave me anyway?"

Rachel started to get upset. Hannah hugged her.

"I'm sorry Rachel, but I just do not trust these Eve's and I can't believe you do!"

"I have to, please understand, I have to give this my all. I'm trying hard to fit in but I need to do this and whilst I want you, I need you by my side if you don't want to be then please at least give me your blessing that you'll understand my reasoning?"

"I do understand but I don't know if I can join you on this journey. Ralph and I have to go but we'll catch up with you once Joshua has finished with us."

Rachel, Willie and Pastor Gore left the tent.

"My children," Joshua said. "I notice you made unwelcome comments or noises during the class."

"We did?" Hannah asked, pointing at herself and Ralph.

"I heard you," Joshua said, directly looking into her eyes. "We are all here to support each other and help the sick get better. You are all sick. I would like all four of you to join Brother James at the PIT at in ten minutes."

"What for?"

"To help you get better," smiled Joshua, placing his hand on hers.

Hannah moved her hands away quickly, almost horrified at the thought of Joshua touching her.

They left the classroom. Rachel, Willie and Pastor Gore were waiting for them.

"What happened?" Pastor Gore asked.

"Joshua said we're sick and the four of us need to go to the PIT to meet James now," Ralph said, almost in fear.

Hannah noticed the look on his face.

"Are you ok Ralph? You look... scared?"

"I don't remember. Did we go outside last night?" Ralph asked Willie.

"Not to my knowledge bro? I was sound asleep all night!"

"I remember... being outside and James was there. I remember seeing the inside of a building. It was so dark, he held up an oil lamp. We were walking down a corridor to a door at the end on the right. I couldn't see what was in the room after he opened the door. It was so dark. I... I remember being held down in a chair then the lights went completely out."

"That sounds horrifying. Sorry Rachel, but I've made my decision, I'm done with this place," Hannah said. "Are you coming or staying?"

"I'm staying Han. I told you," Rachel said, dismayed.

"I'm staying too, there's nothing for me anywhere else now and I wanna clean myself up and help people, same as Rachel," Willie added. "I've had enough of being a bum. I want to make a difference."

"What about you Pastor, are you coming?" Hannah asked. "We can give you a lift back to Jefferson Canyon if you want?"

"I will take you up on that offer Hannah, that's very kind. I have enough information and evidence collected now and will continue to monitor from Jefferson Canyon before deciding on if we need to call for some help to stop Enlightenment."

"Great, so meet y'all at the Chevy at 9am tomorrow?"

"Wait, we have to go to PIT now and see James?" Ralph asked, wide-eyed with fear.

"I'm going with you and those other two guys will be there. James won't do anything to hurt us," Hannah said, smiling.

That didn't calm Ralph's nerves as much as it perhaps should have done.

Hannah said they'd meet the others in the dining hall after they were done. Hannah and Ralph then walked off towards the PIT. Rachel watched them leave then said to the Willie and Pastor Gore that she was tired and wanted to go back to her room for a while. Willie and Pastor Gore decided to go and offer their services to help with finishing off building the additional housing for a few hours before dinner.

Rachel walked with the Pastor and Willie back to the Ashbrook and saw them head around the back then continue to the building site. Once they were out of sight, instead of going up to her room, she turned around and walked back to the Church of Souls. She walked inside the main hallway and through into the inner sanctum. She saw Joshua in the office upstairs on the phone. Once he saw her, he hung up and she saw him leave the office. Within a minute, he appeared through a door at the other end of the inner sanctum, walking towards her.

"Rachel, it's good to see you. I hope you are enjoying your time here with us," Joshua smiled.

"Thank you, Joshua. I am enjoying it so far."

"I can see you look troubled. You do not need to be. I know why you have come here to see me."

"You do?"

"You are concerned about how you've fallen into a dark place within your life and how your use of drugs harmed your friendships. You are also worried that the Messiah will not accept you and help you because of your addictions.

I can put your mind at ease Rachel. The Messiah does not discriminate when it comes to helping the sick. He wants everyone to feel the benefits of his teachings and everyone to feel blessed he is in their lives."

"Thank you, Joshua. But I am not just here about that," Rachel said, nervously.

"I know, my child. I know that you are scared about your friends and that worry that some wish to oppose our work and our vision. I understand that whilst you love them dearly, you also do not want to be associated with their feelings towards our project because you deeply care about what we are doing and want to help us achieve our goals."

Joshua walked over to the right-hand side of the church and looked out of the window.

"I share your same concerns, Rachel. I worry that there are those within our community who are working against us, against me. They will be dealt with in due course."

"You're not going to hurt them?" Rachel asked, alarmed.

"Of course not, my child. However, we must protect ourselves against the demons and those who wish to stop us from making the world a happier and more peaceful place. The Messiah will allow them to leave our community, never to return."

"They have said they are planning to leave tomorrow morning. Whilst I am sad that Hannah is among them and I will miss her every single day, I understand and respect her decision."

"Hannah is important to you, so she is important to us. I am equally sad that it did not work out. However, if I am being truly honest with you my child, you are the Hope we've been looking for." Joshua said, turning to look at Rachel.

"I'm the… what?"

"The Messiah has been looking for a special soul to join James, Joel and I. We feel you are that individual."

"I'm truly honoured Joshua but I've only been here a day?"

"The Messiah has said he will make it his duty to help you overcome your addictions to transform you into his most powerful ally. There are tests you will need to pass and sins you must admit and ultimately atone for, but I have every faith you will become the Hope we have been looking for."

"Joshua, are you the Messiah?" Rachel asked, looking quizzical.

Joshua sat down on a chair facing away from Rachel and bent his head so she couldn't see his face. He started to laugh. Within a few seconds, he stood up again and turned to face Rachel.

Rachel stumbled back in horror at what she saw. This wasn't Joshua. This was someone she knew, someone she'd seen before.

The man she saw in her trip, in her dreams, was standing in front of her.

Chapter Twenty //
21st July 2012 – The Haven, Starr County //

Hannah and Ralph arrived at the PIT. They could see James waiting for them with Todd and Carl.

The PIT was a huge dark house on the edge of the Forest of Eden. The forest was so lush and green it almost looked unreal and because it was so dense, it was impossible to see very far into it. Ralph told Hannah that Joel had explained there were strict boundaries, which stopped the community from venturing far into the forest. Ralph and Willie tried to have a look around that morning before breakfast to see if they could see the Temple of Gethsemane but had no luck.

"So this is the PIT?" Hannah asked as they arrived in earshot of James.

"It is," James replied. "And you are treading on thin ice."

Hannah could tell that what he said was supposed to be as a threat as she could see his stained yellow teeth clenched together as he spoke to her.

"Why are we here, James?" Ralph asked.

"Ralph, you look nervous, a little scared if I may. You have no reason to be afraid, son. Joshua asked me to help further educate you all. Please follow me," James said, softening his tone and smiling.

As they entered the PIT, Hannah could see there were staircases either side which Ralph told her went up to the dormitories. There were also doors on either side of the corridor in front of them.

"James, where are you taking us?" Hannah asked.

James stopped in his tracks, turned around and looked at her.

"How many times do we have to tell you, Hannah? Too many questions!" he snapped.

They got to the end of the corridor and to a door with a keypad. The pad turned green after James entered a code in and the door slide open.

"Everyone walk through please," James said.

They did as James told them. Hannah could see Todd, Carl and Ralph's eyes all light up and say how amazing whatever was through the door was. Hannah walked through last. She couldn't see anything except a long, dark corridor with a few flickering lights.

"Ralph, I think this is the..." she began to say before she felt a blow to the back of her head and everything went dark.

****

"You," Rachel said in amazement. "I've never met you before, yet I feel like I've known you for years. How did you... do that?"

"Do... what?" Joshua asked, looking confused.

"Change your appearance? Ever since we arrived here, you've looked completely different. How have you been so close to both me and Hannah but this is only the first time I've met you?"

"I haven't changed my appearance, my child, let me explain everything," Joshua said, taking Rachel's hands. He invited her to sit on opposite him on one of the pews.

"I had the idea for Enlightenment a long time ago. We started as few and grew into many. James, Joel and I set Enlightenment up in Idaho originally. Some came to us in the past who I had tried to help and asked for their investment in return but they ultimately decided that our project wasn't for them, so they left with our best wishes.

Others have stayed on and become an integral part of our community. As I mentioned, we are looking for someone to work closely with James, Joel and I. I want that person to be you, Rachel. I want you to become our new Hope. I will help you overcome your addictions, face your sins and in return, all I ask is that you commit to our shared vision for the future.

That vision is to bring back peace and harmony, to give the world a sense of normality again. We aim to cure the sick and help as many as we can. Those who choose not to follow us shall be allowed to choose their own path. Those who oppose us will be dealt with."

"I still don't get how I saw you as a different person though? And why did you not say straight away that you are the Messiah?"

Joshua smiled.

"I am Joshua first and foremost, my child. I don't want those who are sick to look on me as anyone different from them. I am not a superior being. I am here to do God's will, to teach us all how we can be better individuals, working together for the greater good.

In order to help the sick, we've been working on a completely organic substance made from plants which we've called the Myst. It gives users a sense of feeling more stable within themselves, feeling normal if you will. We are aware of a massive increase in mental health conditions around the world so we have been very careful refining the substance into something completely natural. One of the side effects that we are working on is that the Myst projects a feeling of euphoria. It tricks the mind into seeing things that are sometimes different from reality. I've always been here as you see me now, dark hair, my aviator's and my beard. I don't know who you saw when we met but I can only assume the Myst must have affected your mind."

"How could I have had any Myst though? We came straight through to see you in the inner chamber when you arrived?" Rachel asked.

"Did you drink the cup of water that the guards gave you at the gates?"

"Yes, it made me feel so much better!"

"So you've had the Myst. Our scientists have refined the substance so it almost clear with a blue tinge to it but there is still a lot of work to do. Once we have atoned for your sins and past transgressions, I'd like you to help us develop the Myst further. I'd like Willie to help us in that area as well. Is that something you think he might be interested in?"

"Willie has said he wants to stay and make a difference, to change the world for the better and so do I. It would be my honour to work with you, Messiah. Once I have passed your tests and proven myself to your cause, may I request help with something?"

"You want me to help you find your brother?" Joshua asked.

"Yes. How did you know?"

"Mason came to me looking to atone for his sins a few days back, but he was aggressive and was asked to leave."

"You didn't hurt him did you?" Rachel said, alarmed.

"No, we asked him to leave us and not return."

"Good. I want to find him myself and when I do, he will pay for what he did to me and what he did to Bo."

****

Hannah opened her eyes feeling groggy. She heard someone slowly tutting behind her.

"Did you really think we wouldn't find out that you haven't been taking your medicine, Hannah? We had such high hopes for you. The Messiah had praised your tenacity and determination but it seems you are using those traits to hinder our work and stop us from helping to free America. So now you will confess."

"What? Where am I? Where are the others?"

"TOO MANY QUESTIONS, HANNAH!" James said, forcefully slamming his hand down on a surface that Hannah couldn't see, which made her jump. "You will confess your sins. If you do not do this willingly, I will extract them from you."

Hannah looked around. She felt her arms tied down to a chair and could see a light shining down on her in an otherwise dark room. The only other thing she could make out was a small metal table but she couldn't see what was on it.

James walked over from within the darkness and pushed the table closer. He brought a chair over and sat down next to her right arm with the table in front of him. He pulled her sleeve up to the top of her arm.

"WHAT THE HELL ARE YOU DOING?" Hannah screamed.

"Scream all you like, no one can hear you," James said, sarcastically.

"I WILL FUCKING DESTROY YOU AND THIS VILE SECT!"

James ignored her. He took a razor to her arm and shaved the fine hairs on covering her triceps area. She couldn't do anything to stop him. Her hands and feet were tied with rope and she couldn't even get them loose, let alone break free.

Once James had finished shaving her arm, he applied some kind of jelly to the area then took a needle off the table. Hannah screamed.

"WHAT THE FUCK DO YOU THINK YOU'RE DOING? WHERE THE FUCK AM I?"

"You have refused to confess your sins. You have undermined us and YOU ASK TOO MANY QUESTIONS!"

"SO YOU'RE GONNA TATTOO ME?" Hannah screamed, incredulously.

"All demons will be marked to show their lack of cooperation. We will help free America and in doing so, the sick that refuse help will be tagged so we can easily identify them when the great reaping takes place."

"THE GREAT WHAT?"

"I've HAD ENOUGH of your incessant questions, Hannah!" James shouted.

He picked up a different needle as she screamed. She felt the slight prick as the needle penetrated her skin then she heard James say "Night Night!" before she blacked out.

****

"So, what happens next?" Rachel asked Joshua.

"There is something everyone who joins us must complete as a first initiation. Tomorrow, we shall visit the holy mountain. First, you must renounce your previous existence as Rachel Walker and become Hope Eve. Please, follow me."

Joshua took Rachel out of the church and over to the Eve's biosphere. It was a truly magnificent circular glass building which rose high above the surface of the ground.

"Your new living space will be the first floor of the Biosphere. You shall have everything could ever want there. James and Joel occupy floors two and three and I occupy the top floor. My door is always open for anything you need. Take a few hours, have a look around and familiarise yourself with your new surroundings. Please also change out of those clothes. We have set you up with the most beautiful dresses money can buy so you will no longer require any other clothing. Tonight, we shall celebrate and say goodbye to Rachel Walker and hello to Hope Eve. We shall also wish Hannah farewell as she leaves our community. I will meet you in the lobby in two hours. Your floor code is 4673. You will need to enter this into the elevator keypad."

****

Hannah woke up feeling awful. She tried to pull her arms up but felt resistance. Her right arm felt like it was burning. She still couldn't see much around the room but it didn't sound like anyone else was in the room with her. Hannah tried to see if she could wriggle free again but the knots in the ropes tying her hands together were far too tight. She heard the door open behind her.

"Hannah?" a whisper came from close to the door. "Are you there?"

"Who is that?" Ralph?"

"Yes, where are you? I can't see too well."

"Why can't you see? Where are Todd and Carl?"

"They drugged me when we walked through those doors. I could see I was in the most stunning garden with the most beautiful women I'd ever seen in my life. I was excited and felt so happy. But the drug quickly wore off. I realised I was actually stuck in a room with Todd and Carl and noticed we were all naked. I got my clothes and then came to find you!"

"Yeah, well, can you help untie me please?"

"With what?"

"Is there a knife or something anywhere?"

Ralph slowly walked closer to where Hannah's voice was coming from. As he moved nearer, he saw the small light that was shining next to Hannah. He also saw the table next to where Hannah was but noticed there was nothing on it. As his eyesight improved, he moved quickly and used the light to see if there was another workbench or table within the room. Luckily there was, to the left of where they were. He walked over to the table, started going through the drawers, and found a knife.

"Found a knife! We need to get out of here tonight, Han. I can't stay here any longer."

"Agreed, we'll grab Rachel and Willie on the way. I can't let them stay here knowing what we know now."

Ralph cut the rope that bound Hannah's feet then her hands. They ran to the door and quickly left the room. They were in the same corridor Ralph remembered seeing the previous night. They got down to the end and tried to activate the door to no avail.

"Try 4673," Hannah said.

The door opened.

"How did you know?" Ralph said.

"4673 is HOPE on a phone keypad," Hannah said. "Joshua is obsessed with me becoming his new Hope. I'm sure it's me, that's why we have to go."

They ran back into the corridor. As the lights were on, Hannah was finally able to look at her arm. She could see James had tattooed the letter 'D' with two lines striking through it diagonally. She then looked at Ralph in horror.

"They've shaved your head as well Ralph and I can see why you were feeling so unwell earlier."

"Why?"

"You've got stitches going right across the top of your head. Like you've been operated on."

"What the hell?"

"I don't think now is the time to ask, let's get your stuff and get the hell out of here!"

Hannah helped Ralph get everything from his room before they left the building and headed back to the Ashbrook. Hannah noticed as they ran that all the lights surrounding the buildings were switched off, making it difficult to see as it was now pitch black outside.

They got back to the Ashbrook and grabbed everything from Hannah's room. They left the building and ran back to the Chevy.

"That was remarkably easy," Ralph said, nervously.

"Too easy..." Hannah replied.

They put their stuff in the back of the vehicle. As they closed the door and locked the Chevy, they saw Joel and James walking towards them from the church. They were carrying logs that were alight and burning. Other members of Enlightenment were approaching them from all different angles with logs on fire.

From a distance towards the entrance to The Haven, Hannah also saw Joshua walking towards them with someone she couldn't quite make out, a woman. She had the most beautiful, floral red dress on.

As they got closer, Hannah realised the woman looked familiar. It was someone she knew and knew very well. It was Rachel.

Chapter Twenty One //
21st July 2012 – The Haven, Starr County //

The lift doors opened slowly. Rachel walked out and saw a circular living room in front of her. The lift was on the far right side. To the left, she saw a couch that was big enough to fit around thirty people. The couch faced a 70" widescreen TV on the back wall. Behind the couch was a bookcase. Rachel walked around it and saw a there was a second bookcase backing on to the first. To the left side of both bookcases was a walk-in bathroom. The right side was clear to walk through to the rest of the apartment.

The glass windows, which surrounded the whole floor, were tinted. Rachel liked the idea of no one being able to see in from the outside but still having full visibility of what was going on externally herself.

She carried on looking around and found a large kitchen behind the bookcases. There were doors on either side of the kitchen that led to her bedroom and closet space. She also noticed that the bathroom next to the bookcases was accessible from the kitchen side as well as the couch side. She walked into the bedroom. She saw a super king-size bed in the room with an en-suite bathroom and a closet which housed the most beautiful range of red dresses with floral patterns on.

Rachel checked the whole floor for hidden cameras and bugs. She wasn't taking any chances after what had happened with Mason. Once she was happy she'd covered every inch of the bedroom, she did as she was told and changed into one of the dresses.

As she still had some time to kill before meeting Joshua, she decided to look through some of the books. She saw a lot of fiction novels and books on American history. But right in the middle of the bookshelf behind the couch, was a book with a completely white cover which just had a symbol on the front, back and spine. She realised she's seen the symbol before, on the news when they were in the hostel in Colter Bay.

She opened the book. The first page simply said 'THE BOOK OF ENLIGHTENMENT'. Rachel left the book on her new bed to remind herself to read and memorise as much as possible.

Once she was ready, she took the elevator down to meet Joshua outside the front of the biosphere. It was dark outside and she felt a bit cold in her new dress but didn't want to show weakness in front of the Messiah so said nothing.

"Hope. You look so beautiful in that dress. It's good to finally call you what you have always been destined to become. Have you brought your old things?"

"Yes, Messiah. I am ready."

"Then we shall go and bid Hannah farewell before having a ceremony to officially welcome Hope Eve."

They walked over from the biosphere to the church. Rachel could see a number of the community were approaching the church with wooden batons, which were on fire.

"Why are they surrounding the church with those?" she asked Joshua.

"The demons are ready to be vanquished, my child. Come."

As they approached the church, Rachel could see Hannah and Ralph standing by the Chevy. The whole of the Enlightenment community surrounded them in a big circle. Joshua and Rachel joined them and walked through to the middle.

"Friends," Joshua projected. "We are gathered here today for a celebration. Not only are we here to crown our new princess of Enlightenment, but we are also here to vanquish the demons who have been plaguing us."

He turned to Hannah.

"We have given you every opportunity to settle and make a life for yourself here. We have given you the chance to confess your sins and atone. You have not taken those chances. You have continually undermined us and called us evil. You have tried to turn your friends against us and have them think badly of what we are trying to achieve here, as you do.

For that reason, you have been branded a demon and you are no longer welcome here. You will leave us and you will take Ralph with you.

Where is Pastor Gore please?"

The Pastor stepped forward.

"Pastor, you have also been working against us. We know about your attempts to try to find out what our scientists are working on. We know about the phone calls to the radio stations we have legally purchased. You shall leave us tonight too.

Willie, have you got the Pastor's things?"

Willie stepped forward with two suitcases.

"Yes, Messiah."

"Tonight, my children, you will be witness to the deaths of Rachel Walker and Willie Sheffield. In their place, we welcome Hope Eve and Roland Ferriday."

Hannah looked at her friend in shock.

"RACHEL! How could you do this? How could you believe this mad man?"

The woman who looked back at her had no expression.

"Rachel Walker is dead Hannah. I am Hope Eve. You have been banished from The Haven. You time here is at an end and you will leave us."

Hannah couldn't believe what she was hearing.

"RACHEL! What the hell? I'm your BEST FRIEND. How can you do this to me?"

"I am no longer Rachel," she said looking into Hannah's eyes in a trance. "You have been banished. Please leave us before the Messiah does something everyone will regret."

"You're threatening me?"

"No. But you have betrayed us. You have betrayed the Messiah. You have betrayed me. You are no longer welcome here."

Hannah stared at her former ally in shock and dismay. She couldn't believe what she was seeing and hearing. She got into the Chevy with Pastor Gore and Ralph, who picked up the Pastor's suitcases to put them in the back. The Haven community made space for the vehicle to back up and drive out.

"Hope, you have done well. Thank you," Joshua said, smiling. "My children, now we have vanquished our demons, it is time to celebrate. We have found our Hope. It is time for you and Roland to fully embrace your new lives."

James and Joel brought forward two more suitcases, which they placed into the middle of the circle.

"These suitcases are the belongings that were brought here by Rachel Walker and Willie Sheffield. As those two individuals no longer exist, their possessions will be burned," Joshua said.

James and Joel took their baton torches and threw them on to the suitcases. They all watched as the fire burned all of Rachel and Willie's possessions.

After the fire had died out, Joshua turned to Hope.

"I will meet you tomorrow morning at the holy mountain for your first trial."

Joshua, James and Joel left to go back to the biosphere.

Hope turned to Roland, surprised.

"How did you know about Joshua?"

"After we left you at the Ashbrook, the Pastor and I went to offer our help to Joel who was overseeing the building project, as you know. When we got there, Joel put the Pastor to work and asked to speak to me separately. He told me that you had gone back to see Joshua and said they were looking for two special individuals to help them with the Myst. He asked me to become their head scientist providing I can pass their trials and confront my transgressions and sins. I accepted.

Whilst I am sad that Ralph and Hannah had to leave, I understand why that was necessary. Have they told you what trials you need to pass yet?"

"Not yet, but my first one is tomorrow morning. Where are you sleeping now?"

"Joel and James have given me a secret property which none of them have told anyone else about yet. It's near your biosphere. I have my quarters upstairs and a full science lab downstairs."

"That's fantastic Willie... sorry Roland," Hope laughed.

"Who is Willie? You look beautiful in that dress by the way."

"Thanks! It's pretty cold, so let's get back. Here's to a new beginning for us," Hope smiled.

****

Ralph drove out of the gates of The Haven, not looking back. He sped through the tunnel then turned towards Owl Creek. Hannah was in floods of tears.

"I can't believe she'd threaten me. How have I betrayed her?"

"You haven't at all, Hannah. She's been brainwashed. The Messiah is very clever and preys on the weak-minded and naïve," Pastor Gore said. "Damn those Ensects. We're going to have an all-out war on our hands in the coming months and years, I can feel it."

"Ensects?" Ralph asked.

"Enlightenment sect. Call them what they are."

"I think you have something there Pastor! That could catch on!"

"I love it," Hannah said. "I need to rest but tomorrow is a new day. Pastor, I'm assuming you're down for joining a resistance?"

"Of course!"

"Ralph? How are you feeling?" Hannah asked.

"Not great if I'm honest. I wanna get checked out as soon as possible to try to find out what they've done to me. But once I'm fixed, count me in."

"Stay with me tonight, there's plenty of room. We'll go to the clinic first thing tomorrow morning to see the doctor."

They dropped the Pastor off in Jefferson Canyon then drove back to Silk Falls. Ralph parked the Chevy at the top of the mountain path then got the suitcases out of the back. Hannah's phone pinged up with a message on Connect.

I'm so disappointed you betrayed us. I hope you'll change your mind one day and understand why I've chosen to trust and believe in The Messiah.

Hope x

"Can you believe that shit?" Hannah showed Ralph before deleting the message.

"Unfortunately, it seems both our friends are been completely taken in by this sect."

"Ex-friends. Rachel can go to hell. Tomorrow is a new day and tomorrow, the resistance begins. They will not win."

Chapter Twenty Two //
22nd July 2012 – Phoenix Mountains, Starr County //

Hope woke at 6am and showered then dressed. She took the elevator down to the lobby and met James who drove her to the Holy Mountain.

"What test must I face today, Brother James?" Hope asked.

"That is between you and the Messiah, Sister. You will not have been the first to undertake this test and you certainly will not be the last. Drink this."

He gave her a bottle with an orange drink inside which looked like Gatorade. Hope did as James asked and drank the contents. It tasted like orange crush but had another taste that Hope couldn't quite work out. It helped her to feel more focused.

"What plans do you have for Roland?"

"Roland must face similar trials to you, Sister. We have big plans for Roland to work closely with you to develop the Myst. I know you have many questions and this must be overwhelming but believe in the Messiah. He will guide us all and we will free America."

James dropped her off at the bottom of the mountain.

"You must climb from here. Good luck. We will see you on your return with the Messiah."

Hope got out of the van and watched James drive off to do his daily supply run then go back to The Haven. She checked her phone. No reply from Hannah to the message she sent last night but she didn't think there would be. She started to climb the mountain. It was a long way to the top but it wasn't too steep.

Hope could see Joshua waiting for her, the closer she got to the top of the mountain. As she approached the summit, he saw her and smiled.

"Come, my child. There is much to achieve. You have reached the summit of the holy mountain but now you need to prove your belief in our cause and walk the path of ascension. Follow me."

In front of her was a statue of the Messiah. Anyone a hundred miles away could see it due to the size. There was a door at the bottom of the right foot, which he opened and went through. She followed him.

In front of them, Hope could see a large circular staircase. Joshua walked to the bottom and started to climb. She followed. There were over three thousand steps before they reached the summit. She was silent as they drifted through the door at the top.

"My child," Joshua said. "You are not the first to undertake the path of ascension and you will not be the last. Some who took the path before you did not make it because they failed to believe in us, in me. The path takes no prisoners. This is the ultimate test of your loyalty and your faith.

I am asking you to trust me, believe that I will look after you and take care of you. What I am asking you to do is to walk across the stone Book of Enlightenment where we now stand. Once you step off, you will ascend, higher than you've ever been before."

"Surely, I will fall to my death?" Hope asked nervously.

"Not if you truly believe, my child. You will rise above me then float to the ground."

Hope did as he asked. As she reached the edge of the stone book, her heart was pounding. She stopped and looked back. Joshua smiled and said, "Go on, my child. I believe in you. Do you believe in me?"

"Yes."

She stepped off the edge of the book.

****

Ralph woke up with an awful headache. He had slept on Hannah's couch for the night, which was comfortable enough, but his head was still hurting when as he pulled himself up.

Hannah was up already and had made breakfast.

"Morning! I've called the clinic and booked you in for a check-up at 10am. How are you feeling?"

"Sore. I can't understand why anyone would operate on another human being without first having their consent and there being a need?"

"Neither can I, but you look sexy as hell bald."

Ralph raised his eyebrow. Hannah laughed.

"We'll get to the bottom of it. I'm sure Doctor Garcia will be able to help."

They walked outside and went to get into the Chevy. As they got to the top of the path that ran down the mountain to Hannah's shack, Ralph noticed something in the distance.

"Han, what the hell is that?"

"OH MY GOD. It's a statue of Joshua. How did we not see that before?"

"There have only been a couple of times we could have noticed it; when we drove to The Haven for the first time and last night when we drove back. On the way, the rain was torrential. I could barely see a hundred yards in front of us. Then on the way back, neither of us were paying a lot of attention to our surroundings and it was too dark."

"True. The Haven is in the middle of some of the tallest mountains in the region so it was impossible to see from the island. That is the perfect place for that vile sect. Unless you know where it is and what it is, you would never go there.

Once we've built the resistance, that statue is first on my list of things to destroy. The last thing I wanna see is that man's face every single time I look up to take in the view."

They got to the clinic shortly before 10am. The Doctor called Ralph in on time. He had a worried look on his face when he came back out.

"What's wrong?" Hannah asked.

"The doctor did an MRI and said that from what he could see, they had opened my head because I had a massive brain aneurysm developing. He said they carried out surgery to remove it."

"That doesn't make sense at all. Why would your head still hurt? Did you see Doctor Garcia?"

"I don't know."

Hannah walked over to the reception area.

"Excuse me, who is the doctor on call today?"

"Hello," the receptionist smiled. "I don't know his name. He's a covering doctor as Doctor Garcia is unwell. I've never seen him before. He had a weird tattoo on his arm though when he came in."

"What did the tattoo look like?" Hannah asked.

"A cross with horseshoes."

"Have you heard of Enlightenment?"

"Should I have?" the receptionist asked, confused.

"Just be very careful. That doctor on call today works for them. They are evil."

"Should I call Sheriff Fowler? We're hopeful Doctor Garcia will be back tomorrow."

"I wouldn't but just keep an eye on him," Hannah said.

She turned to Ralph.

"Further proof Enlightenment is already infiltrating our community. Let's go to the walk-in centre in Great Falls and get a second opinion."

They drove to Great Falls and registered at the walk-in centre, which was a small building in the centre of the city. They had to wait a couple of hours before they called Ralf's name. Hannah went in with him this time.

Hannah described the symptoms to the doctor who then said he wanted to give Ralph another MRI. The doctor let Hannah sit in the room with him whilst Ralph was in the machine. When the images came up, the Doctor turned Hannah with a horrified look on his face.

"You said this doctor at the clinic in Starr County told you they'd removed an aneurysm right?"

"Yes, how comes?"

"He lied. Ralph is developing an aneurysm."

****

Hope initially felt herself fall from the top of the statue but as she fell, she closed her eyes and felt at peace with everything. When she opened her eyes, she could see her body had ascended as the Messiah had promised. She felt weightless as she drifted back up to the top of the statue where Joshua was waiting for her.

"How… how is that possible?"

"You truly believe in us, you trusted me and God repaid that faith as I expected. Follow me, my child."

Hope followed Joshua down to the bottom of the statue. They walked around to the area beneath the stone book. Hope saw a locked cage with some wooden sticks inside.

"I'm glad I don't have to add to that today," Joshua smiled. "One stick for each lost soul who didn't believe in us."

"What other trials must I perform, Messiah?"

"I will take you back to The Haven. Over the next few weeks, we will meet in Sync, walk in the Forest of Eden, and go into the Temple of Gethsemane. You will atone for your past sins, transgressions and make a sacrifice for the greater good."

"What does that mean?"

"All in good time, my child. For the next few days, I'd like you to attend our daily classes as much as you can so you can observe our teachings and eventually take some of the classes yourself. We'll also get you working with Roland, developing the Myst further."

Joshua led Hope down the mountain and to a white SUV. Hope could see the Enlightenment cross symbol was now on the sides of the vehicle.

"The symbol of Enlightenment in all its glory," Joshua proudly said. "It will soon be known throughout the county as a force for all that is good and right. Brother James has been looking into getting all our vans sprayed. What do you think?"

"It's perfect. As you say, once Starr County residents see and recognise the symbol, they'll know we're here for them and to help them. How did you come up with the idea?"

"As soon as we founded Enlightenment, I wanted to use the 'E' and what better way than as a horseshoe, representing our grassroots?"

"It's brilliant."

"I'm glad you think so, my child. We will all be bound by the symbol of Enlightenment soon."

****

"How is that possible?" Hannah said, almost in tears.

"Ralph has a mycotic aneurysm. We can treat it, as it hasn't burst yet so there is no danger to his life. However, there is no way that doctor you saw in Starr County removed it. I'm almost certain that it has developed from an adjacent infection which you can see there."

The doctor pointed to a section of the MRI scan.

"The infection is new. The data indicates it is 24-48 hours old so that would match the timelines you have described. I will get Ralph booked in right away for surgery. We have a slot free this afternoon and I'd like to operate on him as soon as possible. Do you both have health insurance?"

"I do and I'm sure Ralph will."

"Do you know where Ralph has been for the past 24-48 hours?"

"With me, but we were staying with a group of people who kidnapped him and I believe they have infected him."

"You need to inform the police immediately as they can carry out an investigation."

The doctor told Ralph that he'd be booked in for surgery that afternoon. Hannah waited whilst the operation took place. She thought about replying to Hope but decided against it.

A few hours later, the doctor came out of surgery. Hannah stood up.

"Ralph will make a full recovery however he'll need to come back in a few months to have his stitches removed. He may also find he has some side effects such as headaches in the next few weeks but these will subside in due course."

"Thank you so much, Doctor. Will he be ready to go home in a few hours?"

"We need to keep him in for a few weeks I'm afraid."

Hannah looked at him, crestfallen.

Chapter Twenty Three //
18th August 2012 – The Haven, Starr County //

After Hope had passed her first test, she fully integrated herself into The Haven's society and the Messiah's teachings. She spent a lot of time observing the daily lessons in the auditorium that Joshua, Joel and James gave. She also watched how individuals within the community reacted to the content. After a couple of weeks, she began formulating teaching plans in her quarters in the biosphere, as Joshua had told her she would be heading up morning classes every other day.

Joshua and Hope met once a day in his office in the Church of Souls to go over how she was getting on and settling in. Hope also spent a lot of time with Roland working on the Myst, refining and developing the substance further. One morning in mid-August, after a lot of work, Roland asked Hope to come into the lab.

"We've done it!" Roland said, excitedly.

"Done what?"

"We've now managed to change the substance of the Myst so that not only does it retain the feeling of being awake and focused, but now anyone who takes this particular strain can focus their mind by meditating and the Myst will transport you to a different place within a short distance."

"How is that possible?"

"The Myst was originally made up of hibiscus syracuse, wild mushrooms, opium and a few secret ingredients. All we did was add ayahuasca. Once consumed, the user would sit or lie down and focus their mind on a person or place. The Myst will then take them there. At the moment, this will only work for a short period but we are working on extending that."

"Roland, will you keep this to yourself? I'd like to be the sole person to use that strain for the time being. I will tell the Messiah about your amazing work," Hope smiled.

"Of course."

Hope left the laboratory and went to walk over to the Church of Souls to tell Joshua about the discovery Roland had uncovered. As she was walking along the pathway, she met a woman who didn't look much older than she was. The woman was a similar height to Hope with straight blonde hair, which went past her shoulders. She smiled as Hope approached.

"Hey, you're Hope right?"

"I am. How can I help you?" Hope smiled.

"I'm Jess. I just wanted to tell you that you inspire me."

Hope was taken aback. She'd never thought about the effect that the work she was doing would have on others, despite wanting to help as many people as she could.

"Jess, that's the nicest thing anyone has ever said to me. Thank you so much!"

Hope hugged her.

"How long have you been here with us, Jess?"

"Only a couple of weeks, I got thrown out of my parent's house in Valentine. D'ya know it? It's in Owl Creek. We had such a small community there. I loved it so much.

Anyway, I saw an article on Connect about this place and got my uncle to drop me here. It's beautiful!"

"The Messiah has curated such an amazing environment hasn't he? We're working hard to try and help as many people as we can."

"I'm so grateful, Hope. I'd have had nowhere to go if it wasn't for The Haven and Enlightenment. When I got here, James took me over to the Ashbrook. He's nice. Everyone is! I saw you in the auditorium, observing one of Joshua's lessons and wanted to talk to you then but I've been too nervous."

"Oh bless you, Jess. I am here to help everyone and I'm still learning myself. I've been here less than a month but I'm lucky enough that the Messiah has taken me under his wing and is personally showing me the ropes around here. I am determined to make a difference and help as many people as I can. I'd love it if we could be friends and I could help mentor you if you'd like that?"

"Oh my gosh, I'd LOVE that. Thank you so much!"

"Great! Give me an hour and meet me in the Garden of Babylon. Add me on Connect and I can message you if I'm going to be longer."

"Amazing, that's so lovely of you," Jess said, opening her phone and logging on to the social network site. "I've added you so let me know if you're gonna be late. If not, I will see you in an hour."

Hope watched Jess smile and walk away then logged on to Connect and accepted her request. She had created an entirely new profile once she had become Hope Eve and left her old life behind. Her old profile was still active but she didn't use it. She left it there to check any messages she received and to see if her brother had posted anything new. Wade had messaged her a few times, checking to make sure she was ok and asking where she was. She replied to tell him she was fine and was happier now than she ever had been but couldn't tell him where she was. She didn't want anyone from her old life involved with Enlightenment until she had passed all of Joshua's trials.

As she checked her messages on her new account, she saw a notification at the top of the page under 'filtered'. She clicked on the link. There were a couple of new messages in there from accounts she didn't recognise. One was a man she'd never met saying she looked cute and asking where she lived which she deleted. Another was from an account, which said 'unknown'. She clicked on it and saw a link to a voice message. She pressed play and heard a woman's voice.

Hi
You don't know me and I've never met you but I know you have become involved with Enlightenment. I wanted to warn you that Joshua, James and Joel are not good men. I'm sure Joshua has told you all about how Enlightenment started up. I'm also sure he has failed to mention that certain things that went wrong on the way, especially when the project began to evolve in Idaho.

Joshua recruited me. It all started out great. He told me all his plans including how he wanted to make the world a better place and how he needed my help to do it. I was thrilled and wanted to make a difference. Everything was fine until one night, James came to my quarters and told me that Joshua wanted to see me in his temple. I asked what about and was told that it was time to make my sacrifice.

I went and met with Joshua as James had asked. On my arrival, Joshua's voice appeared over an intercom system and told me to go to the confession booth. I walked into the room that had 'confessions' on the door. It felt like I was almost in a police precinct holding room. I couldn't see Joshua, only hear him when he spoke through the intercom. He told me that I needed to confess all my sins.

I went through everything I could think of and atoned for each one. After I finished, Joshua told me that I hadn't confessed everything and started asking me about very private things that were none of anyone else's business. I told him I wasn't comfortable talking about them. He started to get mad, saying it was God's will and that I needed to confess everything otherwise, I'd never be allowed to continue with Enlightenment. So I told him everything because I felt like I had no other option.

A few minutes after I finished talking, Joshua came back on the intercom and told me that it was time to make my sacrifice. It turns out that my sacrifice was Joshua forcing me to have sex with him, with no protection. He walked into the room with an evil smile on his face. I tried to get out but after I'd gotten free of Joshua, James and Joel restrained me. I didn't even realise they were in the room. I felt so alone and like I had no choice. He told me that if I ever told anyone, they'd kill me.

I haven't known what to say to anyone or what to do. I haven't been able to leave my quarters since this happened a few hours ago because I feel so abused and like I'm a terrible person.

But I know that I can't go on like this and can't live here anymore. I don't feel safe. I feel like me even recording this message could leave me vulnerable and open to being attacked. I hope that in saving this and sending this, it will help others but I fear my life could soon be over. Please believe me and please, for god's sake, get out whilst you still can! Do not trust them!

There was no other message underneath. Listening to that recorded message brought back horrible feelings, which Hope had tried to suppress. Feelings about her brother and the kind of things he had done.

The thought of any abuser doing things to someone against their will was completely repugnant and made her sick to her stomach. On the other hand, if what this woman had said was true, perhaps she could use it to her advantage.

Hope never wanted to be involved in any kind of abusive relationship again, but she equally knew that to get to Mason, she needed Enlightenment and needed the Messiah's help. She needed to think long and hard about what she was willing to sacrifice for the greater good to exercise her own demons.

She listened to the message again and wondered what had ever become of that woman who had recorded it. She decided to keep it on her Connect account for the time being and see if she could find out more information about who this person could be from others who had been with Enlightenment since the start.

Hope walked into the back of the Church of Souls and up to Joshua's office. She knocked but noticed he was on the phone so did not enter straight away. He gestured towards her to come in so she opened the door.

"Yes, that's brilliant news. I'll send you over the contract to sign and we can start making the necessary preparations. I'll talk to you soon. Excellent work."

He put the phone down and turned to Hope, excited.

"I have just agreed a deal to buy a fleet of twenty T-1000 white nuclear warhawk planes."

"Nuclear?" Hope asked, horrified. "What are they for?"

"They're just called that," Joshua smiled, seeing her reaction. "We're looking to train a group of individuals who can help us to spread our message further out from Starr

County and then, in turn, they would train others. Flying is an art form and a skill which can help the sick's future prospects once they recover."

"What a brilliant idea. Have you found a base for them yet?" Hope asked, slightly relieved.

"Joel has got an abandoned hospital at the far east of the Phoenix Mountains that we're going to convert into an airstrip. I'm really excited about this. We'll be able to accelerate our plans now. How have you been getting on, Hope?"

"Very well, I am ready to take my first class! I'm very excited to be able to take everything you have taught me and use that to help others."

"That's excellent news. I'm excited for you and I'm looking forward to seeing how it goes. How is Roland progressing?"

"He's doing an amazing job. His developments relating to the Myst are going to give us the capability of teleportation."

"How has he managed that?" Joshua asked, looking surprised.

"He's added ayahuasca and a couple of other ingredients to the formula. They are currently trying to refine it more allow the teleportation effect to become as permanent as the user wants but I feel this is a major breakthrough. Roland said the idea is that the user would meditate; focusing on the place or individual they'd like to be teleported to. Then, after a few seconds, they would appear very close to the person or place they were focusing on. I'd like to request for this to be kept between you and I, Messiah."

"I completely agree. James and Joel have their own style and neither of them has been particularly thrilled with the idea of meditation in the past so I don't believe they'd be bothered about it now. However, I think this is a powerful tool, which I'm very pleased about. Please convey my feelings to Roland and his team."

"I shall, Messiah."

"And now, we need to discuss your next trial. Tomorrow, you will meet me in Sync for confession after dinner. We will go through every part of your life in detail and atone for your sins. Everything must be captured so God knows your atonement is pure and truthful."

"… everything?"

"Yes my child, everything. Every transgression must be atoned, even things you may not be comfortable talking about."

"Everything?" Hope repeated, unsure.

"God does not discriminate, my child and neither should any of us. I am not here to judge you or to upset you. I am here to listen to the sick and help them atone for their sins. The sick all have secrets to hide, we all do. Nevertheless, I am here to help you get better, to help everyone get better. To do that, I need you to trust me implicitly."

"I do Messiah, I proved that when I stepped off the book of Enlightenment. It's just… everything is a lot to try and remember."

"I sensed that hesitation," Joshua smiled. "I will help you through it all and we will atone for your sins together. See you tomorrow morning for class."

Hope smiled and left the office. As she walked over to the Garden of Babylon, thoughts were racing through her mind. Whilst she did trust Joshua implicitly, she couldn't help but wonder if Hannah and the Pastor had been right all along and maybe Joshua wasn't a good person. Then the thought dawned on her. What if that message on Connect was sent by Hannah to try to scare her? She opened her old Connect account and sent Hannah a message.

Hi Hannah

I hope you and Ralph are well. Despite what has happened between us, I have never wished you any ill feeling. I have a new life now and I am very happy... which is why I am messaging.

Please do not send me any more scare story messages as an anonymous account on here. It's so obvious you are trying to sabotage my new life and make me feel like Joshua and the others are out to get me. It won't work, so please stop. You are better than that.

Hope

Hope pressed send and carried on walking. As she turned the corner, she could see Jess waiting for her outside the garden.

"Sorry, I'm a few minutes late, Jess. I had something I needed to sort out."

"No problem," Jess smiled. "You must have so much going on, I'm grateful that you're happy to talk to me. Did everything go well with the Messiah?"

"It did. He's excited by the developments and progress we are making developing the Myst. I have to meet him tomorrow for confession, which is a bit nerve-racking.

"Why?"

"I'm just nervous about what the Messiah is going to think of the sins that I need to atone for. I'm worried that he won't think I'm good enough to confirm my role within

Enlightenment. I've wanted to be accepted and to be able to help others my whole life and I wouldn't know what to do if I couldn't carry on with Enlightenment."

"Hope, you are such an inspiration to me and so many others within this community. I know from talking to people just how much they respect what you've been doing here so far and the impact you've had. I'm sure whatever past transgressions and sins you have committed, the Messiah will be understanding."

"I hope that he will. Thank you, Jess.

So tell me more about yourself. What do you ultimately want to gain from being a member of Enlightenment and how do you see yourself making a difference?"

"So, I'm 18. As you know, I was kicked out of my parent's house in Valentine. I hadn't even done anything wrong. I just came home after a night out with some friends and was drunk. Very drunk... I almost passed out in the garden and this guy I'd kind of been seeing tried to help me but my parents thought he was trying to abuse me and called the cops. They told me that I wasn't old enough or mature enough to be thinking about guys yet. I absolutely am mature enough!

So anyway, they kicked me out. I got my uncle to drive me to here after I saw Enlightenment on Connect and thought I'd see what y'all were about as I needed somewhere to stay. I feel like if I can help and make a difference, I can prove to my parents that I'm not the person they think I am."

"It sounds like you've done nothing wrong at all, Jess. It's always worth remembering that men are usually only ever after one thing and most of the time, once they get what they want, they won't stick around. But, some have amazing hearts who will do anything for you regardless of if you want to be with them romantically or not. You want to keep these kind of guys around.

I've been really lucky in that, I've had two guys fall in love with me in my life so far. One was a guy who lives in the Phoenix Mountains. He's almost double my age and, despite being amazing, I'm not romantically attracted to him. We are friends and he understands that is the limit of what our relationship would ever be. The other was my first boyfriend. I met him at a gig and we did sleep together on that first night, but he stuck around. He was really sweet, caring and the best first boyfriend I could have ever wished for."

"You said 'was'? What happened to him?" Jess asked.

Tears formed in Hope's eyes as Bo's body, lifeless on the ground of the mountain, appeared in her thoughts.

"He was murdered," she said to Jess. "We found him on a mountain near Colter Bay. There was blood everywhere."

"Oh my gosh, that's horrible. I'm so sorry. Are you ok?"

"It's been hard as it's still so raw. I'm trying to cope as best as I can but I have struggled and some of the sins I need to atone for tomorrow were committed after we found him."

"Do you know who… killed him?"

"I do. There is a third man, who is still in love with me, but I have never thought about him like that and I don't ever want anything to do with him."

"Then I want to help you find this person and help bring them to justice," Jess said.

Hope watched Jess's eyes as she spoke and could see she meant every word she said.

"Thank you, Jess. I would love some help with that. I have to pass my trials first and need the Messiah's help and guidance to learn more about the Myst.

If you are interested in helping me for the time being, how would you feel about using Connect to help me find this guy? Just to engage him in dialogue. I need to try and figure out where he's hiding."

"Would it be safe? What would I say though when I add him?"

"Don't say anything. Wait for him to get in touch with you then say you added him by mistake but you're open to getting to know new people and he seems cool. Flirt with him a bit and see how he responds. Most importantly, get him to trust you whatever way you can. If you need to manipulate him, do it."

"What if he wants to meet up? I don't think I'd be comfortable with that knowing that he killed your boyfriend."

"Tell him that you're away for a few months on assignment but you'd be interested when you get back or something like that. I ideally just need someone who can make him think they are on his side and get him to trust them so that when we are ready, we can set a trap."

"I'm in," Jess smiled.

"Amazing! Thank you so much."

Jess showed Hope her Connect account via her phone. Hope switched off Jess's location settings then went to Mason's Connect page and added him as a contact.

"Let me know if and when he adds you and please be careful."

"I will. Thank you for trusting me, Hope."

"Let's meet tomorrow here again and hopefully he'll have replied."

Jess thanked Hope again and then walked back towards the Ashbrook.

Hope got up from the bench they had been sitting on and went to leave the garden but heard a twig snap from over the other side of the topiary wall that surrounded the whole area. Had someone been listening in on the conversation? She ran out of the garden and around to the other side of the topiary but there was no one there. Maybe it was just an animal.

Chapter Twenty Four //
18th August 2012 – Great Falls, Montana //

Hannah hadn't known what to do. The doctor had told her that Ralph would live but would be in the hospital for a few weeks. She had nowhere to go. She couldn't drive and hadn't planned on being away for longer than a night. Luckily, she had some cash with her, so after the doctor told her that Ralph wouldn't be conscious for at least a few days, she went out into Great Falls to find a hotel. She booked a Holiday Inn for a few weeks on credit with a guarantee of a couple more should she need it.

Hannah woke up the following morning and checked her Connect account. She realised she hadn't seen any posts from Rachel's account for a long time. She wondered if her old friend had set up a new account under Hope Eve but decided not to bother looking.

She spent time in the Great Falls library, using their computers and books to find out as much as she could about Enlightenment, particularly about Joshua Eve. He seemed very much holier than thou and like a saint by all accounts from those who had met him. She couldn't believe this was true so she kept digging.

After searching for some time, one afternoon she managed to find a website, tucked deep away from Squirrel or any of the other major search engines. She'd had to go through several different forums to find it. The website was password protected and had an email address with a Connect number underneath. The blog was entitled 'Eve' so she tried putting the Connect number into the social networking search function on the site.

The number took her to a private account, owned by someone called Chloe, which she requested to follow. Within two minutes, the account pinged her a message;

7673Q475A78
He is pure evil. Never trust him.

Hannah entered the password on to the site and started to read a very long and detailed blog about Enlightenment.

I wanted a new start. I needed a new start. I had nowhere else to turn. The Messiah offered me hope. He offered me peace, sanctuary and a new life. I would have been mad to turn him down. Now I wish I'd never spoken to him.

Joshua approached me in the Blue Collar bar in Daytonville, Idaho. He wasn't like the other guys who just wanted to get laid. He took time to speak to me about what I was doing, how I was feeling at the time and genuinely seemed like he wanted to get to know me. He introduced me to his brothers, Joel and James, who told me about a plan they had to build a new society nearby, on a plot of land they had bought in Rivertown off the i90. They said society had become sick and needed healing. I believed that they were in it to help people who have mental illnesses or have fallen on hard times. I could not have been more wrong.

I agreed to become part of Joshua's family in return for a clean slate. Joshua told me that it was time to let go of my past and start again. With that, he said, I needed to burn all my possessions and become his new Hope.

The start was all a bed of roses. Joshua hired a large team to help set up the plot of land and build living quarters, a teaching building, a mediation chamber and a church. When Joshua gave me initial the tour, I could already see there was a building on the plot of land that had trees surrounding it. He called this building his temple and wouldn't allow anyone else in there, saying it was holy and only the Messiah and the sick of his choosing could enter. Funny how it was always younger women that he chose to go in there with him.

At first, Joshua tasked me with social media and getting the word out about what Enlightenment stood for. Once the sick started arriving, he then said I needed to take care of them, listen to their concerns, troubles and issues. Joshua asked me to take notes on each person, as we'd soon look to start curing the sick and help them atone for their sins.

My other task was to start developing a new plant-based drug for Enlightenment, which Joshua said he wanted to use to help heal the sick but told me to add certain chemicals to the formula, which I knew would harm more than help people. I kept those chemicals out because I knew they could lead to people developing mental illnesses who had never had them before and those who had would suffer even worse.

A few months into my time with Enlightenment, Joshua called me to his meditation chamber and told me it was time to atone for all my sins. When I got to the chamber, I sat down on a chair in the middle of a room that felt like a cop cell. Joshua was nowhere to be seen but I heard his voice on an intercom system. He told me I had to confess, so I went through everything I could remember from the start of my life. When I finished, he told me that the list I had just given him was not detailed enough, that God wouldn't accept anything but every single sin atoned for, even my innermost secrets. The way he was talking made me uncomfortable, it was almost… it was almost like he was getting off on the idea of any sins I'd committed that were secret.

I felt that I had no other choice, so I went through a list of the guys I'd slept with. He asked for dates, times and locations, so I told him what I could remember. He asked how it felt. I looked at the intercom completely taken aback. That was when he started to get angry. He told me that if I didn't confess everything, God would punish me. He started to scare me so I told him what he wanted to hear, how it felt, how ashamed I was at some of the places I'd been with my ex-boyfriends, everything.

In the end, I just broke down. I couldn't deal with anyone needing to know that much in-depth information about me and secrets I thought I would carry to my grave. After a couple of minutes, I heard his voice on the intercom. He told me I had done well and that it was now time to make my sacrifice for the greater good.

The lights in the room dimmed and I heard someone open the door, walk in the room and close the door. Then I saw the Messiah's face. He told me it was time. He moved his face closer to mine as if he was going to kiss me. I backed away in horror. He started to get angry again. He told me that if I did not make my sacrifice, God would not allow me to continue with Enlightenment and he would have no option but to terminate my involvement. I asked him what sacrifice I would be making. He smiled and slid his hand up my thigh. I told him that was a sin, that I did not want him touching me like that.

His eyes turned to fire. He pushed me against the wall and told me that I will make my sacrifice otherwise I would not leave the building alive. I had to do as he said. He was so forceful. I knew I'd struggle to get away from him but I realised there was one thing I could try. As he held my arms, I used my left leg and kicked him where the sun don't shine. He fell back and writhed in pain. I ran towards the door without realising there were other people in the room. Joel and James caught me then restrained me on the floor. The Messiah came over after recovering and smiled perversely. He told me that sin would not go unpunished.

After I had 'made my sacrifice', they left me in the room with the lights off. I couldn't move through the fear and the shame of what had just happened. I was petrified, alone and couldn't stop crying. He had just raped me. I felt so abused and disgusted that I just curled up and cried for hours. His sick, perverted smile still haunts my dreams to this day.

Eventually, I got up and opened the door. As I went to leave, I heard his voice on the intercom. He told me I had done well. I screamed and ran back to the apartment block where we all had rooms. As soon as I got there, I locked the door to my room and made sure all the windows were sealed. I knew it wouldn't matter because he probably had a master key for all the rooms but I just couldn't bear the thought of ever seeing any of them again.

I got next to no sleep that night. I was hurting so much from the physical abuse. I was hurting from being mentally tortured. I had nowhere to go and no one I could stay with. It felt like the end of the world for me. I had nothing left. I knew I couldn't stay with Enlightenment at that point and didn't trust anyone there fully to help me escape.

When I woke up the following morning, I was still in so much physical pain but I knew I had to try to get out regardless. I packed what few possessions I had in a small bag I'd kept and I ran. I ran faster than I'd ever run in my life. I knew they'd have the main entrance covered with guards so I ran to the lake side in the hope there was a rowing boat.

No such luck. They'd put barbed wire up at the top of the whole fence so there was no way of getting in or out without swimming. The distance I needed to swim only looked to be a hundred feet or so to get around. I threw my bag over fence and made sure I got the angle right so there was no chance it caught the barbed wire.

The lake was freezing but I knew I didn't have a choice, I had to go. As I went to submerge myself, I heard gunshots from behind me. Joshua was shouting 'STOP HER'. I swam as hard and as fast as I could however as I looked underwater, I could see the fence ran further under the lake. I had to keep going even though the water was bitter cold. I managed to get around the fence after five minutes and swam back to the other side. I could see my bag had cleared the fence but was hanging off the branch of a small tree. Luckily, I managed to reach it, although it took a few attempts.

Just as I got the bag down, I heard James behind me just shouting STOP. I ran again, faster than before, as quickly as I could. Enlightenment's land backed on to the forest that bordered Oregon. I planned to get over the border and seek refuge.

I could hear footsteps behind me but I didn't stop, I couldn't. I ran, deep into the forest and headed for the border. I ran until I couldn't run any further. I stopped to get my breath back but heard voices still behind me, so I decided to climb. I found a tree with a low branch and hooked myself up as far as I could go then tried as hard as I could to say silent.

A few minutes later, I saw Joel beneath me, then James. I heard them say they thought I must have doubled back and ran towards Montgomery, a small town about a mile from the Enlightenment camp. So back they went, towards Montgomery.

I stayed hidden, up in the trees for a few hours, just waiting to make sure no one else was around and getting my breath back. I knew I needed to try to find shelter somewhere before the sun went down so I climbed down when the sun felt at its hottest point and started walking quietly but quickly towards Oregon.

I made it to the border and didn't look back. A few hours later, I left the forest behind me and found a farm. At that point, I was walking a lot slower, exhausted from everything I'd been through over the past twenty four hours. I was still in a lot of pain because of what Joshua had done to me, but it made me even more determined to turn my life around and hold them accountable for what they had done.

I knocked on the door of the farmhouse. An old man answered and asked if I was ok. I just broke down. The old man's wife came to the door and they helped me inside, fed me and gave me a bed for the night. I told them everything.

I stayed in Oregon for a few weeks on the farm. The couple who owned the land were so kind and took care of me. They gave me my own room with a beautiful en-suite, which was private from the rest of the property. They called the police who took down a full account of what had happened to me but at my request, said they would not approach the Montgomery police department until I was safely far away from the area and no longer felt threatened by Joshua. When I was ready, the police drove me across the state up to Tipperary, a small town on the coast where I met my now husband.

The police did as they promised and told Montgomery PD once they had dropped me off in Tipperary. Montgomery PD promised they would monitor Enlightenment's activity and if anything else transpired about Joshua raping or sexually abusing anyone else, they would take action.

I was Enlightenment's first Hope but I know I am not the last. A few months after I left, Joshua met his second Hope, a young woman who had fled home in North Carolina after her boyfriend abused her. What happened to her was truly horrific. She thought she was getting away from all the abuse she had suffered at the hands of ex but she just walked into a trap. Joshua did the same thing to her as he did to me, except she stood up to him and he killed her. From what I heard from a friend I've kept in touch with who has been with Enlightenment since the beginning, after they had murdered her in cold blood, they disposed of her body in acid so the authorities wouldn't ever find out. My contact within Enlightenment called the police who shut the project down and told Joshua he was not welcome in Idaho any more.

Joshua upped and moved to what he now calls The Haven in Starr County, Wyoming. It is the perfect place for him, so secluded that no one could know what they are doing but close enough that he can eventually start to take over the county then the state then who knows.

After they moved and got the first apartment building up, Joshua found his third Hope. She was an African American called Abana who, my contact within Enlightenment says, had the kindest heart of anyone they'd ever met.

This time, Joshua restrained himself. He developed a new technology which allowed him to synchronize his mind with another so instead of relying on others to list their transgressions, he could see every thought that has ever crossed their mind and everything they'd ever done. It's truly terrifying that someone can have that much access to another being's private thoughts.

So he didn't tell Abana what he was doing, he just told her to relax and put his bluetooth device in her ear then told her to close her eyes. All whilst he invaded her mind.

Once he got what he "needed", he let her carry on as normal and told her she would need to make a sacrifice for the greater good at some point before she could become a full member of Enlightenment and full transition to Hope. He didn't give her any idea of what the sacrifice would be so she was almost blissfully unaware.

Two months later, once Joshua had finished building the Temple of Gethsemane in the middle of a forest in The Haven, he called Abana to the secluded temple and told her it was time to make her sacrifice. My contact in Enlightenment says no one ever saw or heard from her again.

I know Joshua has now found a fourth Hope and I have no doubt he will be following a similar path with her. If anyone reading this knows this new Hope, please forward her this blog so she can see the vile monster that she has gotten involved with. For my own safety, I won't tell you where I am now but for anyone reading this, please, for the love of god, do not trust this man. Do not put your faith in him or his ideas. He will destroy you.

Hannah finished reading the entire blog and was shocked. She knew Joshua was evil but rape? Everything she read just made her more determined than ever to stop Enlightenment than she already was. She wanted to get in touch with this woman, 'Chloe' but the Connect account she had was 'send only'.

Hannah decided that, despite her former friend calling her a traitor, she had to pass this information on and warn Hope that her life was in danger. She opened her Connect account. She saw a message suddenly come up from Hope about anonymous accounts and strange messages, where she accused Hannah of making stuff up. She wrote a reply.

Hi Rachel… Hope… whatever you are calling yourself.

I haven't sent you any messages from anonymous accounts so I've no idea what you are talking about.

Secondly, not that you'll care, Ralph had to have brain surgery after what Enlightenment did to him. If you had given me time to talk to you instead of just calling me a traitor, I would have told you James attacked us in the PIT. The others hallucinated that they were their happy places but because I hadn't had any of that water that they had poisoned. I saw what was actually there. A dark corridor with flickering lights. Ralph had described the same dark corridor earlier that day. It was the place where he was taken the night before. Before I knew it, I'd been hit on the head and blacked out.

I woke up, tied down to a chair in a room at the end of that corridor. I heard James' voice. He started acting psychotic, telling me I'd been asking too many questions and that the sect had such high hopes for me but I'd let them down. He got angrier and angrier the more questions I asked and eventually drugged me. After I woke up, James had disappeared. When I looked at my arm, he'd tattooed me with a 'D' which has two lines striking through it. I heard someone come into the room, which, luckily, was Ralph. He untied me and we escaped back to the Chevy. I noticed when we got back into the main dorm area of the PIT that Ralph's head had been shaved and saw why he was feeling ill earlier that day. He had stitches going right across his head. James had operated on him without permission. We drove back to mine and eventually ended up in Great Falls where he has had an operation to remove the infection the sect gave him, which could have led to a brain aneurysm.

I know you won't believe any of this because of the person you have become but I want to share something else with you.

Whilst in Great Falls, I've had a lot of time on my hands. I've spent that time looking into your precious Messiah. Do you know what I found? I found a load of shit. A holier than thou, free of sin, perfect man. However, the beauty of the internet, Rachel, is that if you keep digging, you're bound to find something important. It took me a while but I found something. You need to read it from start to finish because your Messiah is not only pure evil, but he is a rapist and possibly a murderer. I am going to do everything in my power to stop Enlightenment.

Go to http://928732693481343.eve and put in the passcode: 7673Q475A78.

Don't say I didn't warn you.

Hannah hit send then closed the social networking site. She decided to go back to the hospital and see if Ralph was awake. When she got there, she checked with the staff who said she could go up to the ICU and see him.

She walked into his room and saw his eyes were open but looked very weak.

"Ralph! I'm so glad to see you awake. How are you feeling?"

"Hey, Hannah! I'm very tired but a lot better. Thank you for staying and waiting for me. I think I'll be here for a few more days but we'll be able to go home soon."

"I've got the hotel for tonight and can extend for a few more days if I need to."

"I'll call them and arrange to pay your bill. I'm so grateful you stayed."

"It's no problem."

"What's been going on with Enlightenment?"

"I found out some information on the Messiah which is quite shocking. He's a rapist and quite possibly a murderer."

"What?"

"I'm really worried about Rachel. I know what happened, happened but I still don't want to see her life threatened. I found this blog online, which was password protected and included too much information for it to be made up. Someone who said she was Enlightenment's first 'Hope' wrote it.

When you're ready, we'll drive back to Silk Falls via Jefferson Canyon to see Pastor Gore and see what else he's been able to find."

It took three more days to Ralph to recover enough that the doctors in Great Falls hospital were happy to release him. Once he was out the front doors, Ralph went and bought some roses then went to the Holiday Inn hotel that Hannah was staying at. He asked for her room number at reception. They told him she was in room 343. He went up the stairwell and knocked on the door, which was just outside the exit.

Hannah opened the door, half-dressed and a bit surprised. She smiled as soon as she saw Ralph and the roses. She let him in the room. Before he could say anything, she kissed him. His foot knocked the door shut.

Two hours later, they had packed Hannah's stuff and went to reception. Ralph paid the bill and they started the long drive back to Starr County.

"So what else did this blog say?" Ralph asked.

"It gave a full account of how the Messiah treated this girl, Chloe, and what she had to do to get out of Enlightenment's control. She also said that there were other women chosen to become Hope before Rachel and none of them made it out of Enlightenment alive. We are dealing with a very dangerous, sadistic monster. I messaged Rachel the link and told her to read it. I doubt she will but I had to try."

"Do you think there is any way we can stop Joshua from doing something awful to Rachel?"

"I think the best option we have is talking to the Pastor and seeing what else he's been able to find. Do you know how long it'll take us to get back?"

"About an hour to Jefferson Canyon."

When they arrived in Jefferson Canyon, they pulled straight up to Pastor Gore's church and saw he was outside doing some gardening.

"Oh hey Hannah, Ralph. How are you both?"

"Glad to be back home!" Hannah said. "We've been stuck in Great Falls for the past few weeks."

"Starr County is glad to have you back. How are you feeling Ralph?"

"A lot better. Thank you, Pastor. Have you found out anything more about the sect since we last saw you?"

"I have and it's not good. Joshua has just completed the purchase of several ex-military planes that weren't used after being built. No one bar the US government and the military were even supposed to know about them. There is something very very wrong happening with this sect. They've got friends in very high places."

"Yeah well, I've found out more about Joshua and you're not gonna like it," Hannah said.

She proceeded to tell the Pastor about the blog she found whilst in Great Falls. The Pastor looked shocked.

"And you know this is true?"

"I can't be 100% unfortunately, Pastor, but the account is too detailed to be made up. I also believe there must be some way we can find evidence of what happened to the third Hope.

If we can get into The Haven without them seeing us and I can find a way to sneak around into that temple of Joshua's, I think I can find evidence." Hannah said.

"How about a distraction?" Ralph mused. "How about we try and get Willie out?"

"Great idea!" Pastor Gore said. "We don't even have to be successful at getting him out, just so long as we can get as many Ensects chasing us as possible to give you two more time."

"When should we do this?"

"Tomorrow. Why wait? I have ten volunteers who can help us cause a bit of mayhem!" Pastor Gore smiled. "I have a good idea where Willie will be. All we need to do is drive up in a van we stole from the sect and a second getaway car for you two, then we can park up near the lab. We'll wait for you to get clear and give you as much time as we can before we kidnap Willie and drive off. Hopefully, we'll draw a fair few members of the sect away so you can get away easily enough when you need."

"Brilliant!" Hannah said. "Pastor, do you know if anyone has been inside Joshua's temple?"

"Not a clue. Joshua kept everyone well away from the temple the whole time I was there. I don't think anyone even knew where it was. He didn't allow anyone near it."

"We'll just have to take that risk. Let's plan to leave here at 7pm tomorrow so we can hopefully be in and out before dusk. Ralph, are you sure you're up to this?"

"Yes, I wouldn't want you going anywhere near that place without making sure you were ok and I want to get Willie back."

"Just be very careful when going near that temple," Pastor Gore said. "I'm sure Joshua will have taken precautions to visitors. See you both here at 7pm tomorrow."

Hannah and Ralph drove back to Hannah's shack. They walked down the river path and Hannah opened the door.

"I'm both terrified and excited," Hannah said. "All that adrenaline pumping now isn't gonna help me sleep tonight!"

"Well, I can think of a way to release it and likely tire you out enough so you'll get some decent sleep."

Hannah dropped her stuff on the floor and led Ralph into her bedroom, smiling.

Chapter Twenty Five //
19th August 2012 – The Haven, Starr County //

Hope spent the day writing down a list of every sin she could remember. There were so many going back from her earliest memory through to the present day. From punching her brother in the face when he pulled her hair, using swear words, stealing the odd $1 bus fare from her parents' sideboard, impure thoughts about people she'd met throughout her life, sleeping with Bo... the list ran for over ten pages of A4 paper.

Once she finished, she got her things and went over to the auditorium. She checked her phone as she left her apartment, to see if Jess had messaged with her about Mason but she hadn't. She knew she'd see her in a few minutes at school so she didn't send her a message to ask.

Joshua greeted her when she arrived at the auditorium.

"Good morning, my child. You have a packed auditorium full of the sick who cannot wait to hear your teachings. I hope you have fully prepared."

"I will not let you down, Messiah."

Hope's nerves may have made her feel otherwise but she put on an informative, empathetic display that captivated her audience for the whole hour. She related the Messiah's teachings from the book of Enlightenment to her own life and how she's learning to use her errors in judgement and knowledge gained from mistakes to her advantage, becoming a better person in the process.

After the session was over, Joshua, James and Joel came over and congratulated her.

"Hope, you came across so honestly and passionately. We could see how much work you've put into this. I feel like a proud father," Joshua beamed.

"I was suitably impressed. Well done, Sister," James said.

"Your knowledge of the Book of Enlightenment is astonishing considering you've been here less than a month. I particularly liked the way you used what the Messiah is trying to teach the sick and related it to your own experiences," Joel said. "That shows a personal touch and I could see many of the sick relating to what you were saying."

Jess came down from near the top of the auditorium.

"I'm sorry to interrupt but I just have to tell you again how inspirational you are to me, Hope. That was so incredible and I'm so thankful we have you to help guide us. Thank you so much."

Roland was next.

"I'm in awe of how you have developed and come out of the darkness you were facing. You are inspiring so many people in this community and that is something to be so proud of. I'm glad I met you and we are here together."

Hope had tears in her eyes.

"Thank you all so much, you're all too kind. I'm overwhelmed! I know I still have some way to go to improve and get better but all your feedback has been so helpful. I'm glad I made a difference."

"I know you will continue to refine your lessons and you'll work hard to improve every day. This is why we chose you to become our Hope," Joshua said. "I will see you later in Sync for confession."

Joshua, James and Joel left with Roland. Hope turned to Jess.

"What are your plans now?"

"I was hoping to spend more time with you before you have to go to confession. I got a message whilst you were talking from that guy, Mason."

"Shhhh! After you left the garden yesterday, I heard someone or something step on a twig over the other side of the topiary from where we were sitting. Let's talk in private, come back to my quarters."

They walked back to the biosphere. Hope was careful to make sure they weren't being followed.

"How's your day been so far? I'm sorry that I wasn't around to help you, I've spent all morning preparing for the lesson and confession later."

"It's no problem at all. I met this nice guy who said his name was Wes. He was telling me how he had arrived here earlier today with some of his friends. He said their home was shut down by the police after a massive drugs bust or something and they had no place else to go."

Hope felt the colour drain out of her face.

"Did he give names of any other people who were with him?"

"There was a really funny guy, I think his name was Jonny. Also Kayla, Matt and… Emma? No Emily!"

"I know them, Jess. They are good people but they don't like me very much. This is one of the sins I will need to confess to the Messiah later. Before I came to The Haven, I was part of their group FREEDOM for a while with Roland. We were kicked out though because we were both in a dark place and got caught doing things we shouldn't have. But they found us away from the camp and promised not to call the police so I don't understand…"

"Oh, then it wasn't you guys then! Emily was saying that they think someone must have called the police because they came and raided the town."

"I bet that was Hannah, she hated Emily even before they threw us out. I don't think it would be a good idea for me to run into them any time soon though."

"Who is Hannah?"

"She was my best friend. She came here with Roland and another guy called Ralph but just before you arrived, we kicked them out. Hannah was trying to work against us the whole time she was here, calling Joshua, Joel and James evil and making up fake news about them to try to further her own agenda. I think she's also trying to scare me with stories about Joshua from fake accounts on Connect but I can't prove that."

"She sounds horrible. I can't believe anyone would want to be friends with her?"

"She was an amazing friend until we got here. I needed this to work out for me because I had nowhere else to turn to but Hannah has her own place and didn't need to be here."

"Did she not say you could live with her if it hadn't have worked out though?"

"Actually, no she didn't," Hope said, surprised. "I hadn't thought of that. It doesn't matter now. We banished them for working against us and I am glad she is out of my life now. I just want to focus on Enlightenment.

Right, we are here!"

Hope opened the door to the biosphere and entered her password into the elevator keypad. They took the elevator up to Hope's apartment then sat on the couch.

"Now we can finally talk!" Hope said, relieved. "What did Mason message you?"

"The message just said 'A/S/L?' It didn't give a location so I replied '20 / F / Valentine, Wyoming. You?'"

"That's good. Hopefully he'll give us some indication of where he's hiding out."

"Oh he did, he just replied! He said '24/M/Allenstown, Wyoming. He also said I look cute and did I want to meet up."

"Ew. He's 30, not 24. He also has a kid who he's never seen and a wife who left him whilst she was pregnant because he was obsessed with me. Tell him that you don't drive and you're away on business at the moment but that when you get back, sure!"

"Done!"

"Thanks. I will not ever put you in danger and I'll make sure you are protected. Once we have done more work on the Myst, we'll be able to project you any place where Mason is so you won't actually be there or be in any danger."

Hope and Jess carried on chatting for a bit and planning out what was going to happen with Mason before Hope realised that she needed to get ready for later. She took Jess back down to the entrance of the building and said she'd meet her for food shortly. She watched Jess walk towards the Ashbrook then went back up to her apartment to change.

As she showered, Hope thought about what Jess had said about the heads of FREEDOM now being in The Haven. She really didn't want to see them, certainly not until she had finished all her tests.

Hope dressed quickly, realising she needed to leave to give herself enough time to eat before meeting Joshua. She made sure she had her notes with her then walked over towards the dining hall. As she walked in, she heard a voice and looked up.

"Rachel?"

Hope's heart almost stopped but she turned around and smiled.

"Emily! So good to see you again. What are you doing here?"

"It's good to see you too. You look so much better than the last time we saw you. I LOVE the dress as well, it's beautiful."

"Thank You. I feel a lot better. Enlightenment have helped me so much since we last met. The Messiah has taken it upon himself to train me personally and he's helped me overcome my addictions by getting me to focus my mind on helping others.

What happened to FREEDOM?"

"So, just after you guys left, Kayla's hut caught on fire. Luckily, she wasn't inside! I kept seeing this guy hanging around FREEDOM around the same time. He had blonde hair, smoked roll-ups and, to put it frankly, was gorgeous. However, he kept acting real weird and he was asking Wes and Jonny questions about you. I told him you were no longer part of FREEDOM but he just didn't believe me.

A few days after we got Kayla's hut sorted out, we had a drugs bust. I think that guy was the one that called the cops on us and possibly could have been the one who set fire to Kayla's hut."

"That was my brother," Hope said in disbelief. "He was the one that killed Bo. Joshua said that he came to Enlightenment before we did but got kicked out for being abusive. He must have gone back to you afterwards. I'm so sorry. What happened next?"

"When the cops arrived, they found a lot of cocaine stashed in a tent close to our huts. No one knew whose tent it was or what it was doing there. The cops didn't care. They searched every single tent and arrested anyone who had drugs on them then told us we had to shut the entire town down.

Most scattered and went their own ways but the group of town heads didn't have any place to go. Kayla heard about this place online so we decided to take a chance and come here.

I'm so glad you are well. I hope you realise we never had an issue with you? We were just trying to keep our town and our rules in place. Are Ralf, Willie and Hannah here?"

"Willie is here. He is now sober and has become our lead scientist. He goes by Roland Ferriday now. I also don't go by Rachel anymore. The Messiah decided we needed to let go of our old identities to heal. I am Hope Eve."

"Wow, that's so great. What happened to Hannah and Ralph?"

"They were found to be working against us and the Messiah decided it was best for all parties if they left Enlightenment."

"That must have been so hard for you? I know you and Hannah were inseparable."

"Hannah was my best friend. But she knew how important the opportunity was for me here and refused to give it a chance to the point she became obsessed with hating Joshua, Joel and James. She made up false information, which she tried to get us to believe so we would turn on Enlightenment. Even now, she's messaging me from fake accounts on Connect, telling me scare stories about Joshua."

"Wow. I mean, I know she had a real problem with us whilst you were in FREEDOM. It sounds like she has a lot of unresolved issues."

"I'm glad she's no longer here," Hope smiled.

"Well, you are welcome to come and sit with us if you want, Hope," Emily smiled.

"Thank you, Emily. I will take you up on that tomorrow, tonight I have a trial with the Messiah so I need to focus and revise but it was really lovely to see you and please say hey to the others for me."

Emily went off to join Kayla, Matt, Wes and Jonny, who all waived at Hope. She briefly went over to say hi and said she would catch up with them all the following day. She then went and sat at a table on her own, away from everyone else, to eat and focus her mind on her pending trial. Jess came over when she arrived and sat down quietly, as she knew Hope needed to focus fully on her impending confession.

When Hope had finished her food, Jess wished her good luck. Hope looked at her phone. It was time. She took Jess over to where Emily's group were sitting then walked over to Sync to meet the Messiah. As she left the food hall, she saw Roland coming in.

"You'll never guess who is in there, Roland."

"Hannah's not back is she?"

"Nope, but it is someone you know!"

"From FREEDOM?"

"Yes."

Roland thought for a few minutes.

"Nope, not getting anything. I only knew you, Hannah and Ralph. I was too fucked to acknowledge anyone else's existence."

"Emily, Kayla, Jonny, Wes and Matt."

Roland looked shocked.

"No way! What are they all doing here?"

"I'll let them tell you. I have to go! Messiah trial. Wish me luck!"

She kissed him on the cheek then skipped over to the Sync building. Roland smiled as she left.

****

Joshua was waiting as she walked up to the Sync building.

"Come my child, we must begin."

He opened the door and invited her inside. She looked around in amazement. The building on the outside was completely square. Inside, she was in one huge circular room, which was bright white. There were two chairs placed in the middle of the room that were also spherical and had plush cushions covering the whole of the inside.

"Come, child. Please sit," Joshua said, gesturing towards the two chairs.

Hope did as Joshua asked. He walked with her and then asked her to put a bluetooth device into her right ear. He then moved and sat down on the opposite chair.

"I can see you have prepared well for this, but you needn't have," Joshua smiled. "Technology has moved on at such a rate that we can now use these devices to bluetooth into your mind. I will be able to see your memories and see if you truly atone for your sins."

Hope looked hesitant. The thought of another person being able to see her inner most secrets and every thought freaked her out. She thought back to the message she had received on Connect from the anonymous account and what would happen if she tried to hide anything from Joshua. She knew she couldn't say no or do anything to deceive him through fear of possibly being kicked out of Enlightenment or refusing to continue her training.

"It's ok, my child," smiled Joshua, sensing her fear. "I am not here to judge your thoughts, be they pure or impure. God knows everyone has impure thoughts. All I am looking for is purity within your mind that shows me you are repentant of your past transgressions. Are you ready to begin?"

"Yes," Hope said, sitting back and trying to relax.

"Good. Please close your eyes."

Hope did as he asked. Joshua put a similar bluetooth device into his ear then sat back and closed his eyes. Hope felt a tiny clicking sensation, which she assumed, was Joshua's mind merging with hers. She just tried to stay relaxed, focusing on repenting her sins and the work Enlightenment were doing to bring hope to so many.

About an hour later, she felt Joshua take her hands.

"Hope. You can open your eyes. You have passed the trial with flying colours."

"What did you see, Messiah?"

"I saw your entire life. All your memories, all your sins and transgressions. I saw you forgive yourself and atone for every bad thought you had, every action you took which you knew was wrong. For example, your relationship with Bo, the second time you slept together in Pastor Gore's church. I saw you knew that was wrong and were truly sorry that you had desecrated such a holy place. I could see that you have learned from your mistake and would not repeat it.

That is what atoning for sin truly is, my child. Those who refuse to atone for past transgressions will never be truly free or happy."

Hope heard a beeping noise coming from Joshua's shirt pocket. He went to say something but the door of the Sync building suddenly flung open.

"Messiah, Sister, I'm sorry to disturb but its Roland. He's been kidnapped."

Chapter Twenty Six //
19th August 2012 – Jefferson Canyon, Starr County //

Hannah and Ralph arrived at Jefferson Canyon for 6.30pm to give themselves enough time to prepare. Pastor Gore told them they needed to wear balaclavas and dress in the darkest clothes they could find.

The plan was that one of the Pastor's men would drive the stolen Enlightenment vehicle with everyone else in the back and another of his men would drive Hannah and Ralph's getaway vehicle. Hannah could see the van had heavily tinted windows so no one could see inside the back. The Pastor had also created a fake floor for the three of them to hide inside just in case the guards at the gate asked any questions.

"Are you sure you're ok doing this?" Hannah asked Ralph.

"Absolutely. If it gets Willie back and helps us take down Enlightenment, I wouldn't miss it for the world."

"Time to go," Pastor Gore said, walking out from inside the church.

They drove up through the farmlands of Owl Creek and past the ever-winding Emerald River. They could see the Messiah's statue in the distance.

"We need to get that statue taken down as soon as possible," Hannah said, looking disgusted. "The site of that asshole makes my skin crawl."

"We'll get the entire sect shut down soon enough, mark my words," Pastor Gore said. "I won't let them take over our home."

The van arrived at the bridge that connected Owl Creek to the Phoenix Mountains and The Haven.

"Everyone, time to get in position. Hannah, Ralph, we need to lay down here."

The Pastor slid the flooring back to reveal three partitioned spaces that were large enough to fit one person in each. They got in, one at a time then one of the other men slid the floor back in place. The van reached the entrance to The Haven. Hannah could feel the van stop and then heard voices at the gate. Less than a minute later, the van started to move again and flooring above them slid back.

"Perfect!" the Pastor said. He turned to the driver. "The labs are just round back, if you park up a short distance away so no one sees us we'll hang low for a bit to give Hannah and Ralph some time."

The driver pulled up towards the back of the lab buildings quietly. The car stopped behind and the man who had driven it got out and gave Hannah the keys.

"It's time," Pastor Gore said. "We'll wait ten minutes before we go into the labs and get Willie. Keep your balaclavas on and be careful!"

"Will do," Hannah said, pulling her balaclava down to cover her face.

Hannah and Ralph left the others and quietly slipped around the back of the PIT, trying to keep to the shadows so no one saw them. Hannah saw that the Forest of Eden went further back towards the edge of The Haven than she initially realised. They managed to find a gate that led to a pathway into the forest. Ralph said he didn't know about as he and Willie had never been around the back of the building before.

"What should I try as the passcode?" Hannah asked Ralph.

"Keep in mind, the passcodes for each keypad won't be the same. Try Rachel, Joshua or Messiah."

"Last one first," Hannah said, typing in 6377424.

The keypad turned green and Hannah pushed the gate open.

"Amazing call!" Ralph said.

They closed the gate behind them then looked at the path, which weaved left and right with deep, dense and lush vegetation growing on both sides. After a few minutes' walking, the path took them through to a clearing that had massive trees almost towering over the entire area where they stood. There was very little light because of the large amounts of green plants and vegetation. It almost felt like they were in the middle of a jungle.

"Han, look... at... that..." Ralph said, in amazement.

Hannah turned and looked where he was pointing. She saw an Aztec temple, covered in moss and trees stooping over the top. There were two stone staircases that rose high up the sides of the temple and a larger staircase in the middle that led to a stone door. They quietly ascended the steps at the front of the temple and walked up to the entranceway. As they did, the door slid open. Hannah looked at Ralph, almost confused. Ralph shrugged his shoulders. As they walked into the temple, the lights automatically came on in front of them.

They stepped into a corridor and saw another door at the end. The walls and ceiling were completely made of stone and slanted to the centre of the ceiling to make the corridor triangular. The lights on the floor were bright white. As they walked to the end of the corridor, they could hear a slight, deep hum. To the right of the door at the end of the corridor was a keypad. Hannah entered 4673 into the keypad. The keypad turned red, so she tried 722435. The keypad turned green and the door opened.

They walked into the room in front of them. They could see another stone corridor with large stone doors to the left and the right side as well as a door at the end of the corridor. Huge stone panels separated the doors on either side. The panels dropped down from the ceiling, sloping towards where they were standing. Hannah looked around and couldn't see any cameras so they decided to split up after taking their balaclavas off. Hannah took the rooms on the left-hand side, Ralph the rooms on the right.

The doors didn't require any codes, they just slid open on approach. The first room Hannah walked into had a shrine to the original Enlightenment settlement in Idaho. The map of the grounds was a lot smaller than The Haven. Hannah noticed there were only limited buildings but it all fit with how 'Chloe' described everything in her blog. She saw early photos of the mediation chamber and the teaching school. She then noticed a photo of the church. Standing in front of the church were Joshua, James, Jacob and a woman with wavy blonde hair and striking blue eyes who was about 5ft 5 and wore the most beautiful red dress.

"Ralph, come have a look at this," she shouted.

Ralph walked over.

"I think this is Chloe, the woman whose blog I told you about."

"Come see what I've found. I should warn you though, it's pretty insane."

They walked over to the room on the right. Hannah saw a large room with rows of large filing cabinets that she assumed must be full of paperwork.

"What's in the cabinets?"

"All files, files on every single person in Starr County. Look, here's yours."

Hannah read the file. It had details of her whole life; where she lived, what happened to her parents, where she shopped and how likely she was to fit into Enlightenment. It also had photos of her she had never seen before.

"What the actual hell? He's sick, we have to get these files out and tell Sheriff Fowler."

"If he finds out anyone has been in here, he'll tear the entire county apart until he gets his hands on us. You've seen what he's done!"

"We can't let him get away with this!"

"And we won't. But now isn't the right time, we have to be discreet and not touch too much."

They decided to check out the rest of the rooms together. As they got closer to the end of the corridor with the stone door right at the end, Hannah realised that the hum was getting louder.

The other rooms they went in contained recording equipment and CCTV. One set of the CCTV they found was showing images of rooms in the Ashbrook. Hannah felt sick to her stomach at the thought of Joshua watching her when she thought she was alone.

"I think the case we have against Joshua Eve now is more than enough to have him arrested and charged. Spying on women like that, vulnerable or otherwise, is a felony."

"I agree. But we have to play this the right way, we need to find incontrovertible evidence of this other Hope who went missing, then we can have him arrested for multiple charges which will hopefully see him either jailed for life or face the death penalty," Ralph said.

They kept searching the remaining rooms. In the final room on the left hand side, there was a single box on a table. Hannah walked in and had a look. The box contained some random items. Hannah saw a photo of the same woman who was in the first room she had gone in. The woman was with two older people, which Hannah assumed must have been her parents. The next photo was of another younger woman with her arms wrapped around a man on a beach in California. The third was of a young African American woman who was one of the most stunning women Hannah had ever seen. She had such a kind face and beautiful dark brown eyes.

The final photo caused Hannah to put her hand over her mouth and almost start crying.

"Ralph, look!"

"What the hell? That's you, Rachel, Bo and Chad!"

"That was at the gig in Great Falls when Rachel met Bo for the first time. How did Joshua get hold of that? I can't believe Rachel would have given him that, he must have stolen it."

"Do you remember when we got thrown out, I'm sure I heard the Messiah saying how Rachel and Willie needed to burn all their stuff. What if Rachel had kept that photo to remind her of Bo and before the Messiah destroyed her stuff, he took that out? What else is in the box?"

"There are a few pieces of clothing... wait, look. It's Rachel's denim skirt."

"How do you know it's hers?"

"It's ripped in two places, once at the side and once at the top," Hannah said. "Why would he keep this stuff?"

"I don't know but it's really creepy."

"I think we can assume some of this stuff belongs to the other Hope's that Joshua has recruited."

Hannah took photos of the box on her phone, including the photo of the gig in Great Falls and the skirt. She then went back to the room, which had the files in and got a photo of the file Joshua had kept on her.

"Let's see what's in that final room then get out of here."

They walked up to the final door at the end of the corridor. It didn't open. Instead, a hatch appeared with another keypad.

"Don't risk it," Ralph said. "We've got what we need, let's get out of here."

"We need to see what's in there!"

She tried the numeric codes 'Hope' and 'Rachel'. Both times the keypad lit up red.

"Han, we need to go!"

"One more…Enlighten"

Hannah tried '365444836'. The keypad turned red and an alarm went off. They ran towards the exit and managed to get through into the outer corridor and then out of the temple in time before metal doors slammed down and sealed the entrance to both corridors.

Hannah quickly put her balaclava on.

"He'll know someone's been in his temple. We need to find another way back."

"Going so soon, Hannah?"

Hannah froze. She knew that voice. She slowly turned around and saw Hope standing in front of them at the bottom of the staircase.

Chapter Twenty Seven //
19th August 2012 – The Haven, Starr County //

"Messiah, sister, I'm sorry to disturb but its Roland. He's been kidnapped," Joel rushed in.

Joshua turned to Hope and gave her a small device from his shirt pocket.

"Hope, I will deal with the kidnappers and bring Roland back. Go to my temple. Behind the PIT, there is a gate. Enter 6377424 on the keypad then follow the path and wait for the demons who have infiltrated our community and deal with them. Do not go inside the temple."

"You know who they are, don't you?" Hope asked, inquisitively.

"Yes, my child. So do you and you know what you have to do."

Joshua left with Joel. Hope knew she had no alternative and knew she had to go alone. She left the Sync building and walked over to the Temple of Gethsemane. She started to feel a bit nervous knowing who had broken into The Haven and infiltrated the temple without permission.

She got to the gate and entered the code as Joshua had told her to, then she walked down the forest path that twisted and turned until she came to a clearing which was so dense and colourful. The plants and trees were bright green, lush and beautiful to look at. She waited to the right of the main entrance to the temple in case the perpetrators saw her before she wanted them to. She wondered how they managed to get the password to access the path, thinking that they would have likely guessed 'Hope' and 'Rachel' but then must have thought 'Messiah'.

Twenty minutes after she arrived, she heard something move and thought it must be the door to the temple. She listened carefully then a few seconds later, heard someone come out.

"He'll know someone's been in his temple. We need to find another way back."

"Going so soon, Hannah?" Hope asked, walking around from the right of the building.

She saw Hannah freeze and slowly turn around.

"Did you really think he wouldn't know you had broken into our property? Did you really think he wouldn't know the moment you desecrated the Temple of Gethsemane?"

"Rachel!" Hannah said. "So NOT good to see you."

"As I have said to you before Hannah, Rachel is dead. I am Hope Eve. You are trespassing. Please leave our property."

"Rachel, you need to listen to me. The Messiah is evil. Have you seen the message I sent you on Connect?"

"You mean the message from the anonymous account? Yes, I listened to it. Trickery and lies."

"No! What anonymous account? I messaged you from my own Connect account to your account, as Rachel Walker. Look, just go on there and read it. Then go in that Temple and look in the boxes of stuff Joshua has. Stuff he has taken without permission from every Hope he has had in Enlightenment."

"What are you talking about, every Hope?"

"You aren't the first Hope, Rachel. You aren't even the second. The Messiah has been lying to you from the beginning. He has been using you."

"Look, Hannah, I have tried to be nice to you but you need to leave. You are not welcome here and as I have just told you again, Rachel is dead. I haven't looked at that Connect account properly for months because I am no longer that person.

The Messiah told me to deal with you and I'm pretty sure he didn't just mean tell you to leave. But because we've been friends in the past and I don't wish you any harm, I will let you leave this time with a warning; if you ever come back here again, do not expect me to help you. As it is, I will have to answer to the Messiah for not dealing with you in the way he expected."

"What does that mean Rachel? Deal with us? Kill us? Is that what your precious Messiah would have done? You know he has a photo of us with Bo and Chad in there right? He also has your ripped denim skirt in the box as well, the one you loved. Look!"

Hannah walked down the steps, taking her balaclava off. She got her phone out and gave it to her former friend. Hope took the phone and looked at the photos. She looked up at Hannah with tears in her eyes.

"Hannah, I'm so sad that you would make this stuff up," Hope said. "Why couldn't you just be happy for me? Happy that I've finally found peace and found somewhere I can make a difference? You just couldn't do it, could you?"

Hope went through and deleted all the photos Hannah had taken.

"These are all fabricated lies and manipulated photos. Your sick attempts to destroy Joshua's good name will not work. Have your phone back. I have deleted all the photos. Leave and mark my words, if either of you attempt to return, do not expect leniency from of us again. You have ten minutes."

Hannah looked at her former friend incredulously.

"Rachel, I have tried SO hard with you. I have tried to warn you, tried to look out for you but you know what? Fuck you, fuck Enlightenment, you can all go to hell. If you have ANY sense about you whatsoever, you'll check your old Connect account and go to look in that temple. But don't bother to ever contact me again because I'm done.

We will take down your god damn sect and perhaps then you'll realise what a mistake you've made."

Hannah stormed off with Ralph closely behind. After they left, Hope got her phone out and called Joshua.

"They are gone, Messiah. I hope I have now made it clear to them that we will not tolerate any further infiltrations with as much leniency. Hannah took photos, which she claimed were of the inside the Temple of Gethsemane. I have wiped her phone completely."

"You have done well, Hope. I will release the doors to the temple. We have saved Roland and will be back at The Haven within the hour. Please join us in the Church of Souls."

Hope thought about what Hannah had said regarding what was in the Temple of Gethsemane but decided to go to the church as the Messiah had instructed her.

Before Hope started to make her way back, she took a moment to enjoy the beauty of the temple and the surrounding area. She walked up the stairs, sat down by the side of the temple and got her phone out. She logged on to her old Connect account and saw she had several messages from friends and family checking to make sure she was ok. She ignored them all except Hannah's message. She wasn't sure if she should click the link in the message or not as she was worried the Messiah would be upset if she was late to the church, but he had said he'd be back within the hour which gave her enough time.

Hope opened the link and entered the password as Hannah had instructed. She sat and read a horrifying tale of a woman who said she was the first 'Hope' that Joshua recruited. After struggling, she had eventually managed to escape what she described as a tyrannical monster.

After she finished reading through, Hope reflected on the contents of the blog and what she had seen based her knowledge and experience with Enlightenment so far. She thought that whilst there were parts that could have been true, most of it must have been made up because the woman had been in love with Joshua and he hadn't felt the same way. She clicked back to the Connect message Hannah had sent and sent a reply.

Hannah

I hope that this afternoon has taught you not to ever come back or cross us again. I have read this quite fantastic tale of a woman who was clearly in love with Joshua and felt the need for retribution after he turned her down. You need to stop this obsession with Joshua and stop trying to turn me against him because it will not work. Don't bother messaging me again unless you have something positive to say.

Hope

Hope closed her Connect account on her phone. She realised she needed to get back to the church as the Messiah would be back within a few minutes, so she started to walk back. As she got to the PIT, she heard someone whisper her name. She turned around and saw what looked like a woman with facemask and a scarf covering her whole head aside from her eyes, peering around the back of the building.

"Hope, is there anywhere safe we can talk?"

Hope realised she had heard the woman's voice before, on the recording sent from the anonymous account on Connect.

"Who are you?" Hope asked.

"I am you."

Chapter Twenty Eight //
19th August 2012 – The Haven, Starr County //

Hannah stormed off down towards the gate back to the PIT. Ralph was close behind.

"Who does SHE think SHE is? I helped that girl so much and this is how she repays me? I will take down this fucking sect if it's the last thing I do!"

Ralph stayed quiet. They got back to the car and drove back to the Owl Creek.

"Have you heard from Pastor Gore yet?" Hannah asked, impatiently.

"Not yet, but give him a call. He's on speed dial five."

Hannah picked up Ralph's phone and called the Pastor.

"Hello?"

"Hi Pastor, its Hannah. How did it go?"

"We got Willie and got away but Joshua's men came after us. They cornered us at Lexington point. We had no choice but to let them take Willie back. They didn't have guns and they were not forceful but there were too many of them for us to handle."

"Are you ok?"

"Yeah, we're fine. How did you get on?"

"We got inside the temple and found a lot of horrendous things. I took photos and saved them but there was one last door we couldn't access. I tried to enter the code a few times but I got it wrong and an alarm went off. We managed to escape but Rachel was waiting for us at the entrance. She took my phone and deleted the photos."

"What kind of things did you see?"

"Files of every single person in Starr County catalogued like lab rats. Joshua also had a box of stuff, some of which belonged to Rachel. When I told her, she didn't believe me and said was I manipulating the truth. She then told us that if we set foot in The Haven again, she would hand us over to the Messiah who would 'deal with us'."

"So, all that was for nothing? I'm so sorry Hannah. I think we now have to assume that we have royally pissed Joshua off. We need to start preparing for him to come back at us and come back hard.

"Agreed. I think we need to look at involving Sheriff Fowler and more law enforcement too."

"No one outside the county will do anything yet, trust me. Come back to the church and let's talk further."

****

Hope looked at the woman in amazement.

"What do you mean, you're me?"

"Is there anywhere private we can talk? Anywhere they... can't hear us?"

"You sent me that anonymous message on Connect?" Hope asked, surprised.

"Yes, I did."

"Come with me. We can talk by the temple,"

The woman was hesitant.

"Let's go to the biosphere then. I've checked over my apartment. There are no cameras or bugs."

"You just can't see them, trust me, they are there.

I have a boat by the eastern shore. Look, I know this seems a bit much but I cannot trust that they won't overhear us anywhere and I can't face Joshua. Come with me and we can talk there?"

Hope walked over to the boat with the woman and got in. It was a simple rowing boat, tied to a post by the edge of water. The woman followed Hope into the boat and took her mask off but kept her headscarf on.

"I'm so sorry to have to tell you this Hope, but you have been fooled. That article that you read online was real and I can prove it. I'm the woman that wrote it."

"You're Chloe?"

"That's not my real name but yes, I am. My website tracks everyone who comes online. I saw the location come up when you logged in and knew it must have been you. I was out fishing in lakes just off the southern shores of the Phoenix Mountains so I decided to row here straight away. I heard from my source within Enlightenment that the Messiah had chosen a new Hope. I had come here to warn you."

"How do I know you're not a friend of Hannah's who she's using to try and get me out of here? There is no way to get off The Haven except for the road tunnel so perhaps I should assume you came as part of the group who just infiltrated our community?"

"There is another hidden way through the mountains via boat. I found it on Squirrel as I was looking at the overhead maps. I also have no idea who Hannah is.

Look, I know you have no reason to believe me but everything I posted on that blog is true and I think the woman who was Hope before you, who disappeared after going into the temple, is either still locked in there or is dead and Joshua has never removed her body."

"Your blog is so fantastic, it can't be real," Hope said, dismissing the woman's story.

"Are you seriously telling me you've never once had doubts about Joshua's way of doing things?"

"Maybe once but…"

"When?" the woman asked.

"He asked me to meet him for confession and told me I needed to plug a device into my ear which allowed him access to my mind so he could see my thoughts and memories. The idea of another person being able to access that kind of information is frightening."

"What happened afterwards?"

"He told me that I'd passed the test with flying colours. Just after that was when Joel interrupted and told us about Roland being kidnapped. What do you think would have happened had Joel not interrupted us?"

"I think I can make an educated guess. The question is would you have let him?"

Hope looked away.

"Look, I was hoping you'd come with me and move on from The Haven before Joshua did anything that would leave you in the same state of mind as I was but seeing you now and your body language, I don't think you want to leave," the woman said, disappointed.

"I am grateful for you coming and I'm grateful for the information, but you're right, I don't want to leave. As I have said to others, I am in this for the long run. I need this to work out and I need the Messiah's help. I ultimately want to help people feel happier and fulfilled. I believe what Enlightenment are doing will go a long way to everyone living better lives."

"Then I won't stand in your way, but take my number down in case you need to contact me for any help or advice. I am staying in Starr County for another month, seeing family and friends but I won't be around after that again for some time."

"Thank you," Hope said, smiling. "I'm not excusing what the Messiah may have done in the past but I have to look at how he's treated me since I arrived here and based on that, he's given me no reason to leave. Are you feeling better now though? The blog you wrote was quite something."

"It's hard being around here knowing that I could see Joshua again at any point but the most important thing to me is trying to stop him from ever doing touching someone else the same way he touched me."

"Joshua has put me in charge of giving some classes a few times a week. How about if I use some of that time to talk through abuse, what help is available and also run through the feelings, thoughts and emotions that go through your mind after you've been through something like that?"

"As much as I would love that, unless Joshua has added anything about abuse into the book of Enlightenment, I wouldn't. The reason being that if he suspects you have spoken to anyone, he'll shut you down."

"But if he truly wants to make the world a better place, surely teaching about abuse and why it's never acceptable is something vital to improving society?"

"This is the problem, Hope. Joshua wants to heal the sick but to HIS vision of how things should be. Because he is an abuser himself, teaching that kinda thing wouldn't be acceptable."

Hope looked at the woman. She could see a real sadness in her dark brown eyes but also sheer determination.

"I have to go, but I will study the book and will look to incorporate as much about abusers as I can do without raising any suspicion. Are you going to be ok getting back before nightfall?"

"Yes, I will just go back the same way I came in, through the pass in the mountains. You have my number. Take care of yourself, Hope, and please be careful."

Hope got out of the boat and watched the woman row away, not sure what to make of the whole situation. Regardless of what this woman had said, she knew she didn't have a choice but to carry on with Enlightenment to try to help as many of the sick as she could and try to make the world a better place. Then once she had found Mason and he had been brought to justice, she could think about the future.

She turned and walked back towards the Church of Souls to meet Joshua as he had requested. As she approached the building, she could see that there were several vehicles already there. She walked into the hallway and saw the door to the inner sanctum was open. She heard Joshua talking with James and Joel.

"Well done, brothers. Everything is falling into place. God had foreseen Roland's kidnapping as a way for us to move forward with our plan.

Brother James, please go to New Frontier HQ in the morning and collect the order of weapons I placed with them. This has given us the perfect opportunity to arm ourselves and say we were provoked. Once we have the weapons order, we can start making further plans to take over this miserable county and rid the demons amongst us."

"When are you going to tell Hope of our plans, Messiah?" Joel asked.

"Once she has made her sacrifice, Brother Joel."

"Will we be allowed to watch as usual?" James asked, gleefully. Hope could hear a hint of excitement in his voice.

"Yes, brother, from the holding room. I would not deprive you of that pleasure."

Hope carried on listening in horror.

"Once Hope has made her sacrifice, I will help her rid the demons from her life as I promised and she will use a new strain of yellow Myst to start turning all demons in Starr County into an army of Enlightened. We will finally take over this wretched county."

Hope left the corridor, aghast and ran over to the labs. She couldn't believe Hannah had been right after all. How could she have been so blind? She knew she had to be very careful moving forward because she couldn't afford to lose the support of the Messiah. She still needed Enlightenment to help her find Mason.

She got to the labs and went to Roland's apartment, which was at the back of the building. She knocked on the door and heard 'come in'.

She entered the room and saw Roland sitting on his couch watching TV.

"Hey. Are you ok? I heard they got you back after what happened. Did the kidnappers hurt you at all?" Hope asked.

"It was Pastor Gore and a group of men, two of whom I've seen here before who used to be with Enlightenment. They didn't hurt me at all. They said they wanted to get me out to help me but I told them my home was The Haven now and I didn't need saving. Before I knew what was happening, our friends had surrounded the van and forced the Pastor to stop the vehicle. Joshua said that the Pastor had made a grave error in judgement that would have dangerous consequences for the entire county and they wanted me back immediately.

There was no aggressive behaviour from either side, the Pastor didn't stop me from going back. Joshua and the rest of our friends didn't hurt any of the Pastor's men.

On the way back, Joshua asked if I was ok. I said I was. He said that I'd been used as part of a diversion? Is that true?" Roland asked, surprised.

"Yes, you were. The Messiah knew others were trying to access the Temple of Gethsemane. Whilst he went to get you back, he sent me over to the temple to stop them."

"Who was it?"

"Hannah and Ralph."

"But... why?"

"Hannah is obsessed with trying to take us down. She claimed she saw things in the temple that proved that Joshua is not the man he makes out to be. As it is, she might be right."

"What? I thought you loved it here?" Roland asked, not believing what he was hearing.

"I do and I am fully committed to this project, but there are things that have happened which have left me questioning whether Joshua is being completely honest with us.

Hannah told me she had sent me a message on my old Connect account, which had a link to a blog she had read and detailed some quite horrific things about the Messiah. I read it and it was pretty over the top and quite out there, but there was too much information in there to believe anyone could have made the whole thing up.

Then after I told Hannah and Ralph to leave, I started to walk back over to the church as the Messiah had asked but I met someone on the way who said she was me."

"What do you mean? She was you?"

"She was the person who had written that blog. She says she was the original 'Hope' who the Messiah had chosen whilst Enlightenment was in Idaho. She had rowed through the mountains to reach The Haven to find me. She asked me to go back with her. I refused but I took her number in case I felt there was ever any need to call her.

I had wondered if she was someone who Joshua had been with at one point who fell in love with him but he didn't feel the same way. After she left, I walked back to the church and heard Joshua, James and Joel talking inside. Joshua said some awful things and indicated that my sacrifice would be that I would need to sleep with him.

I have a lot I need to think about, Roland. I need to work out whether or not I'd be willing to do be with Joshua in order to carry on working to achieve my goals. I need to figure out if there is any way I can use the book of Enlightenment to start teaching vulnerable women who have come here, about abuse and how they don't have to always say yes to men. Everyone has the right to stand up for themselves."

"If anyone can find a way, it's you, Hope. You are so strong and determined to achieve great things here."

"Thank you," Hope smiled at Roland. "Can I stay here tonight?"

"Of course you can."

"Hopefully, I'll be able to sleep on it and make a decision in the morning and a decision that won't involve me needing to leave The Haven."

Chapter Twenty Nine //
23rd August 2012 – The Haven, Starr County //

Hope spent the next few days with Roland, working on the Myst and trying to stay well away from Joshua, James and Joel. They managed to develop another new strain of the substance which, when tested on lab rats, put them in a complete state of trance.

Roland went out to get food to bring back to his apartment so Hope didn't need to go anywhere.

On the third day, Roland came back and told Hope that Joshua wanted to see her urgently.

"I've been putting it off too long," Hope said, afraid.

"Have you made your decision?"

"I have. I am going with my original plan of staying, even if that means having to sleep with Joshua."

"If you need me, then I will be here for you. We've made amazing progress over the past few days, definitely something to be proud of."

Hope left the apartment after getting dressed for the first time in days. She walked over to see Joshua in the church. She messaged Jess on the way to say she'd meet her later on and apologised for not being around.

When Hope got to the church, Joshua was waiting outside.

"Come in, my child," he said, sternly.

She did as he asked.

"What happened, Hope?" the Messiah asked, looking perplexed. "You were supposed to join us after leaving the temple the other night? Where have you been since?"

"After Hannah and Ralph left I had a long think about everything that had happened and went for a walk along the eastern shore of The Haven. I wasn't sure what to think of what Hannah told me about what she had found in the temple."

"And what was that, Hope?"

"She had pictures on her phone of a denim skirt that I brought here which I thought had been burned in the fire as well as one of a photo of Bo, Chad, Hannah and I on the first night I met Bo. Why did she have a photo of that Joshua? All of my possessions, including that photo, were supposed to have been burned?"

As soon as she asked the question, she knew she shouldn't have. A dark cloud of fury came over Joshua's face.

"You DARE you to question me? I gave you shelter, food, water when you had NOTHING. I gave you a new life in return for asking for your loyalty and THIS is how you repay me?"

The Messiah had fire in his eyes but Hope continued, determined to say her piece.

"I also was sent a blog by an anonymous account online which had some pretty intricate details about Enlightenment's past. Details about how you've had other Hope's in the past and how only one of them has survived."

"I think you should leave now, Hope," Joshua interrupted, turning away from her with his head bowed.

"I'm not finished, Joshua. I heard you the other night, talking to Joel and James about me making my sacrifice and how you're going to let them watch. What sacrifice do you expect me to make? Am I making the same sacrifices as the other women who have been Hope before me? Are you planning to rape me?"

Joshua turned around and moved so his face was right next to hers. She could see he was furious with the assertions she had made.

"LEAVE!"

Hope got up and walked out of the church. As she left the building, she got her phone out to call Roland.

"Hello?"

"Roland, I need you to drive me somewhere. Can you meet me outside?"

"On my way."

Roland met her outside the labs.

"What happened?"

"I confronted Joshua about what he said last night and asked him what he expected my sacrifice to be. He got mad and told me to leave. I need to get out of here for a while and think things over. I'm going to call the other Hope and see if she can help me."

Hope called the number the woman she had met had put into her phone. The woman answered the phone and Hope told her what had happened.

"Of course, come to Angel Pine in Silk Falls. I'll meet you at the front of the lake by the corner of sixth and main?"

"Perfect. See you in thirty minutes and thank you," Hope said, hanging up the phone.

****

Roland drove Hope to Angel Pine, after she had been back to the biosphere to pack an overnight bag with a few items. It took about twenty-minutes to get there from The Haven. When they arrived in town, Roland drove down Main Street to the block where the road met sixth and stopped the van. Hope said she'd let him know what was happening and asked him not to tell Joshua where she was.

As Roland drove off, a woman came over from the other side of the road. She had light brown hair and looked almost identical to the woman Hope had seen in one of the photos on Hannah's phone. The woman smiled at Hope as she approached.

"Hi Hope, what happened?"

"Hi…"

"My real name is Claire," she smiled. "Are you ok?"

"After you left, I walked to the church and overheard them talking about a lot of things that concerned me but also about my sacrifice which I've not yet made. From the conversation they were having, it sounded like he was going to do the same to me as he did to you and the other women. I was so scared Claire, but I had to confront him."

"You're lucky he didn't touch you hun. I'm so glad you're out of there and free of 'em. Do you know what you wanna do now?"

"I have nothing and no one. My best friend won't talk to me and my parents won't take me back. I don't even know if what I did was the right decision. I still believe in the cause and want to help make a difference."

"There are better ways to do that than by being with them. Stay with us for a few days and gather your thoughts."

"Thank you, Claire, that's really nice of you."

"We've got an OxiHome for a month. Never done it before, but it's so easy! Just signed up, contacted the homeowner and agreed dates then paid. They left everything we needed. It's on the corner of fourth and broadway, just up there," Claire pointed to a house in the distance.

"My husband is looking forward to meeting you! He's out of town for a few days but said he should be back by the weekend. I told him about you when we first got to Angel Pine. He pushed me to go and see you to make sure you were ok as neither of us wanted to see anyone else harmed by Enlightenment."

"He sounds like a good man," Hope smiled.

"He is. He's taken care of me these last few years. I'm really grateful."

****

Hope and Claire spent a few days getting to know each other and spending time relaxing next to and in the lake. Angel Pine was located at the very southern part of the Phoenix Mountains, about a two-hour walk from where Hope's parents lived. She thought about going to see them but couldn't face her dad, especially if he still hadn't forgiven her.

Hope found that she had a lot in common with Claire. They both had left home after arguments with their parents. They had both been hooked on drugs. They were both looking for an escape when they joined Enlightenment. They also both had similar interests in botany as well.

On the eighth day after leaving Enlightenment, Hope woke up to the most beautiful clear blue sky and sunshine beaming down. It was September 1st and was her 21st birthday. She got up, showered and checked her phone. Roland had sent her a message.

Hey

Happy Birthday!

Just letting you know that the Messiah has been asking after you. I told him that you needed space for a while. He's been getting more and more upset each time he's been to see me. If you don't come back soon, I'm worried he's going to do something to me.

Jess and Emily have also been asking after you as well. They are worried about you. I've told them you are ok, but you just needed some time away and will be back soon.

You will be back soon, right?

Roland

Hope replied thanking Roland for the birthday message and saying she was fine. She told him she was just evaluating everything but she would let him know as soon as she'd made up her mind.

Claire had said her husband would be back that evening and they could properly celebrate Hope's birthday with a nice meal when he arrived. Until then, they decided to swim in the lake and read. By the time they walked to the lake just after midday, it was around ninety degrees. They found a secluded spot on the small beach down from Ocean Boulevard and laid their towels out.

"How are you finding being away from Enlightenment?" Claire asked.

"I've not felt this relaxed in a long time. It's been lovely, thank you for having me."

"Do you think you might go back to Joshua?"

"Right now, I still don't know. I don't want to think about it today. Let's swim!"

They already had bikini's on so went into the water and swam for a couple of hours before spending some time reading afterwards.

Hope found herself feeling so relaxed and happy. She felt like a massive weight had been lifted from her shoulders and she didn't want the feeling to ever stop. The endless sunshine made her feel so good and even though she wasn't sure what the future held, she felt invigorated to attack it head-on.

Shortly after 5pm, Claire heard her phone go off. She picked it up to look at the message.

"Husband's back! Shall we go freshen up then go for dinner? Our treat!"

"You've done so much for me Claire, thank you. I can pay for myself."

"Absolutely not, it's your birthday! Let's get back."

They walked back up to the OxiHome Claire was renting. Claire opened the door and shouted,

"Hunny, we're home!"

Hope walked through the door behind Claire and pushed it shut behind her. Claire went into her room to change. Hope was looking forward to getting some more clothes on. As nice as wearing a bikini was, she felt a chill as she had walked in.

As she opened the door to the room she was staying in, she saw someone was in there, sitting on her bed. It was someone she knew.

"Hi Rachel, long time no see," he said, with an evil grin.

Hope screamed.

Chapter Thirty //
30th August 2012 – Midtown, Owl Creek //

Over the previous week, Hannah and Ralph had spent a lot of time helping Pastor Gore craft a plan to build up defences against Enlightenment. They went to see Sheriff Fowler in Midtown, Owl Creek to tell him about their dealings with Joshua.

Midtown was a rural village located ten miles north of Jefferson Canyon, and looked like it was stuck in the 1800s. There were very few vehicles around and those that did visit the area were all SUVs due to the town roads being mud. The Sheriff's office was a little way out of town just before roads worsened to the point they became un-drivable.

Ralf had driven Hannah and Pastor Gore to town a couple of days before the beginning of September. They parked in the car park opposite the police precinct. Pastor Gore said he needed to do a few things in town so would catch up with them at a later point during the day. Hannah and Ralph walked into the precinct and looked in awe at the beautiful interior. The walls and roof were all made from redwood with yellow lights hanging down. On the right was a desk that had a police officer sitting behind.

"Can I help you folks?" the duty officer asked, as they walked up.

"We've got a meeting with Sheriff Fowler," Ralph said.

"Ah! You're the folks from Silk Falls about Enlightenment? Right, this way."

The duty officer took them into a waiting room that was equally as beautiful as the rest of the building they had seen so far. Wooden benches surrounded the room with further benches in the middle and a water fountain near the door.

"The Sheriff will be right with you," the officer said, before leaving the room.

They waited for a couple of minutes before Sheriff Fowler walked in. He was a tall, well-built man. Hannah could see he was either bald or the only hair on his head was underneath the light brown hat he wore with his uniform. Sheriff Fowler asked them to follow him through another corridor and into his office. He opened the door and indicated for them to sit in the two chairs facing his desk.

"How can I help you folks?" the Sheriff asked, sitting down opposite them.

"We've seen first-hand what is going with Enlightenment and we're nervous about what their plans are," Ralph said.

"Are you ok, Son? Look like you've had some pretty serious surgery?"

"It's the work of Enlightenment, Sheriff. They infected me with something which the doctors still aren't too sure about but said that if I didn't have surgery, I could have developed a brain aneurysm."

"Do you have proof of this, Son?"

"I can't prove it 100% Sheriff but I sure as hell didn't have these stitches before I stayed with the sect."

"Unfortunately, Son, unless you can provide incontrovertible evidence that Enlightenment were responsible, there is nothing I can do."

"What if I got the doctor who operated on me to write to you?"

"That would help but you'd also need at least three witnesses from within Enlightenment to testify you were missing for that period of time."

"Well I'm one and Pastor Gore would be another. What about everything else?" Hannah asked.

"Such as?"

"You've seen how the sect is slowly infiltrating the county. Is there nothing we can do about that?"

"You mean taking over?"

"You've had a large turn over in deputies recently who have since gone and joined Enlightenment, there are churches around the county are now displaying Joshua's banners and the illegal purchase of government planes?" Hannah asked.

"Deputies come and go all the time, the job is one of the highest turnover positions I know of. I've not seen any churches displaying any banners and I don't know anything about any government planes that have been sold recently.

Look, I appreciate you folks' concern, but unless you have some evidence that cannot be disputed, I can't just go and raid private property."

"So there is nothing you can do at all? Not even go to The Haven to speak to him?"

"Not unless someone can present some solid evidence of a crime. I will keep all this noted down and we will keep an eye on things. Now, if you'll excuse me, I've gotta interview some new jail guards this afternoon," Sheriff Fowler said, getting up from his chair.

"Jail guards?"

"Yeah, haven't you been by the new Starr County Jail? It'll be finished in about a month. The state got permission six months ago and demolished Gator Stadium days after. They've done an exceptional job to get the building up so quick."

The Sheriff saw the look on Hannah's face.

"I'm real sorry, I guess Gators Stadium meant something to y'all then?"

"Yeah, we used to love going down to games. There's precious little else to do around here." Hannah said.

Hannah and Ralph thanked Sheriff Fowler for his time then walked into Midtown to grab some food and meet Pastor Gore.

"That was a total waste of time," Hannah said. "If he's not going to do anything, we're literally on our own."

"I can't believe they are so blind to what is happening,"

"I guess looking at it from their perspective, The Haven is secluded on an island in the middle of the mountains. Why would they ever need to go there? We need to find some way of getting hold of evidence surrounding these planes and maybe that will be enough for the Sheriff."

As they got to the corner of first and north, Hannah noticed police officers approach from all angles with their guns pointing at her.

"Hannah Taylor, you are under arrest for murder. You have the right to remain silent. Anything you say may be used in a court of law. You have the right to consult an attorney before speaking to us and to have an attorney present during questioning now or in the future."

A police officer handcuffed Hannah.

"Sir, you are free to go," the officer said, looking at Ralf. "Miss Taylor will be held at the local precinct before standing trial and being transferred to a maximum security facility."

"What the hell is going on? Who have I murdered?" Hannah asked the officer, looking perplexed.

"You are under arrest for the murder of David and Mary Taylor."

"Huh?" Ralph said. "Who are David and Mary Taylor?"

"My parents," Hannah said.

Chapter Thirty One //
1st September 2012 – Angel Pine, Silk Falls //

Hope stared in horror as Mason smiled at her sadistically. She wasn't ready for to see him again so soon. She had planned for Jess to talk to him on Connect then to lure him out before dealing with him for what she hoped would be the last time. All the feelings she had after finding Bo and realising it was her brother who had killed him, came flooding back. She thought about lunging for Mason and trying to hurt him but realised that wouldn't do any good at all as she had no kind of weapon to use, so instead she decided to try and get out of the apartment. She turned around to leave the room.

"Where do you think you're going, missy?" Claire was standing right behind her.

"What... I don't..."

"Aw, you don't understand? Well, let me explain," Claire grabbed Hope's wrist and forcefully pulled her into the main living room.

"You're hurting me!" Hope said, aghast.

"How lovely to see you, Rachel," Mason sneered, walking behind them.

Hope managed to wriggle free of Claire's hold and kicked Mason's groin. He collapsed on the floor in pain. Hope spat in his face.

"You bitch, just you..."

"Hunny, remember what we discussed," Claire said to Mason, who was writhing in pain on the floor.

Claire turned and slapped Hope across the face. Hope recoiled onto the couch, crying.

"Touch my husband again and it'll be the last thing you do, bitch."

"What the hell is going on?" Hope cried.

"Oh, you really don't get it, do you? Let me explain something to you, missy. This man looked over you and looked after you as you grew up. He kept you proper and off a bad path. He stopped you from mixing with the wrong crowd. What did he ask for in return? For you to love, appreciate and respect him. You just couldn't do it, could you?"

"Why are you doing this? I don't understand."

"Of course you don't," Mason chimed in, after finally recovering from the pain. "Princess Rachel, the apple of Pop's eyes, couldn't do anything wrong, perfect in every possible way."

"You have NO RIGHT to talk to me after killing Bo," Hope screamed, tears streaming down her face.

"That hurt me more than it hurt you, trust me."

"How could that POSSIBLY have hurt you more?" Hope said, aghast.

"Because he LOVES you," Claire interrupted. "He doesn't want to see you upset or in pain, especially because of something he's done. He's protected you in more ways than any other brother would and you repaid him by sleeping with the first guy you laid eyes on. How could you? Why couldn't you just love him back?"

"Because he's my BROTHER?" Hope said, incredulously.

"You don't deserve him. You don't deserve anyone. Did you know he used to look in on you to make sure you were ok every day?"

"He watched me showering through peepholes he drilled through to my bathroom, Claire. HOW is that normal? Why are you protecting him?"

"Because I love him, I married him, through sickness and in health. That's what we promised on our wedding day. Nothing will come between us. You couldn't even be bothered to show up."

"I wasn't even invited? I didn't even know you. Did he tell you he was already married? Did you know he ran away from his pregnant wife because he was spending all his time following me?" Hope sneered, looking at Mason.

"Yes. I know everything because he is completely open and honest with me. I also know what happened after that night you met Bo for the first as well. The night you thought your dad was abusing you."

"So you know he raped me?"

"He didn't rape you, Rachel. He got what he deserved after all the years of looking after you and protecting you," Claire said.

"You're sick in the head, the pair of you! Claire, as a woman, how can you stick by an abuser and rapist? How little you must think of yourself.

Mason, you struggled to meet anyone until you were in your mid-twenties when you met Abi. What kind of stuff fucked you up so badly you thought it was ok to rape your own sister and make it look like our dad was the one who did it?

Both of you quite clearly have serious unresolved issues and blame others for their successes because you believe you deserve to be where they are, but you're unwilling to work hard to get there,"

"How do you not get this, Sis? I didn't rape you. I LOVE you. I got what I deserved and Bo got what he deserved. He's dead. Get over it." Mason said, dismissing his sister's comment.

"Get OVER it? You KILLED my boyfriend. So now what Mason? What's next? What are you planning to do to me? Huh? You know it's my birthday."

Mason couldn't stop staring at his sister's chest. Hope realised she was still in the bikini she had worn down to the lake so she covered the area of her body with her arms and crossed her legs in pure disgust.

"We're going to give you the birthday you so richly deserve," Claire smiled, licking her lips.

"You… were never with Enlightenment, were you?" Hope asked.

"Wow, the penny has FINALLY dropped! No, Rachel. I was never with Enlightenment. I've never met Joshua."

"So you made everything up? The message on Connect, blog post, everything you said when you came to The Haven was a lie?"

"Wasn't it all perfect? It lured you here."

"You look so similar to the woman in the photo Hannah had on her phone though?"

"I know, isn't it great? She was my twin. She died of natural causes whilst she was with the sect. Joshua never touched her, he never abused her and he never asked her about her darkest secrets."

"Was anything you wrote in that blog was real? This mysterious contact you had within Enlightenment was obviously a complete lie."

"All the boring nice stuff and all the stuff about the other Hope's except their names. Oh and I don't know if Joshua killed the second one. Probably not. But I don't care," Claire sneered. "My sister was in a relationship with Joel, he told her everything, even after she died. I saw all his letters to her, even the ones he wrote her after she died."

"You made me question my loyalty to the Messiah when all he was trying to do was help and protect me. You made me leave my home." Hope sobbed.

"Never to return. Tie her up in the bedroom, Mason. I'm going to freshen up before the fun really starts."

Claire walked into the bedroom she shared with Mason and shut the door. Mason slowly got up.

"What does she mean, Mason? What are you going to do to me?"

"You know what, Sis? When I told Claire all about that night whilst Pop was in Murphy's, it turned her on. She said all she could think about was being with both of us. So here we are, the perfect birthday present. A night neither of you will ever forget."

Hope saw a large vase on the table next to the couch she was laying on.

"You know what, Mason? I've been... suppressing something for a while that I think you should know about."

Hope slowly stood up from the couch and let her arms drop to her sides. "That night outside Murphy's felt so good. I didn't know how to handle just how incredible it felt."

She licked her lips and massaged her body with her left hand. Mason looked dumbfounded.

"What?"

"Well, look at you. Those muscles are enough to turn any girl on. I just... couldn't control the feelings I had, so I suppressed them. But I see it now. I see that body and it's just making me feel so... Then the night you killed Bo, I was heartbroken, yes, but I think part of me almost... wanted it to happen so that one day, this could become a reality."

"Really?"

Mason's eyes were transfixed on her chest and were so wide, Hope could see his veins popping out. She grabbed the vase with her right hand and in one quick move, smashed it over his head.

"No, not really you sick pervert!" Hope shouted before running to grab her red dress and overnight bag from the room she had stayed in then smashing the front door open.

Claire heard the vase break and ran out of the bedroom completely naked. She saw Hope run out of the front door.

"DAMN IT MASON, GET AFTER HER!"

Mason didn't respond. He was out cold. Claire grabbed some jeans and a top from her room, threw them on, then ran out of the apartment, down to the lakeside but it was too late. Hope was nowhere to be seen.

.

Chapter Thirty Two //
1st September 2012 – Angel Pine, Silk Falls //

Hope watched from behind the back of the apartment block as Claire zoomed out and down towards the lake. She turned and looked down the alleyway she was standing in. There was no one around so she put her dress on then walked down the alley towards the road at the end. She looked left and saw a bus stop. She always kept a small bag of change on her for emergencies.

Hope jumped on the first bus that arrived which terminated near her parents' house. She struggled keeping her composure the entire way after everything that had just happened. Half way to her parent's house, the heavens opened and it started to rain heavily.

She got off where the bus terminated then made her way down to the Emerald River. Hope stood there, alone in the pouring rain, tears spilling down her cheeks. She couldn't stop thinking about how she ended up like this or what the future might hold. So much had happened over the past few months. She felt overwhelmed trying to make sense of it all.

She drifted slowly along the darkest parts of the Emerald River. Her wavy blonde hair was soaked, her crystal blue eyes were bloodshot red from the tears but she didn't care. She wanted a new start. She wanted the world to swallow her. Again.

As she got to Kiwi Point, she saw her old house from a distance. She couldn't let her dad find out what she'd done to Mason through fear of how he might react. His temper could change instantly and she knew he wouldn't understand, even though it was self-defence.

Things were so different less than a year ago. She had so much to look forward to. Then it all changed after that one night out in Great Falls. It led to so much suffering, so much hurt, so many tears. She was determined to make sure that no one else ever had to go through anything similar. She was determined to do what she could to change the world.

Just as she turned the corner near Alder Lake, she saw a man walking towards her. As he got nearer, she knew exactly who he was. She couldn't turn back and she couldn't hide because somehow, someway, if she did, she knew he would find her. She remembered what Hannah had told her. She knew she wasn't the first and likely wouldn't be the last. She knew she had to put her heart and soul into the future, into his vision otherwise, she could end up like the others.

Without realising, she had started singing as she drifted towards the Messiah.

Amazing grace
Once lost now found
A wandering soul
My heart now bound.

Chapter Thirty Three //
1st September 2012 – Silk Falls, Starr County //

Hope studied Joshua's eyes as she sang, moving ever closer towards him. She couldn't tell whether he was angry with her or not. The tears were rolling down her face as she walked into his arms.

"Hope, my dear Hope," Joshua said, hugging her. "I'm not angry, I'm not upset and I'm not disappointed. Every relationship has setbacks along the way. This was a setback. We will move past it. Let's go home."

He walked her back to the van, which he had driven to find her and put a dry towel around her to stop her shivering.

"How did you find me?" Hope asked.

"Roland told me where you had gone. He was worried about you. I guessed you would come this way at some point so I prayed and God told me where to find you. What happened in Angel Pine?"

"Someone came to The Haven, pretending to be the original 'Hope' who joined you when you were in Idaho. She told some quite fantastic stories about what you had supposedly done to her and the story of how she said she managed to escape. She tried to get me to leave with her but I refused to at the time. She gave me her number so after our conversation in the church, I gave her a call.

When I got to Angel Pine, she was kind, welcoming and generous. She said her husband was out of town on business. Today, we got back from swimming in the lake, I walked into the room I was staying in and found Mason sitting on the bed. I tried to escape but this woman was standing behind me in the doorway. I told her all about what Mason had done to me in the past. She said she already knew, didn't care because she was in love with him and they were married."

"What did she say her name was, Hope?"

"On the blog I was sent, she went under the name Chloe but when I met her in Angel Pine, she said her name was Claire."

"We have never had anyone join us called Claire or Chloe who I trusted enough to become part of my inner circle. There have only ever been three Hope's before you and there will be none after."

"What happened to them?"

"The other Hope's? One died of natural causes, another decided Enlightenment wasn't for her so she moved on with our best wishes. Their names were Genesis, Ruby and Peyton."

"Why did you say to James and Joel about being able to watch my sacrifice in the church when I overheard you all talking? What is this sacrifice I have to make?"

"All in good time, Hope, things have changed now. Roland has uncovered something quite extraordinary and we are going to move our plans forward. We will discuss everything when we get back to The Haven. I will tell you everything, I promise."

"I'm sorry I doubted you, Messiah," Hope said, ashamed.

"It's ok, Hope. I can see in your eyes how much you have suffered because of what happened. We all make mistakes. I have also atoned for getting angry with you. I am sorry we were not there to stop Mason from hurting you again. Once we are ready, all the demons in this county will be converted and we will all finally be free."

Joshua drove Hope back to The Haven. When they got back, Hope went to her apartment in the biosphere to change then walked back to the Church of Souls. Joshua was waiting for her in the inner sanctum.

"Sister, the time has come for the great revealing. I have invited James and Joel so we can be as one."

James and Joel came into the room and sat down.

"We have been working hard on a plan to end evil and corruption, to absolve the human race of sin and improve all our lives. The world has become a dangerous and corrupt place. Fossil fuels have left the planet starving and we, as a species, need to start giving back instead of just taking.

We need to rid the world of sin and the only way that will happen is to purge sin from the human race. Roland has done some exceptional work developing the Myst, which will allow us to start the great reaping. This process will not be easy, as many people we all love shall be sacrificed for the greater good.

"What do you mean by this? You're not planning to kill anyone?" Hope asked, concerned.

"Absolutely not. We are offering them a re-birth. A chance to change their lives for the better and start again with a passion to live, free of sin and free of corruption. The Myst will help us revolutionise the world, starting with Starr County and your sacrifice, Hope."

"What is to be my sacrifice Messiah? What must I do?"

"There are things in my past, like everyone else, which I'm not proud of," Joshua said. "I am not going to ask of you what you think I am. I am not the person others have told you. I have repented for the sins I have committed in the past.

What I am asking of you is far greater than anything I asked of any of the previous Hope's or James and Joel. You must go and seek your parent's forgiveness for what happened with your brother and help them to understand our cause. You must free them from sin, using the Myst and they will become our first Enlightened."

"I shall do as you ask, Messiah."

"It will not be easy, Hope. Nevertheless, this is the final test of proving your undying loyalty to our cause.

The time has come. We will soon start to enact our plans and rid this county of all demons who oppose us and heal the sick who will then work with us to build a brighter future for all mankind."

As soon as the Messiah had finished talking, he turned to Hope and slapped her across the face with the back of his hand.

"Don't ever question me again."

Chapter Thirty Four //
1st September 2012 – Silk Falls, Starr County //

Hannah's parents died in 2010. They had been driving across a large bridge when her dad had lost control of the vehicle, which then crashed through the barriers and over the side of the bridge. Hannah had always assumed it was an accident and the coroner had ruled as such after their autopsies. To hear the police now accusing her of their murder came as a shock.

The police walked Hannah back to the precinct in cuffs after taking all her possessions, including her phone, away from her.

"What evidence do you have that Hannah killed her parents?" Ralph asked, aghast. "When do we find out what is bail set at?"

"Bail will be set after Miss Taylor's first court visit on Tuesday next week. There is evidence placing Miss Taylor's DNA under the vehicle that her parents were driving when their brakes failed and their vehicle catapulted off Buffalo Bridge. As I'm sure you know, Sir, Buffalo Bridge is one of the highest in the United States of America. We do not doubt that Miss Taylor either wore the brake pads down or changed the brake line with a worn alternative so it snapped. She is a danger to us all sir, I suggest you stay well away."

"I wouldn't even know how to identify what cable related to the brakes!" Hannah shouted, incredulously.

The police officer raised his handgun.

"I suggest you keep quiet ma'am, otherwise we'll be forced to use this here weapon."

Ralph walked back to the police precinct with Hannah and the officers. Sheriff Fowler was out in interviews so the officers placed Hannah in a cell until he returned.

The officers told Ralph he could only wait with her for ten minutes but would then have to leave.

"Find the Pastor and get to the bottom of this. I bet this is that damn sect," Hannah whispered angrily.

"Do you really think Rachel would do something like this?"

"No, but if Joshua found out, he might well have. It can't be anyone else. I wouldn't have killed my own parent's Ralph, you have to believe me! They were all I had left in the world."

Hannah broke down crying.

"Of course I believe you. Let's see what bail gets set at and hopefully, I'll be able to pay to get you out."

He kissed her forehead.

"Sir," one of the police officers came over. "Sir, you need to leave now."

Ralph turned round to face the officer.

"Can you show me this evidence you have against Hannah Taylor?"

"I'm not at liberty to disclose that information, Sir."

"You don't have it, do you? Who has provided you with this supposed evidence?"

"Sir, if you don't leave I will be forced to arrest you for criminal trespass."

Ralph held his hands up and walked towards the exit of the precinct. As he did, he saw Sheriff Fowler who had just walked out of an interview, looking perplexed.

"Sheriff, have you seen this phantom evidence against Hannah?"

Sheriff Fowler looked over at Ralph.

"Sorry, I don't know what you are talking about. Why are you back here?"

"Your deputies arrested Hannah on suspicion of the murder of her parents. They died over a year ago, Sheriff."

"I need to catch up on my paperwork, but if my team has asked you to leave, please do so. I have your details and will be in touch with you as soon as possible."

Ralph left the precinct as asked and walked into town to find the Pastor. He was shaking with anger, determined to find out who had set Hannah up. He thought about contacting Willie to see if he could help investigate but thought better of it in case Willie told Joshua.

Ralph found the Pastor having a quiet drink in the local Saloon Bar.

"Where's Hannah?" the Pastor asked as Ralf walked in.

Ralph told him everything that had happened. The Pastor looked shocked.

"Sit down here. I'll get you a whisky."

"What are we going to do Pastor? How are we going to get her out of this?"

"I suggest you contact Willie to see if he can tell us any information or find out anything from Joshua, or we can send word to the sect and see if we can arrange a meeting?"

"Joshua won't allow us back into The Haven. I did think about contacting Willie but wasn't sure if it was a good idea. What if he went and told Joshua after we'd spoken to him?"

"Do you think he'd do that?"

"I don't know. We didn't see him at all whilst we were there. How did he seem to you?"

"He seemed fine. Didn't seem like he'd been brainwashed at all, his speech was less slurred from when I first met you all and he seemed happy. But it's hard to say, especially if he has been solely working on this Myst substance."

Ralph sank his whiskey and got his phone out of his pocket.

"Maybe I should try and contact Rachel. She would never have deliberately sabotaged evidence just to spite Hannah, even after everything that's happened."

Ralph opened the Connect application on his phone and opened a new direct message.

Hi Rachel

Hope you are keeping well and I hope Joshua is treating you well.

Something awful has happened. Hannah's been jailed for the murder of her parents. I know she didn't do it! Her folks died over a year ago in a car crash which was ruled an accident. There was no evidence of foul play at all after the original inquest. Suddenly, the cops say they've been given new evidence showing her DNA was found underneath the vehicle hours before her parents' death.

Can you help me find out if Joshua or anyone else within Enlightenment knows anything about this? For Hannah's sake?

Ralph sent the message then turned to Pastor Gore,

"I've asked Rachel if she can find out any more information. I don't see who else could or would have done this though other than the sect?"

"Hopefully she'll come back to you," Pastor Gore said.

Chapter Thirty Five //
2nd September 2012 – The Haven, Starr County //

Hope was still feeling the effects of the Messiah's slap the previous night as she walked over to see Roland. It scared her thinking about what Joshua might be capable of but in coming back to The Haven, she knew she had now committed herself fully into Enlightenment. She arrived at the lab and saw Roland was already hard at work.

"Oh hey, good to see you back! How was your birthday?"

Hope burst into tears.

"It was horrible. Has Joshua not told you what happened?"

"I haven't seen him since yesterday morning,"

Hope told him everything, from Claire betraying her with Mason then how she escaped and saw her parents' house before the Messiah finding her walking along the river.

"So this Claire wasn't ever part of Enlightenment at all?" Roland asked.

"No, but she looked so similar one of the women in the photos that Hannah showed me. She said she was twins with her and her twin was the one who became the first Hope."

Hope felt her phone vibrate in her pocket. She got it out, looked and saw a new notification.

"Speaking of Hannah, I just got a message through from Ralph. He's saying Hannah's been arrested for the murder of her parents? I know she couldn't have done that because she was with me the whole day."

"What? What does the message say?" Roland asked, looking shocked.

Hope showed him the message.

"I know what she's said to me and what she has done to us, but we have to help her. I'll go and see Joshua."

Hope went to the Church of Souls but Joshua wasn't there so she checked the Sync building then the Auditorium. No luck in either of those either. She then doubled back around to the biosphere and called up to his penthouse suite. No answer. She knew he hadn't left The Haven as all the trucks were there. The only other place she thought to try was the Temple of Gethsemane.

She walked over to the gate by the PIT and put the password in then opened the gate. As she walked around the final section of the winding path, she heard a scream. She ran the last bit up to the temple and saw the door was open. She ran up the stairs outside the front of the temple. There was another scream.

Hope ran inside, through the first corridor and saw Jess standing in a stone room ahead. There were stone doors to the left and the right then a door at the end, which was open.

"Jess, are you ok?"

"In… in there," Jess stammered, pointing towards the door at the end.

Hope walked towards the end door and peered around. She saw a square room with three animal carcasses propped up, one in each corner. In the middle of the room was a chair, facing away from her. Something was sitting on it. It looked human but had blue smoke emanating from its skin and was bald. There was a hum coming from inside its body. It slowly got up and turned around, staring at Hope with its crystal eyes transfixed on hers. She was mesmerised as she walked into the room.

"HOPE!" A voice shouted from outside. "Get away from the door NOW."

Hope slowly backed away without taking her eyes off the creature, which didn't move but now had a sick, sadistic smile. She backed through the door and into Joshua who was standing just outside with a dead boar. He threw the carcass into the room and entered a code, which closed and locked the door.

Hope turned to Joshua.

"Wha… what is that thing?" Hope stammered.

"That was an experiment gone wrong," Joshua said, quietly. "We developed a red strain of the Myst which we used on a willing member of Enlightenment who the turned into that; a savage, evil monster. That is the opposite of what we are hoping to achieve. I had wanted to show you under controlled conditions, Hope. Why did you come here?"

"I was looking for you, I need to talk to you about something that's happened to Hannah so I came to see if you were here then I heard Jess scream. Wait, where is Jess?"

"She is outside. Did you bring her here with you? You know this is sacred ground, Hope." Joshua asked, his eyes narrowing.

"Of course not! She was already inside the temple when I got here. I assumed she must have been with you?"

"We'll deal with that later. For now, come back to the church. We will talk there."

The Messiah ushered Hope out of the temple and told her to wait out front. Hope did as he asked. Jess was waiting at the foot of the staircase leading up to the entrance to the temple. Hope walked down and hugged her.

"What was that thing?"

"I don't know. The Messiah said it was an experiment gone wrong. It looked like it could have been female in the past but I can't be sure. The hum coming out of it was weird. The blue skin and lack of hair freaked me out. It was almost as if the substance that thing was injected with turned it into a zombie.

What were you doing in the temple anyway Jess? The Messiah has forbidden anyone from going in there without his express permission."

"He brought me here," Jess whispered. "He told me he needed my help with something urgent so I came with him. He pressed a load of numbers on the small device he carries around and both the outside door plus the door that connects the first and second corridors opened. We walked inside and he told me to wait in the main corridor. He disappeared through a door on the right side then two minutes later that end door opened. As soon as I saw that thing, I screamed. I'm so glad you were nearby and heard it."

"Ok, go back to your room at the Ashbrook, I'll come and find you as soon as I can."

Hope got Jess to leave quickly before the Messiah came out of the temple.

"Walk with me, Hope. Where is Jess?"

"She was terrified, she's gone to calm down and I said I'd speak to her properly later."

"That's good, thank you. That creature in the room you found was our last Hope. Her name was Peyton. She volunteered to trial a red version of the Myst we had developed. Unfortunately, the side effects of that particular strain were not expected and the substance did things to her that we couldn't reverse. We had to lock her down for her safety and ours. The substance changed her brain pattern, turned her skin blue and produced that humming noise you heard. It seems to get worse the hungrier she gets so I try to go in to feed her every few hours.

What did you need to talk to me about?"

"It's Hannah."

"What has she done now?" The Messiah asked, his face darkening in mood.

"She's been arrested for murdering her parents. Except, I know she didn't do it because I was with her the whole day when they died. The police say they've been sent new evidence which proves she tampered with their car. Is there any way you can help me find out who did this?"

"I'm sorry to hear that Hope. I truly am. My time must be focused on doing everything I can to help the sick, but I understand we have recently had some new members of Enlightenment who you previously knew from before you arrived? Talk to them. I will ask Brother Joel to assist you."

"Thank you, Messiah. I will find Jess to make sure she is ok then gather the sick you mentioned. We will find the people that have framed Hannah and will get her out of jail. I'm hoping this will also go some way to gaining her trust that we are here to help."

"Do as you need to, Hope. I will make all the resources I can available to you. Whilst we have branded Hannah a demon, I do not want to see anyone suffer for sins they have not committed. Brother Joel will meet you shortly."

Joshua headed off towards the church. Hope watched him walk away then went to the Ashbrook. She called Jess on the way who then met her outside.

"Are you ok?" Hope asked, as she approached her friend.

"Yeah, I don't understand what just happened. The whole thing was weird. The Messiah asked me to come and meet him at the back of the PIT because he needed my help with something so I did. When I got there, he didn't say anything else except to follow him. So we walked, in silence, to the Temple of Gethsemane. He opened the doors using his device I told you about then we walked through the first corridor and into the second with those rooms in. He then told me to wait. After he disappeared, the door to the other room opened. I saw that thing inside and screamed. I couldn't help it, it looked so evil. It started walking towards me so I screamed again. Then you rushed in. When you went into the room, the Messiah reappeared and told me to go outside. I'm so confused."

"I wonder why he wanted you to go there in the first place," Hope pondered. "He told me that thing in the room used to be a previous Hope who had volunteered to try a new red strain of the Myst substance which had done things to her that they couldn't reverse. He said that for the safety of everyone else in Enlightenment and her own safety, he had no choice but to lock her away in that room."

"Awful," Jess shuddered.

"He had that dead boar with him though to feed it. Did he have anything with him when you both walked into the temple?"

"Not that I remember."

"Has the Messiah ever spoken to you before today?"

"No. That's what made this even weirder," Jess said, confused.

"Let me know if he ever asks to see you again. How've you been anyway? Sorry I haven't been around."

"Yeah, I've been good! I've been hanging around with the FREEDOM lot mostly. Oh yeah, Mason messaged me to see if I was back yet. I didn't know what to tell him so I just said that work needed me to work away longer and I'd let him know."

"Yeah, well, I saw Mason whilst I was away from Enlightenment," Hope said, shuddering.

"What?"

Hope told her friend all about what happened after she met Joshua in Sync up to Mason surprising her on her birthday.

"What the hell? That's horrendous, Hope. What you've just told me has made me more determined to help you get some revenge on this guy."

"I think there is only one way I can get rid of Mason otherwise he's never going to stop until I submit to his every wish, his every desire. He's leaving me no choice.

The Messiah has told me that my sacrifice is going to be the hardest thing they've ever asked anyone to do. It's to do with my parents. I'm really scared, Jess. I haven't seen my parents in months and I have to get them to believe in Enlightenment's cause. I don't think they'll understand."

"What did the Messiah say would happen if that's the case?"

"I know what I have to do in that instance," Hope said, looking at her friend forlorn.

Hope saw Joel walking towards them from the Church of Souls.

"Jess, I have to go but I will catch up with you tomorrow?"

"Sure."

Hope walked over and met Joel near the forest.

"Sister, I have gathered the sick you talked to the Messiah about. They are in the auditorium and have some information that may interest you regarding your friend's arrest."

"Thank you, Brother Joel. Walk with me?"

"Of course."

"What did you know of the other women who Joshua chose to be Hope and were with Enlightenment before me?"

Joel looked at her with sadness in his eyes.

"Genesis was one of my closest friends, although I never knew her family. The Messiah told me what happened to you in Angel Pine. I'm sorry we were not able to provide you with more protection against Claire and your brother, but I will help you find them. Genesis was nothing like her sister. She was kind, caring, considerate, and beautiful."

Hope could see tears form in his eyes.

"You were in love with her, Brother Joel?"

"Yes, we were together for a while before she passed."

"What happened if you don't mind me asking?" Hope asked.

"She had bowel cancer. She suddenly starting losing weight and complaining of cramps. We tried everything we could to help her. The Messiah paid for the best treatment available but she passed a few months after the initial diagnosis."

"I'm so sorry." Hope said, putting a hand on Joel's shoulder.

"Thank you, Sister. She was an amazing Hope and a beautiful spirit. But others have come since who have brought their own attributes to our society."

"Ruby and Peyton?"

"Yes, Ruby was one of the most gentle and beautiful women any of us had ever met but ultimately her kindness meant she couldn't agree with how the Messiah wanted to proceed with those who oppose our vision. She wanted to help every single soul and we all realise that is beyond the realms of possibility. Some just do not want to help or to save themselves from their own sickness.

Peyton was the third Hope. She was doing well at integrating into our culture and ways of living before she agreed to be the test subject for a red strain of Myst that was developed. The Myst altered her DNA and she became a danger to not only everyone in Enlightenment but herself as well. The Messiah has kept her locked away until we figure out what to do with her."

"I saw her, Brother Joel. I went to look for Joshua, as I had to let him know what happened to Hannah. I couldn't find him anywhere so I went to the Temple of Gethsemane. The door was open. I heard screaming inside. I went in and found Jess, standing petrified looking at the cell where Peyton was. The door was wide open so I looked inside. I've never seen anything which has scared me more in my life. I thought she was going to attack me until I heard the Messiah's voice."

"Why was Jess in the temple?"

"She says the Messiah took her there and left her outside the cell where Peyton was then disappeared. He asked me if I brought her with me when I came to find him, which I know I didn't."

Joel looked perplexed.

"I've seen him do this before..."

He stopped mid-sentence as he saw Joshua approaching them.

"I come bearing excellent news. We are now able to protect our Haven properly as James has brought back the shipment of weapons from New Frontier that we had expected to receive a few weeks back. We will finally be able to move our plans forward.

Hope, I'd like to make your sacrifice soon. I am happy to come with you if you feel you need support." Joshua said, excitedly.

Hope looked at Joshua with no emotion on her face.

"I will do as you ask, Messiah. I would like Roland to accompany me to see my parents."

"As you wish, Hope. I'm happy you and Roland have such a... good relationship."

He looked at her sternly then walked off.

"What was that about?" Hope asked Joel. "He sounded... jealous?"

"You are our Hope, Sister. Joshua holds us all to the same degree of expectation in that we devote ourselves to him and his teachings. He expects nothing less than 100% devotion to him once you have made your sacrifice, in every part of your life. That includes your personal relationships."

"So he expects us to show him pure obedience and loyalty towards him but he is allowed to be polygamous?"

"He is the Messiah. Someone has to lead us and in return, he expects us to be completely faithful."

They arrived at the teaching school. Joel opened the door for Hope who walked inside. The ex-heads of FREEDOM were sitting chatting in the auditorium.

"Hey guys! Joshua told me you had some information about what happened to Hannah regarding her arrest. I know we've all had our differences with Hannah, but she doesn't deserve to be locked up for something I know she didn't do," Hope said.

"I have an idea who planted the information," Wes said, standing up. "After you all left FREEDOM, this guy was hanging around asking questions about you all. Emily said he's your brother?"

Hope nodded.

"Well, he was asking us about your relationship with Bo and Hannah's relationship with Chad. We told him that we didn't know you that well and you'd been removed from the town due to breaking the rules. He asked which rules you had broken. We told him that was confidential. He then started asking if what had happened to Bo and Chad had affected the relationship between you and Hannah. We again said that we hadn't had many conversations with you and didn't know. He then walked away and muttered that it didn't matter anyway because Hannah would be gone soon too."

"What?"

"That's not even the full story," Jonny piped in. "Em told you about what happened and why FREEDOM got shut down right? Well, after the police left and took the drugs away from the tent that no one knew anything about, we searched the rest of the tent. There wasn't much in there, but we did find this."

Jonny handed Hope a clear plastic bag with a piece of paper in.

"We think the police dropped it. It's a drawing of a 1970 Dodge Charger, specifically the underneath of the car and if you look at the bottom of the drawing, there's a small picture."

"That was the car Hannah's parents were driving when their brakes failed, but how did you...?"

"Joshua met us when we arrived here and asked us about where we were from. When we told him, he asked us to bring anything we had relating to FREEDOM with us into the community and keep it safe. When Joshua told us to meet you earlier today, he said that it was about Hannah and that we should bring any items we saved from FREEDOM with us. This is all we could think of that might be of any use. I've no idea how he knew we had it or how he knew it would even relate to what happened to Hannah."

Hope looked at Joel who shrugged his shoulders.

"Are you happy for me to borrow this?" she asked Jonny.

"Sure, do want you like with it. We don't need it back," Emily smiled. "Please pass our best wishes on to Hannah if you see her."

Emily, Wes, Jonny, Kayla, and Matt left the auditorium. Joel took some plastic gloves out of his pocket and opened the document on the table.

"Exactly what they said it would be," Hope said. "We need to get this to the police right away. Will you drive me, Brother Joel?"

"Certainly, Sister."

They left the auditorium and walked back over to the Church. Just as they arrived, Joshua came outside with something in his hand.

"I hope that helped you find out more about who was behind your friend's arrest. I have been to see Roland who has provided me with something that I would like you to take to your parents, Hope. If they are unwilling to invest in our vision, they must be sacrificed for the greater good. This is a new strain of yellow Myst, which Roland has been working on. It is a stronger version of a previous development, which takes hold of a demon and turns it into a new hybrid creature we are calling the Enlightened.

If your parents stand against us, they will become the first of the Enlightened. Many more shall follow until the county starts to understand they must admit their transgressions, atone for their sins and become well again."

Hope studied him, feeling crestfallen. The last thing she ever wanted to do was to hurt her parents but she knew that if she did not obey the Messiah's instructions, he'd punish her and likely find a way to give them the Myst anyway. She took the bottle from him.

"I will do as you ask, Messiah."

"Good. First, travel to deliver the document provided by the sick, which should exonerate Hannah of any wrongdoing. Then travel to see your parents. Let me know when it is done."

"I am to go to my parent's now? I had hoped you would allow Roland to come with me as we had discussed, Messiah?"

"Roland is busy. You will go tomorrow with Brother Joel."

"As you wish, Messiah."

Hope decided to go back to the biosphere. It had been a long day and she just wanted to relax. She also needed to prepare herself for seeing her parents.

As she left Joshua and Joel, she turned around and saw them deep in conversation.

As Hope got closer to the biosphere, she saw Roland was waiting for her.

"Hope! I've been looking for you but I saw you were with Joel and the Messiah so didn't wanna disturb. Has Joshua spoken to you about the Myst?"

"He has. He wants me to take the new strain he says you gave him and use it on my parents if they react negatively to our plans. I know my dad won't be at all receptive. I don't know if I can do it, Roland," Hope said, with tears in her eyes. "I wanted you to come with me but the Messiah said you were too busy."

"I need to let you know, it's worse than that. This version of yellow Myst will kill off any resemblance of the human being and turn them into a completely new hybrid. I've never seen anything like it. It turns their skin blue, all their hair drops out of their entire body. Their eyes become bloodshot red, all day, every day. They lose all sense of individuality and just… exist."

"I can't… kill my own parent's Roland? I just can't!"

"What do you think the Messiah will do if you don't go through with it?" Roland asked.

"I'll be kicked out of Enlightenment at the very least…"

Roland moved his head closer to her ear and whispered,

"That creature in the temple did not volunteer. He did that to her by making her ingest the Myst."

"How do you know this?" Hope said, looking at Roland wide-eyed.

"I overheard the Messiah talking in the Church of Souls. He said that if you didn't go through with giving your parents the Myst, he'd make you take it and you would become the first of the Enlightened."

Hope looked at Roland in horror.

"So I've no choice? I have to kill my parents to save my own life?"

Chapter Thirty Six //
3rd September 2012 – Midtown, Starr County //

Hope arrived at the Church of Souls at 10am and met Joel. She opened the passenger side of the van and as Joel opened the driver's side.

"Yesterday when I left you and Joshua, I saw you both deep in conversation. Was there anything else Joshua needed me to do today, Brother?" Hope asked.

"He gave me additional instructions for you which we will discuss once Hannah has been released from jail."

Hope decided not to push Joel to give her any more information until later.

They arrived in Midtown just after lunchtime. Joel parked the van in the precinct car park.

"Do we have everything we need, Sister?"

Hope took the plastic pouch out with the document inside. She had made sure not to touch the document itself at all. Joel nodded and got out of the van. Hope followed and they walked into the precinct. Hope looked around but couldn't see Hannah anywhere.

"Can I help you folks?" the officer on duty asked.

"We need to see the Sheriff urgently please, officer. Hannah Taylor is innocent and we can prove it," Hope said.

"Oh can you now? Just you wait there, Miss."

The officer got up from his desk and walked around the corner, into a room behind him. Thirty seconds later, Sheriff Fowler appeared and asked Hope and Joel to follow him around to separate room through the precinct. They walked past cells holding prisoners and Sheriff Fowler opened a door to a room at the end of the corridor.

"Rachel? What are you doing here?" a voice came from behind them.

Hope turned around and saw Hannah standing up, holding the bars to her cell.

"Getting you out," Hope said, smiling at her old friend.

"PLEASE do not talk to the criminals," Sheriff Fowler said, ushering Hope and Joel into the room in front of him. He followed them in and closed the door.

"I understand you folks have evidence which exonerates Miss Taylor of any wrongdoing?"

"Yes your honour... wait, Sheriff," Hope said, looking confused.

She got the plastic sleeve out with the document inside.

"This document was found by the heads of FREEDOM right after Colter Bay PD shut the town down. It was located in a tent, owned by someone who was not part of FREEDOM. Run fingerprint scans on this document, I guarantee you won't find Hannah's on there."

"What is this here document, ma'am?"

"It's the underneath of a 1970 Dodge Charger. The same car that Hannah's parents were in when they died. Whatever evidence you have been given has clearly been forged as this is the original."

Sheriff Fowler got up and took the document.

"Stay here."

He walked out of the room, without closing the door behind him. Hope waited for a minute then peered around the door. She couldn't see any officers in sight down the long corridor which veered off to the right at the end. She quietly sneaked out over to the cell Hannah was in.

"Why are you here, Rachel?" Hannah asked, confused.

"To get you out! I know you didn't kill your parents, you were away with me the whole time. You couldn't possibly have!"

"But I can't prove that."

"We can. It turns out shortly after we left FREEDOM town, Colter Bay PD shut it down. They carried out a drugs bust. After the police left, Emily and Kayla searched a tent that they didn't recognize where the cops said they found the drugs. They found a document inside a plastic envelope that one of the police officers dropped. It was a document of a 1970's Dodge Charger."

"Wait, that's the same car my parents were driving? Who left the document?"

"Jonny said that Mason was snooping around town shortly after we'd gone and was asking about our relationships with Bo and Chad. Particularly if their deaths had affected our friendship. Jonny said that they didn't know us that well and wouldn't have told Mason even if they did. He said that Mason muttered that it didn't matter anyway because you'd be gone soon too."

Hannah was shocked. It took her a few minutes to compose herself before asking,

"How did you find this out, Rachel?"

"Emily, Kayla, Jonny, Wes, and Matt came to Enlightenment after FREEDOM was shut down. We got chatting. Once I found out you had been arrested, I asked Joshua if he could help get you out because I knew you hadn't killed your parents. He told me to meet the FREEDOM heads with Joel who then gave us that document and told us what happened. They said they hope we get you out today and asked me to tell you that they never had any issues with you or any of us. "

"How could Joshua possibly have known?"

"Hannah, if you'd have given the Messiah more of a chance initially, you'd have seen what a generous and kind man he is to those who genuinely need help."

Hannah didn't reply.

"I have to go as the Sheriff will be back soon and I don't want him to see we've been talking to you but keep the faith. We will get you out of here today."

Hope walked back into the room and sat down. A few minutes later, Sheriff Fowler walked in looking confused.

"I've run this here document through several tests and the document does not have the accused's fingerprints on it."

Hope smiled.

"So that's good, right? She can go?"

Sheriff Fowler continued, "I then inspected this here document with a magnifying glass and you can see a tiny name at the bottom of the reverse side of the document."

He took the document and placed it on the table then gave Hope a magnifying glass.

"Before you look at this here document, look at this."

He produced another identical document and turned it over.

"This here identical document clearly says the accused's name on the back and when we checked our databases for fingerprints, the accused's were all over it."

Hope looked at both documents. She scanned the document that said Hannah's name at the bottom first. She then scanned the document she had given to Sheriff Fowler. The other document gave the name of the automobile garage in Angel Pine.

"Mason!" she said, quietly.

"Sorry ma'am?" Sheriff Fowler asked.

"Have you called the garage on the document I gave you, Sheriff?"

"I have indeed ma'am. They said this here document was sold to a tall young man with blonde hair who smelt heavily of cigarettes. Didn't keep a name on record for the young man."

"It was my brother, Sheriff. Mason Walker. We've been searching for him for some time. He murdered my boyfriend and raped me."

"You have evidence of this ma'am?" Sheriff Fowler asked, raising his eyebrow.

"Doctor Garcia at the Starr County Clinic will have records of the tests I had to undergo after the rape took place. There is also Mason's mobile, which I handed over to Colter Bay PD. It was found at the scene where my boyfriend was found dead."

"I will get in touch with Colter Bay PD and we will co-ordinate the search for your Brother. I'm real sorry for the wrongful arrest of the accused ma'am. I will arrange to release her immediately."

"Did Mason bring you the document himself, Sheriff?" Hope asked.

"No. It was a gentleman ma'am. He was just shy of 7ft tall, had brown hair and an odd moustache, looked like an ex-convict. Said he'd been told to give it to us and that we needed to pick up the accused as she was a danger to society."

Hope turned to Joel, her eyes wide as if she couldn't believe what she was hearing.

"That sounds like Roland?"

"He said his name was Willie, ma'am," Sheriff Fowler said.

"When did he come into the precinct, Sheriff?"

"Hmm… let me see now. It would have been just a few days before the accused came in. Said he'd just come back from Angel Pine. The officers looking at the evidence did not finish their initial investigations until just after the accused left the precinct after initially coming to see me, which is why the accused was arrested shortly after she left the precinct."

Hope thanked the Sheriff for his time then walked out of the room with Joel. Hope noticed Hannah's cell was empty. They walked through back into the lobby and she saw Hannah waiting.

"Just got to have you sign this here document ma'am," the officer on duty said to Hannah.

Hannah did as she was asked then the officer gave her everything they had confiscated from her upon arrest.

"What the hell is going on, Rachel?"

"It turns out that Roland seems to know Mason. Roland brought the document with your details on to give to the police which he must have done on the way back to from Angel Pine."

"Why was he in Angel Pine?"

"It's a long story, but Midtown PD are now coordinating with Colter Bay PD to search for Mason and arrest him for murder. I'm just glad you're free."

"Thank you, Rachel. I'll call Ralph to come and get me."

"No it's fine. We'll give you a lift back home. I'm going to see my parents afterwards so it's kind of on the way anyway."

"Thanks," Hannah smiled coldly.

They walked back to the van. Joel got into the front. Hope and Hannah opened the back and got in. Whilst Joel drove back to Hannah's, Hope explained everything that had happened, from meeting the other Hope to Angel Pine then finding out what had happened to Hannah.

"Rachel, I'm grateful for you getting me out, but I still can't forgive you for sticking with Enlightenment and I am still going to do everything I can to stop Joshua."

"Even after everything I've told you? I wouldn't have been able to rescue you if it wasn't for Joshua!" Hope said indignantly.

"Enlightenment gave Ralph a life threatening illness. He could have died! I know what Joshua has planned and I cannot and will not allow it to happen to innocent people."

"Then this is the last time we will speak because I'm done trying, Hannah."

Joel stopped the van. Hope opened the back doors.

"Wait, we're not even in Silk Falls yet!" Hannah said, alarmed.

Hope pushed Hannah out of the back of the van then threw her bag out afterwards and closed the doors. Joel drove off, leaving Hannah on the side of the highway.

Chapter Thirty Seven //
3rd September 2012 – Walker Conservatory, Starr County //

Joel stopped the van a few hundred yards from Hope's old house. They got out of the vehicle and stood at the side of the road.

"You know what you need to do, Sister."

"I don't know if I can go through with this, Brother Joel," Hope said, tears forming in her eyes.

"The Messiah predicted this might happen. He understands how difficult this must be for you and the pressure you must feel right now. He has given me a sample of the blue Myst that Roland has produced just for you to use. Do not be afraid, Sister. If you look at this bottle compared to the strain that the Messiah asked you to give to your parents, they are very different."

Hope compared both bottles and noticed the Myst that Joel asked her to take was light shade of blue and the bottle Joshua gave her to give to her parents was yellow. She took the bottle of blue Myst Joel had and drank the contents. Suddenly, she lost all of her anxieties, worries and fears.

"I am ready, Brother Joel. Wait for me here."

Hope walked towards her parents' house in a trance like state. She drifted down the driveway and knocked on the front door. Earl opened the door and looked shocked when he realised who was outside.

"Rachel?"

"Hello Daddy."

"What are you doing here? Where have you been? We've been worried sick."

She looked at him, devoid of emotion.

"Is Mother home?"

"Yes, but…"

"Can you both meet me in the kitchen? We have a lot to discuss."

Hope drifted into her parents' kitchen. As Earl went upstairs to fetch Susan, she made them two mugs of coffee, pouring the yellow Myst into both.

"What's going on Rachel? We haven't seen you for months and you just turn up unexpectedly with no explanation, looking like… that? Where are your shoes?" Susan asked, as she came down stairs.

Hope looked at both of them, knowing what she was about to do. She sat on one of the armchairs. Earl and Susan followed and sat down on the couch.

"First of all, I'm sorry I accused you of raping me, Daddy. I now know it wasn't you. I know it was Mason. I found out he had also been spying on me here whilst I showered. I found my boyfriend slumped in a pool of his own blood because Mason killed him. I managed to escape before he tried to rape me again, after kidnapping me."

Her parents were shocked. They sat in silence, unable to comprehend what their daughter had just told them.

"I've been working with a group called Enlightenment who took me in and have helped me become a better person. They are looking to help all of us improve our lives and get better from the awful sickness we've developed as a society.

We all have sin we need to atone for. We all need to start believing in a greater good for humanity. We must stop the fake news, stop the pollution, stop the war and fight to become a better species for the sake of the whole planet."

Earl put his hand up to stop her from saying anything else.

"You've been brainwashed. I can see it in your eyes. All this talk of greater good and atoning for sins, the kind of talk that comes from crazy religious sects.

You had no right to accuse me of touching you inappropriately without any kind of evidence. Now you come back home after over six months with no remorse? No emotion? What have they been feeding you?"

Hope looked at him, expressionless.

"I made you coffee."

She handed them both a mug each.

"Rachel, why is blue smoke emanating from your skin?" Susan asked.

Hope looked at her mother, expressionless.

"I have been raped and abused by my brother whilst the world turned a blind eye. I have been through more in the past six months than most people go through in their lifetimes."

"Look, I'm real sorry we didn't know about Mason and weren't able to help stop him but none of what has happened is an excuse for you coming back here acting like this. Damn it Rachel, you're scaring us!" Earl said, exasperated.

Hope watched her parents' take mouthfuls from their mugs of coffee.

"Do you even know where Mason is?" Susan asked.

"We are tracking his movements. We will find him when the time is right," Hope said.

Earl got up from the couch, walked over to the front door, and locked it.

"Now you're back, I'm sure as damn hell not letting you leave again."

"You can't keep me here, Daddy. My life is with Enlightenment now."

"It damn well is not. I've heard some creepy things about that sect and I will not have my daughter being part of it."

Hope looked at her father, expressionless.

"How's the coffee?"

"Delicious, thank you," Susan replied.

Hope smiled with her mouth, but still showed no emotion in her eyes.

"What has happened to you, Rachel? What have Enlightenment infected you with? Someone who has been through what you are claiming would be a wreck," Earl said.

"I have learned to control my emotions since you last saw me, Daddy. Joshua has taught me many things that we will use to help the sick and root out the demons infecting our world with their plague."

"Help the sick? Root out the demons? Are you hearing yourself? Who even speaks like that? I've a good mind to drive over there tomorrow and give this Joshua a piece of my mind!"

"I think you should, Daddy. I think you should come too, Mom. I want Joshua to meet my parents and I want you to see what an incredible man he is. He has such a brilliant mind. He was tracking me for a long time, knowing that I would one day become his Hope."

"Has he touched you, Rachel?"

Hope looked at him with anger in her eyes.

"No, Daddy. He has not touched me."

"Well I'm damn sure still going down there tomorrow to give him a piece of my mind. No one brainwashes my daughter and gets away with it!"

"Drink your coffee, Daddy," she said, looking at her father with a sadistic smile in her eyes.

As Hope saw her parents finish their mugs of coffee, she stood up, closed her eyes and concentrated on Joel. She saw the van where he was waiting and saw him smoking a roll up on the other side of the road near the Emerald River. She opened her eyes and looked at her parents.

"I'm going now, but I will see you both real soon."

"You're not going anywhere until your father says so," Susan said, sternly. "Why are your eyes glowing blue now?"

As Susan looked, she saw her daughter disappear in front of her, surrounded in blue smoke.

Chapter Thirty Eight //
4th September 2012 – The Haven, Starr County //

Joel finished smoking his roll up and stubbed it out on the floor. When he looked up, he saw Hope standing in front of him.

"How did you…"

"The Myst worked perfectly. Once my parents finished their coffee, I closed my eyes and focused on you. The Myst transported me from the couch to where I stand now."

"Did you do as the Messiah requested?"

"I did, Brother Joel. They will come to us in due course. Let's go home."

****

Hope was woken up the following day by the sound of her door buzzer. She answered it via her mobile phone. Joshua was standing in the lobby, asking to see her. She told him she'd be five minutes.

She quickly rose from her bed, showered and put a dress on, then went down to the lobby where Joshua was waiting.

"Hope! The most amazing thing has happened. Follow me."

Hope followed him out of the biosphere as he asked. Two individuals stood in front of them. Their hair had completely fallen out and their skin was blue. Hope realised straight away who they were. Tears formed in her eyes.

"Hope, you have sacrificed more than any of us could ever have imagined. I am so grateful for your loyalty and putting your trust in me," Joshua said, beaming. "Your parents have become the first of the Enlightened. They will now help us in our quest to achieve the greater good. They will want for nothing, they feel nothing and they no longer have any power to communicate. They will no longer need sleep, food or water. All they will do is obey our instruction."

Joshua turned to Earl and Susan, looking deep into their eyes.

"You will obey me."

Hope burst into tears, overwhelmed at seeing her parents transformed in such a horrific way, knowing that she had done this to them. She walked away from the Messiah who shouted after her to come back. She needed to be alone.

As she walked past the labs, Roland came out.

"Hey. How did it go last night?"

Hope looked at him, tears streaming down her face. She knew she couldn't trust him after finding out he was working with Mason. She equally knew that she couldn't let on she was aware of anything he had done. Yet.

"How much of that blue Myst are you able to make, Roland?"

"As much as you need, why?"

"I need enough for me to take every day and for it to last all day."

"You want to be… permanently Enlightened yourself?"

"Roland, I just killed my parents. What is standing over there with Joshua is not my parents. I cannot deal with what I have just done. I need the Myst."

Roland went back inside and re-appeared a couple of minutes later.

"Drink this, it will help. I'll get some more to you later."

"Thank you," Hope said, taking the mug and drinking the contents. "Can you refine the substance so my skin doesn't give off steam as much? Or change it so the steam is clear?"

"I'll get to work on it right away," Roland smiled.

Hope thanked Roland, drank the contents of the bottle he gave her, then walked over to the edge of The Haven and sat next to a small hill with her legs in the water, looking out to the edges of the mountains surrounding her. It was another beautiful day with the sun beating down on The Haven and no clouds in the sky.

She wondered which way Claire had rowed in to the island or what she said was even true. Perhaps she'd managed to sneak past the guards on the front gate after Mason had driven her to the Haven?

The Myst took hold as she sat there crying. The emotions she felt started to go away and her head cleared. A few minutes later, Joshua walked up and sat next to her.

"I know what you did has taken its toll on you. It would on anyone. I am truly grateful for your faith in our cause and your faith in me. The Enlightened are exactly what we expected and wanted them to be. We will start to further our plans and start expanding past the confines of The Haven.

I am putting plans in place for Joel to run our Phoenix Mountains' chapter and James to run our Owl Creek chapter. I'd like you to run our Silk Falls chapter and expand the Myst manufacture out there."

"As you wish, Messiah."

"How did the Myst work that Joel gave you?"

"It worked perfectly thank you," Hope smiled. "I drank it before I went in to see my parents. I was able to control my emotions and focus on the task you asked me to perform. When I was ready to leave, I focused my mind on Joel and the van where I had left him. When I opened my eyes, I told my parents I was leaving and the next thing I knew, I was standing in front of Joel.

Roland is working to produce a constant supply for me. If I am to continue to remain focused, I must be able to have constant access."

"As you wish, Hope.

We will start sweeping through Silk Falls first. I have already put teams in a number of churches. Radio stations across the county will soon spread our message of peace, love and harmony, whilst equally encouraging our comrades to root out any who oppose us and mark them as demons so we can deal with them in due course.

Once we have swept Silk Falls, Owl Creek will follow then the Phoenix Mountains. None shall stand in our way."

PART FOUR

Interlude //
4th July 2016 // Angel Pine, Starr County //

Darkness Falls

They stood, in a line, in front of the gathering of soldiers, looking at the three prisoners. Relief flowed through their bodies, having finally defeated the evil that had infected their home for so long.

"How is she?" Ralph asked.

"Alive. She should be grateful for that as it is," Hannah said, callously.

"What do we do now?" Pastor Gore asked.

 "Find a way back to how we used to live?" Ralph replied.

"Not sure I can, Ralph," Hannah said. "They've destroyed my compassion, destroyed my home, and destroyed all my relationships. I don't know if I can ever go back to how things used to be."

She took the gun out of her holster, pulled the trigger and shot her former friend in the head before turning to walk out of the graveyard.

Chapter Thirty Nine //
12th February 2013 – Silk Falls, Starr County //

Things had moved quickly over the next six months. Enlightenment maintained its base in The Haven but spread rapidly over the entire county, taking over gas stations, shops, bars and gun stores. Once they had completed sweeping Silk Falls, they furthered plans to move to Owl Creek and then to the Phoenix Mountains as Joshua had prophesised.

Many of the Starr County residents agreed to work for Enlightenment and rallied to Joshua's cause, however plenty also refused and were branded demons. Joshua had ordered all the capture of all demons in groups and told Hope, James and Joel to inject all demons with the yellow Myst to turn them into more Enlightened.

Joshua tasked Hope with turning her old house and conservatory into a Myst manufacturing plant. Once numbers of Enlightened grew, Hope arranged for help to clear out both the house and the conservatory. Roland moved in to the house and got the Enlightened to clear the maze and gardens before building a much larger laboratory.

In February 2013, Hope brought Joshua over to the old Walker premises for a tour. The Messiah was very happy with the progress made.

"Hope, the time has come to discuss Mason."

"How do you mean, Messiah?" Hope asked.

"I made you a promise that we would deal with your brother once you had completed your sacrifice. I am a man of my word. I know you have been working with Jess to find out Mason's location. He is in the Phoenix Mountains."

"I have sensed him, Messiah. What would you have me do?"

"I see your perception levels have increased through use of the blue Myst. Well done, Hope. Move on with your plans to have Jess meet Mason in two days. James will bring a small group of our best women and men as back up."

"What about Jess's safety?"

"Roland has come up with an even stronger strain of the blue Myst, which he says will allow the user to transport a copy of their physical persona to a different place for however long the user needs. Providing the user mediates in solitary confinement and doesn't have their focus broken, anyone interacting with that person will not realise they actually aren't there, unless they try to interact with them physically. Roland will give you a small crate's worth of bottles of the new super strength blue Myst shortly."

"What happens if the user's focus is broken during use?"

"They will vanish from where they are focusing on. If they are harmed in any way, that harm will not transfer back to their physical body, providing they don't die. The only way the user would not survive if they are not able to focus on their body quickly enough to transport their consciousness back in time before death takes hold.

Go to the Temple of Gethsemane and the spare room to the right of the Peyton's chamber. No one will find or disturb you meditating in there. Focus on the railyard in Lexington and tell Jess to get Mason to meet her there. The railyard isn't used anymore and is remote. It also has a disused bunker. Lure Mason in there and James' soldiers will do the rest."

"As you wish, Messiah. What is to become of Roland?" Hope asked.

"I know Roland has betrayed you. I will leave it to you to decide his fate," Joshua said. "Congratulations on turning this into a manufacturing plant fit for our needs. We have almost completed sweeping Silk Falls. Rather than individually giving each demon a Myst injection moving forward, I propose we take over the Richmond processing plant and feed the yellow Myst into the water supply."

"Will this not affect those who have said they are with us?"

"All who are with us will not be affected. I have produced a serum which will protect them."

"I will make the necessary preparations, Messiah," Hope said. "Concerning Roland, I have asked his second in command to produce a strain of Myst that will turn him into an Enlightened but not cause his brain capacity to fade. He will still be able to work however, I want him to transition to become Head of the Enlightened."

"As you wish, Hope."

Joshua gave Hope a bottle of the super strength blue Myst he had told her about then said his farewells and drove back to The Haven.

Hope went to her old bedroom in the house and locked the door. She took her phone out and called Jess. Her friend answered and told her she'd be at the Garden of Babylon in five minutes. Hope said she would meet her there.

Hope took the bottle of the super strength blue Myst Joshua had given her. She poured a small amount into a glass of water, then drank the contents and closed her eyes. She focused her mind on The Haven and on the Garden of Babylon in particular. After a few seconds, she found herself walking into the garden and sat on the bench to wait for Jess. Her friend appeared shortly after.

"Hey Jess! How are you?"

"I'm really good. It's so good to see you! How's everything over at the conservatory?"

"Progressing really well. The Messiah is very pleased and wants us to start to expand so we can stop needing to inject the demons with the Myst. He is planning for us to take over a water plant here in Silk Falls and dilute the yellow Myst so any who oppose us drink it naturally.

However, that's not why I'm here. I want to talk to you about Mason."

"Oh yeah, he messaged me again. He's desperate to meet up. What should I tell him?"

"Tell him to meet you in the abandoned railyard in Lexington in the Phoenix Mountains on the evening of February 14th. Tell him you'll meet him outside and there is a bunker you can use which has a bathroom, shower and queen size bed. I will find you tomorrow at The Haven and we will plan the details."

"What do you mean, find me at The Haven? You're here sat next to me?"

Hope looked at her friend and smiled.

"I'm glad you think that. What you are looking at is not me. It is a projection of my body. The strain of blue Myst that Roland developed and I have sole control over, gives me the ability to meditate and focus all my thoughts and energy into finding a person or place. If I am in meditating in a room that no one else is in, with my focus not broken, it allows me to project my body and make it seem like I am really with you, even though I'm not."

"That is amazing! So are you proposing we use that to meet Mason?"

"Exactly. The Messiah has said we can use the Temple of Gethsemane to meditate in a room out back which will be perfect as no one will find or disturb us."

Jess looked hesitant.

"It's just... after what happened with that thing. I don't wanna go back there."

"Don't you trust the Messiah?"

"Of course, but I don't know if I want to be in the same building as that thing again."

"How about you come here and I'll make sure Roland is over at The Haven for the next few days? I'll ask Joel to drive you over tomorrow."

"Perfect."

Jess messaged Mason on Connect as Hope watched. They arranged to meet Mason at 6pm at the rail yard on Valentine's Day. Hope then told Jess to arrive at the conservatory at 2pm on February 13th. They said their goodbyes then Jess watched as Hope vanished in front of her, leaving a residual blue mist.

Hope opened her eyes and decided that it was time to give Roland a dose of his own medicine. She went down to the kitchen and brewed a mug of coffee, as she had for parents, then walked over to the new laboratory.

"How's everything coming along, Roland?" Hope asked, as she walked in, smiling.

"Very well thanks, we are looking into ways to getting the yellow Myst past the water filtration when we take over the Richmond processing plant and I think we've come up with something."

Hope gave him the mug of coffee.

"Thanks Hope, that's so kind!" Roland smiled, taking a sip.

"Great news about the processing plant. The Messiah will be so pleased. He has guaranteed anyone who has not been branded a demon will be safe from the Myst affecting them. All demons will become then become part of the Enlightened without needing an injection.

I've a favour to ask, I need to do something private here tomorrow for the Messiah. Can you work from The Haven tomorrow afternoon through Thursday? James has also told me that he needs your help on Thursday evening with an important task."

"Sure, I need to go back over there at some point to get more equipment so may as well be now."

Hope watched as Roland drank his coffee.

"The Messiah talks so highly of you, Roland. I never thought when I met you that you had the skills to become such an incredible scientist."

"Thanks, Hope. That means a lot, I'm really glad we ended up with Enlightenment. It's given me a new lease of life, a new focus and purpose."

"I also never thought you'd betray me."

"Say what?" Roland asked, shocked.

"This whole time, did you really think I'd not find out?" Hope replied, her eyes changing from smiling to anger in an instant.

"I… I… don't?"

"Save the bullshit! I know you were the one who picked the document up from Mason after you dropped me off in Angel Pine. I know you then took it to Midtown and gave it to the Sheriff to have Hannah arrested.

Well, guess what? Mason's plan has backfired because Hannah is not in jail. We got her out, with the Messiah's help. He led us to incontrovertible proof that Mason was behind her parents' murder."

Roland tried to run out of the lab, but Hope grabbed his arm.

"Run all you like, Willie.," she hissed. "You will soon find out that deception doesn't pay. Don't try and contact Mason. You won't be able to as we've blocked your mobile phone and your social media accounts.

Go back to The Haven and see the Messiah. He will discuss your new role with you further."

"Mmmmyyyy new role?"

"As head of the Enlightened," Hope smiled, sadistically. "Did you enjoy your coffee?"

"What have you done to me?" Roland said, wide-eyed.

"Just given you a dose of your own medicine. Don't ever cross me again."

Chapter Forty //
13th February 2013 – Silk Falls, Starr County //

The following day, Hope made sure the living room on the first floor of her parents' old house was clear and the lock on the door was working. Roland had been staying in her old bedroom and Hope had moved into her parents' old room on the top floor.

The previous afternoon, Roland had run out of the conservatory after Hope had drugged him with the special yellow Myst. She had followed him back into the house. He ran upstairs into his room and locked the door. As Hope followed him up the stairs, she heard him frantically packing his stuff into a bag. She walked up to the top floor and watched him as he eventually ran out of the house and get into his van. She could see that he was already losing his hair.

Once Roland left, Hope opened the room he'd been staying in and told some of the Enlightened to clear out the rest of his belongings and burn them in the yard.

On the Wednesday, Hope got a call from Joel to say that he and Jess would be there within ten minutes. She went outside to meet them.

"Jess, so good to see you!" Hope called out, as the van drove up with the windows wound down.

Jess got out and gave her friend a hug. Joel also got out.

"Brother, thank you for bringing Jess here. I am truly grateful."

"You are welcome, Sister. The Messiah asked me to send his best wishes regarding your journey to find Mason and says he will see you in the Temple of Gethsemane when you are done."

"Joel, we're not going to the temple to meditate. That is why I asked if you'd be able to bring Jess here. We have an underground bunker a few miles downriver that we're gonna use. Can you swing by here early on February 15th to pick us up?"

"Sure."

"Thank you. If the Messiah asks why we didn't use the temple, just tell him we didn't have chance to get back to The Haven in time."

Joel bid them farewell, got back in his van and drove off.

"How do you feel about tomorrow, Jess?" Hope asked, as they walked into the house.

"Nervous. Do you think he'll know that I'm not really there with him?"

"Did you have any idea I wasn't with you back in the Garden of Babylon?"

"None at all."

Hope smiled.

"The only time that Mason will wonder is when he tries to touch you but James will be there way before that happens."

"Can we test the Myst tonight before I meet Mason tomorrow?"

"Sure. Have you heard back from him at all?"

Jess opened her phone, logged onto her Connect account and showed Hope the message she had received from Mason.

Can't wait to finally meet you and looking forward to seeing that gorgeous body ;). 6pm, Valentine's Day cannot get here quick enough. I will make all your dreams come true. Will make sure I get to the rail yard early. See you soon baby x

The message made Hope feel sick.

"I promise, I will not let him touch you, Jess. Come up to my old living room on the first floor of the house. I've set it up so that we can totally relax and meditate without distraction. There is no way anyone will be able to get in to the house, let alone the room, so we'll be able to focus solely on the task at hand."

Hope took her friend upstairs. Jess dropped her stuff off in Hope's bedroom then came back downstairs to the room Hope had prepared. She saw the windows locked and blacked out. The room was completely clear aside from two mats on the floor with some padded backing behind to keep their backs straight and stop them from falling whilst they meditated.

Hope had prepared two mugs of water. She got out a small bottle of the blue Myst and poured equal amounts into each mug.

"Where do you want to go, Jess?"

"Can we go to Ruby Falls? I've always wanted to see them and have never had the chance."

"Of course! All we need to do to focus on the same area near the falls. Here, have a look at this."

Hope used her phone to bring up an image of a totem pole, which was located five minutes' walk away from the falls.

"Once you've had the Myst, focus your mind on the left hand side of the totem pole. I will focus on the right hand side." Hope said.

"What happens if something goes wrong whilst we are meditating?"

"What do you mean?"

"What happens if I was to accidentally slip and fall down a cave or fall off a bridge?"

"Providing you wake yourself up quickly enough from meditating, nothing will happen. If you aren't able to then you will suffer the same effects as you would if you had fallen from the bridge in real life."

"You mean I'll die?" Jess asked, aghast.

"Yes. That is why it is so important to maintain focus throughout."

They both drank the contents of their mugs and laid down on their mats on the floor. As she had said she would, Hope focused on the right hand side of the totem pole near Ruby Falls and within a couple of minutes she saw herself walking towards the object. She looked to her left and saw Jess walking next to her.

"Well done Jess! How do you feel?"

"I feel like I'm actually here and seeing this in person."

"It's amazing isn't it?"

They walked through the beautiful forest up to Ruby Falls. Hope could see so many different species of flower, blossoming all around in so many vibrant colours. Trees surrounded the paths through the forest, with sunlight seeping through at points.

They criss-crossed the river bridges leading up to the falls. As they walked over the last bridge from right to left, Hope saw the path curve to the left hand side and figured they must be almost there. As they turned the corner, Hope noticed the vegetation, plants and flowers were all changing colour from green to orange then dark red. She looked at them in awe before looking up and seeing Ruby Falls.

"Look… at… that, Jess!" Hope said gobsmacked.

In front of them were four separate waterfalls, covered in dark red and pink flowers. The trees at the top also had deep red leaves on. The sun was setting to the east of the falls and had a deep red hue.

"I've never seen anything so beautiful in my life," Jess said, getting her phone out to take a picture. "Can we just stay here forever?"

Hope laughed. "For few minutes, but I don't want to stay too long just in case. This was just a test."

"It's just so pretty, I'm amazed more people aren't here taking in the view."

"It's quite a distance up here from Dakota Valley. A lot of people probably don't even know about it. I wish Bo was here right now."

"He's at peace," Jess said, squeezing her friend's hand. "He is with you in your heart and that's what matters."

"Thanks Jess."

They watched the sun go down sitting over the side of the cliff face then helped each other to stand and started to walk back.

"Seeing as this is a test, why don't we test the theory you mentioned earlier?" Jess asked.

"What do you mean?"

Before Hope had realised, Jess turned back and ran off the cliff edge.

Chapter Forty One //
13th February 2013 – Silk Falls, Starr County //

"JESS!" Hope screamed, running back towards the edge of the cliff and looking over. She couldn't see anything at all as there were low clouds that had started to form and the sun was too low in the sky. She focused back on her body in Silk Falls and within a few seconds, she was opening her eyes.

She immediately looked to her right and saw there was no one there.

"That was so much fun! And it worked exactly how you said it would" Jess was standing up, beaming.

Hope got up, ran over to her friend and hugged her tightly.

"Don't ever do that again, Jess! You scared the life out of me!"

"Sorry Hope, but I had to know! It was real easy though. I did exactly what you said and just focused my mind back here."

"I could have lost you! I can't go through losing anyone like that again."

"I won't do it again, I promise. I just needed to know."

Hope composed herself and they went down to the kitchen to get some food.

"So tomorrow, we'll start by focusing on the gas station which is a minute out from the disused rail yard. I will make sure I can see you at all times, just in case. Please stay in sight at all times until you get to the bunker. James and his team will be down there, waiting. Get Mason to go down first and they will do the rest."

"Got it. What if Mason doesn't show up?"

"He will, I know he will," Hope said. "If anything does go wrong, get yourself out of there immediately."

****

They woke up late the following day and went for a walk along the banks of the Emerald River to finalise plans. As they were on the way back to the house, Hope got a call from Joshua.

"Hope. How are plans for tonight coming along?"

"Everything is set. We will arrive at the rail yard shortly to meet James and his men before they drop into the bunker. I will keep hidden away in the gas station next door so I can see everything that is going on and buzz Jess if I see anything unexpected."

"Good. The Temple of Gethsemane is all set for you."

"We won't need that, Joshua. Thanks though."

"Why not, Hope?" Joshua asked.

"We have found a location nearer to the conservatory which suits us better, plus we won't have time to get back to The Haven now. Sorry, I would have told you, Messiah, but I didn't think it would be a problem?"

"We will discuss it later, Hope. Just get this done."

Joshua hung up the phone.

"He sounded mad," Hope said. "He wants to talk to me about us not using the temple when we get back to The Haven."

"Why is he so insistent on us using that temple?"

"I don't know, but my number one priority is protecting you and if you don't feel safe in that temple, then we aren't using it."

"Thank you, Hope. It's almost time for us to go, are you ready?"

"Yes, are you?"

"Ready as I'll ever be," Jess smiled.

"Do you have the binoculars?" Hope asked.

"Yes, why do you need them again?"

"Just in case, I don't trust Mason and I want to make sure we are prepared."

Hope made a couple of sandwiches, which they wolfed down before heading up to the meditation room. Hope grabbed a large bottle of the blue Myst on the way up, along with a couple of glasses. They drank a large dose, diluted in water, laid down on the mats and closed their eyes.

Hope opened her eyes and saw Jess standing next to her. They were across the road from the gas station and could see the rail yard next to that. Hope scanned the area and saw no one was around. She waved at Jess to follow her as she crossed the road and walked into the gas station.

"Pass me the binoculars please, Jess."

Jess did as Hope asked.

"I need to scope everywhere to make sure…"

Hope moved through the office to a window on the left hand side. She looked through the binoculars and saw everything was exactly the way she had expected, the rail yard had a large entrance and tracks leading in from direction she was looking in. There was one empty train car at the end of the line. Hope could see the bunker hatch was to the right of the empty train car.

She looked at the surrounding area and saw there was a cliff edge behind the rail yard, to the right of her. There were trees all along the cliff and hills behind. She adjusted the binoculars and saw one particular section that looked to be a perfect for anyone wanting to watch what was happening down below. Scanning the entire area, she couldn't see anyone else around or anything that made her think there was someone hiding nearby.

They heard the door of the office swing open. Hope turned around and saw James walk in with a group of men.

"Sister. How are you?"

"Well, thank you, Brother."

"Is everything set and ready?"

"Yes. Jess is planning to wait for Mason at the entrance then take him to the bunker. He'll open it and go down first where you will be waiting for him."

"I will be in the bunker with Michael. I will also station two soldiers hidden near the entrance to the rail yard and a couple who will keep an eye on proceedings from the cliff above to make sure he doesn't run."

"Excellent, Brother. I was going to ask you about that. Where is Roland?"

"Secured in our truck with the Enlightened. He will not be allowed out until it is done."

"Good. Thank you, Brother."

James left a semi-automatic M4 on the counter, even though Hope said she wouldn't need it, then moved his soldiers out and set them up as he and Hope had agreed. He gave Hope and Jess devices to put in their ears, which kept them in communication with each other and his soldiers.

Jess stayed with Hope in the gas station until it was time for her to go and meet Mason. Before she left, Hope scanned the area one last time to make sure everything was as she had planned. She saw James' soldiers were in place on the cliffs behind the rail yard. She saw one hidden away near the entrance and saw the hatch to the bunker closed as expected.

"Are you sure you are ready?" Hope asked.

"Yes. I'll be careful, I promise."

"If you feel in danger, just press on your right ear and say the word 'Alpha'. We'll get you out."

Hope hugged her friend then watched with trepidation as she left the gas station and walked to the entrance of the rail yard.

It got to 6pm and there was no sign of Mason.

"Something's wrong," Hope said, pushing on the device in her ear.

"What do you mean, Sister?" James replied.

"He's not shown up."

She looked into the binoculars, moving them around the yard. James' man near the entrance was still there. She moved the binoculars to the cliffs and trees behind the rail yard. She didn't see anyone there at all.

"Where have your men gone who were posted to the cliffs at the back?"

"They're not there?"

"No. James, stay in position. I'll find him."

Hope knew he was nearby. She grabbed the M4 and closed her eyes. She focused on her brother and saw him lying down on the ridge above the rail yard, using a pair of binoculars to look down at Jess. Less than ten seconds later, Hope was standing a few metres behind him on top of the cliff. She looked around and saw the bodies of the two soldiers James had sent up to keep watch.

She approached him quietly.

"Mason."

He froze then pulled himself up.

"I knew you were behind this, Rachel. Did you really think I would meet this girl without taking precautions? Your guards are dead and so is Jess. Look."

Hope moved over to the edge and looked through her binoculars. She couldn't see Jess anywhere in the rail yard. She looked around frantically to see if she could see her near the gas station or in the forest over the other side of the road, but she wasn't there.

Suddenly, out of the corner of her eye, she saw Mason try to lunge for her. He went to grab her and take her down, but he fell through her. He had a look of shock on his face, unable to get his balance. He lost his footing then fell from the cliff edge. As Hope looked over, she saw him hanging to a branch just below the cliffs.

"Rachel! Help me!" Mason screamed. "I can save your friend, just HELP ME!"

She stared into his eyes.

"No."

She took the M4 and aimed it at his head.

"RACHEL! WHAT ARE YOU DOING?"

"You killed Bo. You raped me. YOU RUINED MY LIFE. It's time YOU were made to pay."

She shot the branch he had grabbed. He was forced to let go and he fell straight down the cliff edge, screaming until he hit the ground below with a thud.

Hope stood back then collapsed on the ground. She had finally avenged Bo. Relief flowed through her body as she started to well up with tears.

JESS.

Hope touched the device in her ear.

"Jess, can you hear me? Are you safe?"

"I'm ok, Hope. A woman approached me. She tried to kidnap me but James' men saw and shot her. She's alive, we tied her up. We're in the gas station."

"That must have been Claire. I'm coming down from the cliff side."

"What happened to Mason?"

"I'll explain everything in a minute."

Hope closed her eyes and focused on the gas station. Within a few seconds, she was outside, near the entrance to the office. She saw James emerge from the bunker as she went in to the gas station. As Hope opened the door, she saw Claire tied up on the ground. Jess was sitting down, looking shaken.

"Well, well, well, what do we have here?" Hope said, looking at Claire.

"You fucking bitch! Just you wait until Mason gets his hands on you!"

"Oh that won't be happening, Claire. Your precious husband is dead."

Claire lunged for Hope, trying to attack her but fell through where Hope was standing.

"What the hell? Bitch, I'll kill you!"

"No, Claire, you won't," Hope said smiling. "I'm not here. Jess isn't here. You thought you were so clever taking our men out but you didn't realise that we had taken extra precautions ourselves. What you are looking at is a projection. Our bodies are twenty miles away, in a house in Silk Falls. Your husband tried to grab me, to no doubt assault me again but he fell. Just like you did. Except he fell off that cliff up there."

Hope pointed outside to the edge of the cliff.

"Bring her," she said to James's soldiers, signalling them to follow her to the rail yard.

As they walked out of the gas station, she saw Roland approaching her. He was completely bald and his skin had turned yellow.

"What have you done to me?" he asked, with tears in his eyes.

"Did the Messiah not tell you, Roland? You are head of my Enlightened. You answer to me. Your precious friend Mason is dead. You made the wrong choice and it has cost you your freedom."

She watched as Roland started to wail, then she signalled to James to bring all the Enlightened to the rail yard with them.

As they walked in, two of James's soldiers had brought Mason's body and had left it on the ground next to them.

Hope approached them and stood over the body feeling ambivalent. She felt pure relief that it was finally over but equally sad that it had to come to this. She had searched for Mason for months to no avail but as her mind had become clearer and the Messiah had trained her to use the Myst to her advantage, she had sensed his presence numerous times before tracking him down and laying a trap she knew he couldn't refuse.

The awful things that he had done to both her and those closest to her would scar her for the rest of her life. She would never forgive or forget.

Hope turned to Roland and said, "Burn the body."

Roland signalled to two of the Enlightened. Hope watched as they did as they were told; firstly getting logs from the pile at the back of the rail yard, stacking them to form a table then picking up the body and placing it on the pile of logs. Finally, they lit the ends and the bottoms of the logs with lighters.

Watching them closely, Hope could see tears in their eyes and she understood why. The body was that of their son.

Claire was incandescent with rage and inconsolable with grief as she watched Mason's body burn.

"I'LL FUCKING DESTROY YOU, RACHEL. YOU'LL NEVER SEE IT COMING. MARK MY WORDS, YOU'RE DEAD!"

Hope turned to Claire, signalling to James at the same time.

"Oh Claire, trust me, you won't. You're going to become something very important and special to us. You see Roland over there, you know, Mason's friend? He's been working on numerous strains of our Myst but there was one particular strain that I wanted to get hold of, just in case. A strain that was made before we joined Enlightenment. A strain that the Messiah is very proud of. A strain that he was never going to use again but I convinced him to let me have a small amount, just for you."

James took a red bottle out of his pocket and took the lid off. He then forced Claire's mouth open, pouring the contents down her throat and forced her mouth closed so she couldn't spit it out again.

"WHAT HAVE YOU JUST INFECTED ME WITH? FUCKING PSYCHOPATHIC BITCH!"

"You'll see," Hope said, pacing back and forth. "If there is one thing that incident with you and Mason taught me, Claire, it's never to fully trust anyone again. Your trust in Mason has led to this. Once the Myst has taken hold, you will be taken to the Black Caves in Silk Falls and left to roam for the rest of your existence."

"The FUCK are you talking about, Rachel? You're fucking crazy!"

Hope signalled to the men holding Claire to take her back to the office. She followed behind. As they walked in, Hope opened a desk drawer and found a mirror, which she put in front of Claire's face.

Claire screamed as she saw what was staring back at her.

PART FIVE

Interlude //
Unknown Date // Unknown Location //

The End

She opened her eyes. All she could see was Myst surrounding her everywhere. She stood up and tried to walk but realised she couldn't move. She saw the Myst start to clear in front of her slightly. As she looked, she saw The Haven getting closer in front of her. She saw the Garden of Babylon covered in Myst. They were waiting for her, sitting in the centre of the garden, watching as she drifted closer to join them.

"What the hell is going on?" she cried, tears streaming down her face.

"I saved you. After all this time, I saved you again. I saved you from the prophecy."

"What do you mean? What happened? WHAT IS GOING ON?"

"They're all dead. They didn't listen and now they are dead. He truly wanted to help people and save the sick. Now he can save no one, so no one lives. But I saved you."

Chapter Forty Two //
1st July 2016 – Silk Falls, Starr County //

Years had passed since Hannah last saw Hope. She had been waiting for the right time. They had been quietly planning and plotting a full resistance to rid the county of Enlightenment for good.

The sect had taken over. Every shop, bar, business were all under their control, as were the majority of the buildings in Starr County.

Hannah thought back to the day Hope had thrown her out of the moving vehicle and left her for dead. How times had changed since. Wade, who was out tracking wild buffalo, found her. He took her back to her shack on the Emerald River where Ralf vowed he would make sure Hope did not get away with hurting her. He got down on one knee and proposed to her at that moment. Hannah cried with joy as she said yes. They decided not to think about the wedding until after they had ridden the county of the evil that had been infecting them all for so long.

Enlightenment had initially taken over Starr County Jail but had been driven out after the inmates started to riot and killed a number of the Enlightened. Sheriff Fowler and his men were forced out of Midtown and took refuge in the jail along with the majority of those who Enlightenment had identified as demons but hadn't been converted. Hannah and Ralf mainly worked from the jail, travelling to Jefferson Canyon, when needed, to talk to Pastor Gore who had developed his church into a refuge centre for anyone hurt by the sect or any new resistance members.

Hannah watched Hope had infiltrate every area of Silk Falls. She had seen the sect take over the Richmond water plant and infect the county's water supply including the Emerald River, which now flowed bright yellow instead of clear. Enlightenment had destroyed the brewery and numerous other businesses and the Enlightened had taken over the remnants of the buildings.

Shrines had gone up in Silk Falls, which were all dedicated to Hope. There were rumours that Hope invited male suitors to these shrines, allowing her to control their lusts before infecting them with the Myst and turning them into more Enlightened. Hannah had heard from those who had escaped the sect that Hope now lived in the Myst herself and no one knew where her physical form was.

The Pastor said that similar things were happening in Owl Creek with James, who had become a maniacal dictator. He was cleansing any who opposed his tyrannical rule in the Myst infested rivers and if they still didn't conform, he'd take them back to his work room, have them tattooed and marked as demons before having them shot.

In the Phoenix Mountains up north, Wade told Hannah that Joel was behaving differently to the others. He based himself in a military camp in the far north of the area and let the majority of citizens go about their daily lives but if anyone or anything got out of hand, he would deal with the perpetrators and have them turned into Enlightened for Hope.

The Resistance decided to attack both Hope in Silk Falls and James in Owl Creek at the same time. Hannah was worried that finding Hope would be impossible. She knew that they needed to find her actual body so sent scout parties to look in places that were not obvious throughout the area. However, despite thorough investigations, they got no closer to finding out where she might be.

One night, Hannah had been working in the Jail, planning another scout party. She was exhausted and decided to sleep in one of the beds brought in by the Sheriff's team. A few minutes after she lay down in the room and shut her eyes, she heard a whisper.

"Hannah."

Hannah opened her eyes and saw Hope standing in the room, looking at her.

"I know what you are doing, Hannah. It isn't going to work. However hard you try, however many times you try, you will not find me. He protects me and looks after me. He'll never let you anywhere near me."

Hannah sat up on the bed.

"Your precious Messiah will not protect you forever, Rachel. He is pure evil. He has taken away our freedoms and our joy. We will never forget and we will never give in. He will be taken down and you with him."

"All these words are meaningless, Hannah. It would be so much easier for you if you join us and become part of the solution, not part of the problem."

"You have murdered innocent civilians. You promote the glorification of violence and work to appease a false god. You have forgotten what it is like to be a good person, Rachel. I would never join you. But mark my words, I will find you and I will destroy your vile sect."

Hope shook her head, listening to what Hannah was saying.

"You have been brainwashed into believing this nonsense. The Messiah promotes peace and harmony. We are not here to hurt anyone. We are here to help the sick get better and free America."

"I've been brainwashed? Do you hear yourself speak, Rachel? You're literally repeating the lies that maniac Joshua is feeding you. Your precious Messiah is destined to fail and soon, you and your vile sect will be gone from this county forever."

Hope looked at her former friend callously.

"Declaring war on us would not be wise, Hannah. Are you sure that is the route you want to take?"

"If war is what it takes to get our county back, so be it."

Hope vanished in front of Hannah's eyes. Hannah didn't attempt to figure out how Hope had got into her room. She picked her phone up and messaged Ralph asking him to meet her early tomorrow then took a mouthful of water in the glass on the sideboard before moving back to her bed, laying down and falling asleep.

****

The following day, Hannah woke up and met Ralph in the large office at the front of the jail. She told him all about what had happened the previous night with Hope. They then contacted Pastor Gore and agreed it was time to move.

The Pastor and the Sheriff had both tried to get additional help in from outside the county but no one was interested, telling them they had to deal with the issue themselves.

They agreed a two-pronged attack. Sheriff Fowler would take a group of soldiers and start taking back the buildings that the sect had over run in Silk Falls. They'd start at the water plant then move to the brewery, the conservatory and so on. They said they would take out any members of the sect who refused to join them.

The Pastor, Hannah and Ralf would take down The Haven with a smaller group of men, working quietly and carefully. They'd enter via the lakes, using a passage through the mountains they found. The plan was to destroy the Messiah and find out where Hope was hiding.

They all wished each other luck before departing.

Ralf had arranged to get hold of a few large rowing boats from the dock based at in the southern area of the Phoenix Mountains. They drove over from Silk Falls and got all their gear in the rowing boats.

"When we get to The Haven, remember that the primary objective is to find the Messiah and force him to give up Rachel's location. Alpha team, with me. We head straight for the Church of Souls. Beta team, with Pastor Gore. Quietly eliminate all threats and release anyone being held captive by the sect," Hannah said.

They rowed out to the edge of the mountains and found the gap. It took them a while to get through as the boats were fairly wide, fitting eight people in each. The path was also very narrow so it wasn't easy rowing through.

Once they had traversed their way onto the lake where The Haven was located, Hannah signalled for three boats to slow down. They watched as the fourth boat arrived at the east side of The Haven and the soldiers inside disembarked. The third boat then followed. The second boat with the Pastor's team was next, followed by Hannah's boat last.

"Right, Pastor, head towards the south of the island first. You shouldn't come in to too much trouble as the majority Enlightenment are now scattered throughout Starr County."

"Call us if you need any help. Good luck!" Pastor Gore said, before he and his team started to move south.

"Ok, Ralph, we need to head to the church. Should we check the temple first seeing as we are pretty much there anyway?"

"Do you think he'll be there?"

"If he is, it'll be easier to get to him."

"True. However, what if he's changed the passcode to the gate? I think we probably need to go there last."

They headed on to the Church of Souls as planned. They remained quiet and stealthy, making sure they waited until any Ensects within the vicinity had left before moving closer. As they reached the back of the church, they saw James and Joel leave and head towards two vehicles parked out front. They sneaked in to the back of the church and could hear voices upstairs in Joshua's office.

Hannah signalled to the soldiers with her to guard the all entrances and make sure there was no way out of the building. Two of the women swept through the ground floor of the church except for the inner sanctum. They reported that there was no one in building except whomever was in Joshua's office. Hannah slowly crept up stairs and heard Hope and Joshua in the office. She crept downstairs and whispered to Ralph.

"She's there with him. We can get both of them at the same time."

Ralph grinned then signalled to the resistance soldiers guarding the back of the building to follow them. Hannah climbed the stairs first then, once the others were at the top, she burst in and saw the Messiah across the room from her. She pulled a knife out of her back pocket and lunged towards him but heard a shot at the last second before she got to him. She looked across the room as her body fell towards the ground. Hope was standing there with a gun pointed towards her.

Hannah felt blood seeping out of the side of her stomach. She heard Ralph scream then saw him try to attack Hope who disappeared into a cloud of Myst before he could get to her. She saw Joshua run across to the left side of the room and through a door in the wall, which she'd never seen before. As soon as he was through, the door shut and disappeared. She could hear Ralph bark orders at the others to find out where that door went. He told them to make sure they captured Joshua, before coming over to Hannah.

"HAN, HAN! Can you hear me?"

"Just... get... after... him. We... have... to... stop..."

"Don't speak. I'll be back in two minutes. Put this on the wound and don't you dare close your eyes."

Ralf wrapped the jumper Ralph had given her around her stomach, particularly the area where the bullet had penetrated. As he left the room, Hannah thought about Hope. She couldn't believe her best friend had shot her in cold blood. She couldn't stop crying as she saw her life flash before her eyes.

Ralph ran outside and around to the front of the church. He met up with the rest of the resistance.

"Did you get him?" he asked one of the soldiers.

"No but no one has left the building. I don't understand where he could have gone?" was the reply.

"Keep searching. I need to make sure Hannah is ok."

Ralph ran back into the Church and up the stairs into the office.

"Han, are you ok? I've got something that might help with the blee..."

He looked up as he entered the room. There was no one there.

Chapter Forty Three //
3rd July 2016 – Black Caves, Starr County //

Hannah woke up surrounded in total darkness. She remembered what had happened in the Church of Souls and immediately felt her stomach. There was no pain. She felt the other side just in case but no pain there either. She didn't understand how this was possible as she distinctly remembered Hope shooting her.

Hannah used her hands to try to feel around her but there was nothing there aside from the surface she was lying on, which felt like stone. She felt in her trouser pocket and pulled out her phone, which had plenty of battery left but no 3G. She sat up and turned the torch function on to look around.

Hannah was in a large dark cave. There was a door to the right hand side. She ran over to it and pushed on the handle. The door opened so she ran outside into a corridor, which had more doors to the left and the right. She looked in the first door with her phone's torch but couldn't see anything inside.

In the second door, she saw a smaller cave. Inside was a woman lying on the stone floor. She had a red dress on, wavy blonde hair and was barefoot. Hannah thought she was looking at Hope but couldn't be sure as the lighting was poor. She tried to open the door but found it locked. The doors were made of thick titanium steel so there was no way of getting inside.

Hannah walked to the end of the corridor and opened the door. She walked in and saw another large cave. She closed the door and heard it click. Suddenly, she saw lights come on above her head. With the cave now lit up, she saw just how vast it was in all directions. The only door she saw was the one behind her that she'd used to access the cave.

As the lights came on, Hannah thought she heard a noise.

"Hello? Is anyone there? Can anyone hear me?"

Her voice reverberated around the cave. There was no reply so she crept to her right. She heard another sound, a sound that was closer that the last. It was almost like a low growl of a large dog or wolf. Then she heard another sound she knew she'd heard before, a low hum. The sound she had heard in the Temple of Gethsemane, coming from the door they couldn't get access to.

"Is anyone there? Can you help me get outta here?"

The lights suddenly went out and darkness enveloped Hannah once again. She heard another growl, this time almost next to her. She slowly took her phone out again and turned her torch on then pointed it in front of her. From the darkness, she saw what looked like a female standing in front of her. Except, she had blue skin, no hair and was shaking. The humming sound she had heard from coming from this woman.

Hannah was struck with fear and didn't know what to do.

"Hannah. Do not turn around until I say. When I tell you, run to the end of the cave behind you."

She didn't dare look around to see who was there but she knew whose voice it was. The creature standing in front of her started to move closer.

"NOW!"

Hannah turned and ran down to the end of the cave. She saw a bright flash of light behind her but did not turn back. She kept running. She saw another door at the end, which slid open as she arrived. She ran through then it shut immediately and she heard it lock. She looked back through the pane of glass in the centre of the door and could see the creature was pressing against the door, trying to get through.

"Hannah."

She turned around and saw Hope standing in front of her.

"Rachel, what the hell is going on? You shot me in The Messiah's office. I thought I was dying and then I wake up in these caves. What the hell was that… thing?"

"Do you remember hearing that low hum in the Temple of Gethsemane?" Hope asked.

"I was thinking about that."

"That thing is the by-product of an experiment with the Myst that went wrong. There have only ever been two subjects tested with that strain. The first is still locked up in the temple. The second is the woman you saw in there. She used to be Mason's wife, until Mason died in a very sad accident at a rail yard in Lexington a few years ago."

"I'm… sorry to hear that?"

"I'm not. I killed him," Hope said, smiling sadistically. "He deserved everything he got and so did she."

"So what happened in the office?"

"I saved your life."

"No, you tried to kill me!"

"Hannah, if I had wanted to kill you, I would have done it a long time ago. I saved your life. Do you remember when I came to see you in Starr County Jail a few nights back? Well, I may have slipped some Myst in to your water."

"Why?"

"Because I foresaw what was going to happen and I couldn't let you kill the Messiah. But equally, I didn't want you to come to any harm."

"So you drugged me?"

"I saved your life, Hannah. As soon as you were asleep, I got the Enlightened to bring you here so you were safe. The version of the Myst you had allowed me to focus your mind on waking up in the jail as you would have expected to."

"How do I get out of these caves?" Hannah asked, ignoring Hope's explanation.

"Down the end of this corridor, turn right and you'll see the cave opening."

"Thanks," Hannah said, coldly before walking off.

"Oh and Hannah," Hope shouted behind her. "Not everything is as it seems, we will know if you tell anyone what you saw here."

Hannah turned around.

"Is that a threat, Rachel? You know what? I'm sick of your threats. I will get a team, come down to these caves and take out your whole operation."

Hannah saw her ex-friend disappear in a cloud of Myst in front of her. She screamed in frustration then turned around followed the directions provided to leave the caves.

As soon as she got to the exit, she phoned Ralf.

"Hey, where are you? Are you ok? I've been so worried," he said, after picking up the phone.

"I'm fine. It turns out Rachel drugged me by feeding me a strain of this Myst. What you saw yesterday morning wasn't me but a projection of me. When she shot me in the church office, all I could think about was her as the life drained out of me. I guess after you left, I must have closed my eyes and a few minutes later, I woke up in a cave. When I got out of the cave, I saw her body locked behind a titanium door a few caves down from me.

We have to get a team down here and clear these caves out quickly before she has time to hide the evidence. Did you find Joshua?"

"No, he escaped but we've cleared out the rest of The Haven. All the remaining Ensects have either fled in vans or have agreed to join us."

"Great work!"

"I know where the Black Caves are but you might wanna move away in case Rachel tries to attack you again. I'll meet you at the abandoned shack just off the i35 in twenty minutes."

"I know where Joshua is hiding," Hannah said, suddenly.

"What?" Ralf said, confused.

"That damn statue. I guarantee that's where he'll be."

"Right. Once I've picked you up, we'll get back to the jail, speak to the Sheriff and Pastor Gore and get that statue destroyed!"

Chapter Forty Four //
4th July 2016 – Silk Falls, Starr County //

Hannah woke at break of dawn. Once everyone was up and ready to move, they loaded up with plenty of guns and ammunition before setting off for the statue.

Hannah had asked the Pastor's teams to separate and sweep the caves, destroying everything down there then to move on and start clearing out the individual buildings within Owl Creek to rid them of any Ensects. She told the Pastor to make sure that they captured Hope alive when they swept the caves.

They got to the base of the mountain at midday. Ralf had spoken to Mike Raye from Owl Creek and enlisted his help in piloting an upgraded helicopter. He told Mike to make sure he arrived at the statue at 1pm with as much ammunition as the helicopter could carry.

Hannah and Ralf told their team to move up the mountain quietly. As they got close to the top, they heard a number of guards patrolling the area. Ralf signalled for two soldiers to have a look and let him know how many guards were there. The soldiers came back and said there were ten in total. Hannah gave instructions to take the guards out quietly. Luckily, none of the guards realised what was happening until it was too late.

Hannah approached the door at the base of the statue. She quietly opened it and looked inside. The Messiah was sitting with his back to her, talking to someone on the phone. She closed the door again and went back to crouch down near Ralf, who was on the path near the top of the mountain. She felt her phone vibrate in her pocket. It was Pastor Gore.

"Pastor? Are you ok? How did the cave sweep go?"

"The only things we found were a woman who had blue skin and had a hum coming from her body, which was also shaking the entire time. She attacked a number of my team so we had to shoot her. We then found a younger girl in a smaller cave who had a red dress on, she looked similar to Rachel. She said her name was Jess and had been sent to feed the blue thing."

"Wait, Rachel wasn't there?"

"Not that we could see."

"What have you done with Jess?"

"She said she would not betray Rachel so one of the guards has driven her to the maximum security facility near Dakota Valley."

"Thanks Pastor. We're about to attack the statue. I'll get back to you once we've taken Joshua out. When your teams are clearing through Owl Creek, make sure they capture any Ensects and kill any Enlightened. Have you heard from the Sheriff?"

"Not yet but I know he's working to capture James and Joel."

"Excellent. Speak to you later."

Hannah put the phone down and turned to Ralph.

"Rachel wasn't there. She's got to be here with the Messiah."

"Did you see her?"

"Not at first but where else is she going to be?"

Hannah got the soldiers to surround the statue then remembered something before just before they were going to attack.

"Ralph, I can take this from here. Go back to the bottom of the mountain and see if there is a symbol down there. I remember Rachel saying she had a dream about jumping off this statue. If she's in there and hears us capture the Messiah, she'll try to escape. The only way will be from the top with a parachute. We need to make sure someone is waiting for her."

"Done. Good luck!"

She kissed him before he left.

After giving Ralph time to get clear, Hannah signalled half of the soldiers to follow her as she went to open the door. She walked inside and saw the large staircase in front of her, leading to the top of the statue. She saw the Messiah still had his back to them and was still on the phone.

She pressed the gun against his neck and pulled the trigger.

****

Hope heard the gun shot from the top of the staircase. She stood up, looking down the stairs and saw Hannah standing over his body. She started to scream before realising they'd come for her too. Hannah looked up and saw her at the top of the staircase. The group of soldiers she was with were already climbing the stairs.

"You can't run forever, Rachel!" Hannah shouted.

Hope knew there was only one option. She grabbed the last bottle of blue Myst she had on her and quickly put her parachute on before running out to the top of the statue and jumping off. She floated down to the ground, unclipping her parachute as her feet touched the surface and started to run. She heard him behind, following her. She knew he was intent on bringing death and destruction to all who opposed him in Starr County and despite her best efforts, she wasn't sure that she had enough Enlightened in the region to help stop him. The Messiah had told her about what they had done to him when they opened up his brain. She realised he must not be aware of exactly what he had become.

She looked behind and saw him a few hundred yards back through the trees. The only way she could lose him was by hiding in the White Caves. She had to use everything the Messiah had taught her, so she concentrated her mind on the caves and almost felt the Myst envelop her but heard a huge explosion at the last second. She looked around, breaking her concentration, and saw the statue of the Messiah was on fire, with parts of the stone head falling to the ground. She knew she didn't have time to mourn, she had to keep going to get to the caves. Not far now.

She arrived at the White Caves within a couple of minutes. She went deep into the darkest cavern, taking the most complicated route she knew in order to lose him. She waited until dusk then crept out of the caves slowly and carefully, making her way to the border of Silk Falls and the Phoenix Mountains. She knew if she could make it across the border, Brother Joel would protect her the short distance she then needed to travel to get to The Haven.

She could see her brothers and sisters guarding the checkpoint. She closed her eyes as she ran and prayed the Messiah would keep her safe to the border but as she carried on running, she heard a shot from a distance.

She fell to the ground. She could see blood start oozing out of her shoulder. She was in agony, trying to crawl closer to the checkpoint and trying to shout to her brothers and sisters. But it was no use. No sound was coming out of her mouth.

He walked up and stood by her side, looking into her eyes as she lay on the ground, crying.

"Goodbye Hope," he said, pointing the gun to her forehead.

"Wait!" Hope heard a cry behind him. "I told you not to kill her!"

She saw Hannah run up and stand next to him.

"You really still trust her? After everything she's done to you?"

"Hell no! You know that!"

She grabbed Ralph's gun and shot both of Hope's legs.

.

Chapter Forty Five //
4th July 2016 – Silk Falls, Starr County //

Hope screamed in agony as she felt the bullets pierce her skin.

"Oh shut the fuck up, Rachel. You'll survive," Hannah said, rolling her eyes.

She turned to Ralf.

"It wasn't him. It wasn't Joshua."

She heard a maniacal laugh from below.

"You'll never find him, he knows every move you're about to make. He's going to destroy you."

Hannah pointed her gun at Hope again.

"If you don't shut up, Rachel, I'll shoot both your arms as well.

Ralph, there is only last thing I can think of. He never left The Haven."

They picked Hope up. Ralf slung her over his shoulder and they walked back up to the van that the soldiers had driven close to their location. Ralf dumped Hope in the back and used some old clothes to apply pressure to her legs where the bullets had penetrated.

They drove back to The Haven, which was now completely empty. Hannah walked into the Church of Souls and up to Joshua's office. There was no one there. The door she had seen him walk through after Hope had shot her, hadn't reappeared. She looked around the entire wall but couldn't see anything obvious. She pressed on the top of the area she thought the door had been and heard a click. She pressed again. The wall slid back and revealed a passageway with a door.

"Let's go," she said to Ralph, opening the door.

They walked down the passage, which led to an underground chamber. The chamber extended almost a mile in every direction. They could see another temple in the centre, which looked identical to the Temple of Gethsemane.

Hannah walked right up to the Temple. The door opened and she walked inside with Ralf. She saw one triangular, white room with Joshua sitting, facing them and dressed head to toe in white gowns. He had his head bowed.

"I knew you would come for me, my children. But know this, if you strike me down, I will become more powerful than you can ever imagine."

Hannah didn't pay any attention. She waved her soldiers to grab the Messiah and take him back outside to The Haven. She then followed the guards out of the Temple with Ralph.

When they got outside, the soldiers tied Joshua up and put him in the back of the truck with Hope. They bound both their mouths so they couldn't speak then drove off The Haven Island and back to the graveyard in Silk Falls where they had agreed to meet the Pastor and the Sheriff.

As they drove up to the graveyard, they saw Roland, James and Joel had been captured and were lying, face down with their hands and feet bound.

Ralph and the soldiers pulled Hope and Joshua out of the truck and placed them next to their brothers and Roland. All the soldiers, the Sheriff and Pastor Gore watched as Ralph positioned the Eve's and Roland on their knees.

"You have brought pain, suffering and misery to the people of this county. All of you will now pay the price. This will be the last sunset you ever see," Ralph said, pointing to the dark red hue in the sky. "Sheriff, take James and Joel to Starr County Jail and lock them away."

The Sheriff grabbed the two men, put them in his van and drove off. As he was driving out, Joshua managed to loosen one of his arms enough to pull a knife out of his trouser pocket. He then lunged for Hannah, stabbing her in the leg.

Hannah cried out in pain. As soon as Ralph heard the scream, he turned and shot Joshua in the head.

Hope and Roland both wailed in agony, seeing their Messiah lying motionless on the ground. Ralf looked at Joshua and saw the twisted, sick grin, forever etched on his lifeless face.

Ralph turned to Hannah, smiling. "Are you ok?"

"I'll be fine, he didn't penetrate very deep. It's just a prick."

They stood, in a line, in front of the gathering of soldiers, looking at the three prisoners. Relief flowed through their bodies, having finally defeated the evil that had infected their home for so long.

"How is she?" Ralph asked Hannah, looking at Hope.

"Alive. She should be grateful for that as it is," Hannah said, callously.

"What do we do now?" Pastor Gore asked.

"Find a way back to how we used to live?" Ralph replied.

"Not sure I can, Ralph," Hannah said. "They've destroyed my compassion, destroyed my home, and destroyed all my relationships. I don't know if I can ever go back to how things used to be."

She took the gun out of her holster, and shot Roland in the head before turning to walk out of the graveyard.

As she went to leave, Hope suddenly broke free of her bounds and jumped on Hannah. Her weight was enough that Hannah fell to the ground. Myst enveloped them both and they disappeared. Less than a second later, Ralph heard an explosion. He turned around. The last thing he ever saw was a mushroom cloud rising from the surface, less than a mile away.

Epilogue //
Unknown Date and Time - The Myst //

Afterlife

Hannah opened her eyes. All she could see was Myst surrounding her everywhere. She stood up and tried to walk but realised she couldn't move. She saw the Myst start to clear in front of her slightly. As she looked closer, she saw the graveyard where she had been just a few seconds ago. She saw Ralph, the Pastor and all the resistance were dead, their bodies scorched from an atomic explosion that must have happened after she disappeared. She broke down in agony looking at their faces, twisted with fear.

She looked up again and now saw The Haven getting closer in front of her. She saw the Garden of Babylon covered in Myst. Hope and Joshua were waiting for her, sitting in the centre of the garden, watching as she drifted closer to join them.

"Rachel? What the hell is going on?" Hannah cried, tears streaming down her face.

"I saved you Hannah. After all this time, I saved you again," Hope said softly.

"Where are we?" Hannah asked.

"In the Myst. I saved you from the Messiah's prophecy. I saved you from death."

"What do you mean, Rachel? What happened? WHAT IS GOING ON?"

"They're all dead, my child. All your friends, your fiancée. They're dead. They didn't listen to me and now they are dead. Hope saved you. We are together for all eternity, living in the Myst," Joshua said, opening his arms to Hannah.

"Ralph is... dead?" Hannah burst out crying.

"The Messiah warned us all, he told you not to under estimate him. He told you that if you struck him down, he'd become more powerful that any of you could imagine. He wasn't lying. He truly wanted to help people and save the sick. Now he can save no one, so no one lives. But I saved you," Hope said.

Hannah collapsed in agony, unable to comprehend the enormity of everything that had happened.

Hope drifted over to her friend and put her arm around her before slitting her throat with a knife and walking away, hand in hand with the Messiah.

FROM THE AUTHOR

Unfortunately, not everything in life turns out as we expect. Equally, not everyone who we see as being a good influence on our lives ends up being so. Keep those who mean something to you close and tell them you love them.

Treat people with kindness, even in the face of adversity.

This book took ten months to write and three more to edit. Whilst I initially struggled to figure out how I wanted to end the book, I decided that one of my goals in writing was to do something that I've not seen in many, if any, books and that was to finish the story with the main character as the main antagonist.

Special thanks to everyone who has given me tips whilst writing this book, particularly Lottie Newings. Also thanks to my mother and brother for their never-ending love and support.

Printed in Great Britain
by Amazon